Aubrey De Vere

The Sisters, Inisfail, and Other Poems

Aubrey De Vere

The Sisters, Inisfail, and Other Poems

ISBN/EAN: 9783337206789

Printed in Europe, USA, Canada, Australia, Japan

Cover: Foto ©Andreas Hilbeck / pixelio.de

More available books at **www.hansebooks.com**

THE SISTERS, INISFAIL,

AND OTHER POEMS.

BY

AUBREY DE VERE.

LONDON:

LONGMAN, GREEN, LONGMAN AND ROBERTS.

DUBLIN: McGLASHAN AND GILL,

SACKVILLE STREET.

1861.

PREFACE.

THE poem entitled " Inisfail," which occupies the greater part of this volume, is an attempt to represent, as in a picture, the more memorable periods of Irish history,—a history as poetical as it was troubled. In old times poetry and history were more nearly akin than they have lately been. In England, in Spain, and in other countries ancient and modern a collection of ballads had early grown up, out of which rose the later literature of each ; ballads that recorded many a precious passage of old times, and embodied the genius as well as the manners of the past. Irish history does not stand thus related to letters. For many centuries before the Norman invasion of Ireland, and for several after that event, the Bards occupied a more important position in Ireland than they have enjoyed in any other part of the West : their dignity was next to the regal ; their influence with the people unbounded ; and they possessed all the secular learning then existing. The Gael required that even the maxims of law should be delivered to him in verse, as well as that the lines of the chiefs and princes should be thus

and the course of which reveals an increasing sig-
nificance.

" Inisfail" may be regarded as a sort of National
Chronicle cast in a form partly lyrical, partly narrative, and of which the spirit is mainly dramatic. The
plan will account for the necessary exclusion of
modern political subjects, however momentous. Its
aim is to record the past alone, and that chiefly as
its chances might have been sung by those old
Bards, who, consciously or unconsciously, uttered
the voice which comes from a people's heart, and is
heard in festive hall, and in the village circle, in
the church-porch, and on the battle-field. That
voice includes many tones besides its sadder or
more solemn ones :—it changes also at different
periods of a nation's history ; and this diversity I
have endeavoured to mark by a corresponding
change of tone in the three parts of the Poem. A
National Chronicle in verse would necessarily, so far
as it was true to the spirit of history, include what
may be called the Biography of a People—its
interior as well as its exterior life. The annals of
Ireland were stormy and strange after the lapse of
those three golden centuries between her conversion
to Christianity and the Danish inroads. But there
were also great compensations—Religion :—natural
ties so powerful that they long preserved a scheme of
society almost patriarchal : an ever-buoyant imagi-

nation; and the inspiring influences of outward nature on a temperament as susceptive as the heart was deep. After the storms had rolled by, there still remained a People and a Religion. So long as its life is mainly from within, a People works out its destiny.

CONTENTS.

INISFAIL; OR, IRELAND IN THE OLDEN TIME.

PART I.

INISFAIL; OR, IRELAND IN THE OLDEN TIME.

PART II.

INISFAIL; OR, IRELAND IN THE OLDEN TIME.

PART III.

THE SISTERS; OR, WEAL IN WOE.

FROM nine to twelve my guest was eloquent
   In anger, mixed with sorrow, at the things
He saw around us—lands half marsh, half weeds,
Gates from the gate-posts miserably divorced,
Hovels ill-thatch'd, wild fences, fissured roads—
" Your people never for the future plan ;
" They live but for the moment." Thus he spake ;
A youth just entering on his broad domains,
A senator in prorogation time
Travelling for knowledge; Oxford's accurate scholar ;
A perfect rider, clean in all his ways,
But by traditions narrow'd.   As the moon
Turns but one side to earth, so show'd that world
Whereon he gazed, for stubborn was his will,
And Ireland he had never loved. " You err,"
I answer'd, taking in good part his wrath,
" Our peasant too has prescience ; far he sees ;
" Earth is his foreground only, rough or smooth ;
" In him from seriousness the lightness comes.
" Too serious is he to make sacrifice
" For fleeting good ; the battles of this world
" He with the left hand fights, and half in sport ;

" He has his moment—and eternity."
" Ay, ay," exclaim'd my guest, " your Church, she
          " does it !
" Your feasts and fasts and wakes and social rites,
" With ' Sir,' and ' Ma'am,' and usages of court :—
" I've seen a hundred men leave plough and spade
" To take a three weeks' infant to its grave,
" A cripple pay two shillings for a cart
" To bear him to the Holy Well—Sick Land !
" Look up ! the proof is round you written large ;
" Your Faith is in the balance wanting found ;
" Your shipless seas confess it ; bridgeless streams ;
" Your wasted wealth of ore, and moor, and bay.
" Beneath the Upas shade of Faith depraved
" All things lie dead—wealth, comfort, freedom,
          " power—
" All that great nations boast !" " Such things,"
          I answer'd,
" The Gentiles seek ; and you new texts have found,
" ' Ecclesiæ stantis vel cadentis,' friend,
" ' Blessed the rich : blessed whom all men praise.'
" New Scriptures these ; the Irish keep the old !
" Say, are there not diversities of gifts ?
" Are there not virtues—Industry is one—
" Which reap on earth, whilst others sow for heaven ?
" Faith, hope, and love, and purity, and patience,
" Humility, and self-forgetfulness,
" These too are virtues ; yet they rear not States.
" What then ? Of many nations earth is made :
" Each hath its function ; each its part for others :—

" If all were hand, where then were ear or eye?
" If all were foot, where head? You rail, my friend,
" Not at my country only but your own.
" The land that gave us birth our service claims,
" The suffering land our love. Yet England, too,
" They love, and they the most who flatter not.
" A thousand years of nobleness she lived
" Whereof you rob her ! In this isle are men
" By ancient lineage hers. Such men might say,
" ' My England was entomb'd ere yours had birth'—
" Dates she from Arkwright only ? Rose the nation
" With Alfred, or those Tudor Kings who built
" The Golden Gate of England's modern time,
" But built it upon liberties annull'd,
" Old glories quench'd, the old nobles dead or
        " quell'd—
" Ay, wrecks more sad ?" His host, I could not use
Words rough as his albeit to shield a land
For every shaft a targe ; so changed the theme
To her he knew—thence loved.

                    He loved his country ;
An older man than he for things less great
Had loved her less. Yet who could gaze, unmoved,
From Windsor's terraced heights o'er those broad
        meads
Lit by the pomp of silver-winding Thames
Dropping past templed grove, and hall, and farm,
Toward the great City ? Who, unthrill'd, could mark
Her minsters, towering far away, with heads
That stay the sunset of old times ; or them,

Oxford and Cambridge, England's anchors twain,
That to her moorings hold her? Fresh from these
Who, who could tread, O Wye, thy watery vale
Where Tintern reigns in ruin ; who could rest
Where Bolton finds in Wharf a warbling choir,
Or where the sea-wind fans thy brow discrown'd
Furness, nor love and wonder? Who, untouch'd,
When evening creeps from Scawfell towards Black
  Combe,
Could wander by thy darkly gleaming lakes
Embay'd 'mid sylvan garniture and isles
From saint or anchoret named, within the embrace
Of rural mountains green, or sound, scent, touch,
Of kine-besprinkled, soft, partition'd vales,
Almost domestic? Shadow-haunted land !
By Southey's lake Saint Herbert holds his own !
The knightly armour now by Yew-dale's crag
Rings loud no longer : Grasmere's reddening glass
Reflects no more the on-rushing clan ; yet still
Thy Saxon kings, and ever-virgin Queens
Possess thee with a quiet pathos ; still,
Like tarnish'd path forlorn of moon that sets
Over wide-water'd moor and marsh, thy Past
A spiritual sceptre, though deposed, extends
From sea to sea—from century-worn St. Bees
To Cuthbert's tomb under those eastern towers
On Durham's bowery steep !

     He loved his country :
That love I honour'd. Great and strong he call'd her;
But well I knew that had her greatness waned,

His love had wax'd.
           As thus we talk'd the sun
Launch'd through the hurrying clouds a rainy beam
That smote the hills.   My guest his pipe cast by,
And, issuing from its wreaths, exclaim'd, " Come
      forth—
" We waste the day! You ridge my fancy takes;
" Climb we its crest." The wolf-hound at our feet,
Our drift divining, bounded sudden on us
In rapture of prospective gratitude.

    We pass'd the offending gate; three planks for
      bridge,
We pass'd the offending stream which dash'd its spray
Contemptuous on us, proud of liberty.
I laugh'd.—" Our passionate Ireland is the stream ;
" Seven hundred years at will it mocks or chides ;
" You have not made it turn your English mill ! "
We scaled the hills ; we push'd through miles of trees,
Which, sire and son, had held their own since first
The tall elk trod their ways. Lightning and storm
Had left large wrecks :—election wars, not less,
Or hospitalities as fierce, when home
A thousand helot clansmen dragg'd the bride,
Or danced around a cradle,—ah, brave hearts !
Loyal where cause for loyalty was scant !
Vast were those woods and fair ; rock, oak, and yew,
Grey, green, and black, in varying measures striking
That three-string'd lyre, which charms not ear but eye.
Long climbing, from the woodland we emerged

And paced a rocky neck of pale green pasture.
The limit of two counties.   Full in face
Rush'd, ocean-scented, the harmonic wind.
Round us the sheep-bells chimed: a shower late past
With jewelry had hung the blackberry bush,
And gorse-brake half in gold.   On either side
Thin-skinn'd, ascetic, slippery, the descent
Down slanted toward the creeping mists.   Our goal
We reach'd at last—a broad and rocky mass
Forth leaning, lordly, unto lands remote,
The lion's head of all those feebler hills,
That cowering slunk behind it.   Far around
Low down, subjected, stretch'd the sea-like waste
Shade-swept, unbounded, like infinity.
An hour before his time the sun had dropp'd
Behind a mountain-wall of barrier cloud
Wide as the world: but five great beams converged
Towards the invisible seat of his eclipse;
And over many a river, bay, and meer
Lay the dull red of ante-dated eve.

    That summit was a graveyard.   Cross-engraven
Throng'd the close tomb-stones.   Each one had its
            prayer;
And some were raised by men whose heads were white
Ere selfless toil had won the hoarded coins
That honour'd thus a parent.   In the midst
A tomb-like chapel, thirty feet by ten,
Stood monumental, with stone roof and walls
The centuries slid from.   At its door we sat,

While, by the polish'd angle split, the wind
Hiss'd like a forkèd serpent.   Silent long
My friend remain'd; his sallies all had ceased,—
A man of tender nerve though stubborn thought.
The scene weigh'd on him like a Prophet's scroll
Troubling some unjust city.   Round and round
He scann'd the desolate region, and at last
Pray'd me the hieroglyphic to expound.
" You tower which blurs that lonely lake far off,
" What is it ? " And I answer'd, " Know you not ?
" He built it, he that Norman horsed and mail'd,
" Who, strong in Henry's might and Adrian's bull,
" Rent from the Gaelic monarch half his realm ;—
" The rest came later, dowry of the bride."

      Once more he mused ; then, westward pointing,
            spake :—
" Yon lovely hills, yet low, with Phidian line,
" That melt into the horizon :—on their curve
" A ruin'd castle stands ; the sky glares through it,
" Red, like a conflagration ! " I replied :
" Four hundred years the Norman held his own :
" He spake the people's language ; they in turn
" His war-cry had resounded far and wide ;
" Their history he had grown, impersonate.
" The land rejoiced in him, and of his greatness
" Uplifted, glorying, on a neck high held
" The beautiful burden, as the wild stag lifts
" O'er rocky Torc his antlers.   Would you more ?
" The Desmond was unloved beside the Thames ;

" The right of the great Palatine was trampled ;
" His faith by law proscribed. O'er tombs defaced,
" In old Askeaton's Abbey, of his sires
" He vow'd unwilling war. Long years the realm
" Reel'd like a drunken man. Behold the end !
" Yon wreck speaks all ! "

                              Thus question after question
Dragg'd, maim'd and mangled, dragg'd reluctant forth
Time's dread confession. Crime replied to crime :
Whom Tudor planted Cromwell rooted out ;
For Charles they fought ;—to fight for kings, their
          spoilers,
The rebel named rebellion ! William next !
Once more the nobles were down hurl'd ; once more
Nobility as in commission placed
By God among the lowly. Loyalty
To native Princes, or to Norman chiefs,
Their lawless conquerors, or to British Kings,
Or her the mother church that ne'er betray'd,
Had met the same reward. The legend spake
Words few but plain, grim rubric traced in blood ;
While, like a Fury fleeting through the air,
History from all the octaves of her lyre
Struck but one note ! What rifted tower and keep
Witness'd of tyrannous and relentless wars,
That shipless gulfs, that bridgeless streams and moors,
Black as if lightning-scarr'd, or cursed of God,
Proclaim'd of laws blacker than brand or blight—
Those Penal Laws. The tale was none of mine ;
Stone rail'd at stone ; grey ruins dumbly frown'd

Defiance; and the ruin-handled blast
Scatter'd the fragments of Cassandra's curse
From the far mountains to the tombs close by,
Which mutter'd treason.
                    That sad scene to me
Had lost by use its pathos as the scent
Which thrills us, while we pass the garden, palls
On one within it tarrying. To my friend
It spake its natural language: and as he
Who, hard through habit, reads with voice unmoved
A ballad that once touch'd him, if perchance
Some listener weeps partakes that listener's trouble,
Even so the stranger's sorrow struck on mine,
And I believed the things which I beheld
There sitting silent. When at last he spake,
The spirit of the man in part was changed;
The things but heard of he had seen: the truths
Coldly conceded now he realized.
Justice at last, with terrible recoil,
Leap'd up full-arm'd—a strong man after sleep—
And dash'd itself against the wrong! I answer'd:
" Once more you speak the words you spake this
            " morn,—
" ' Look up, the proof is round you, written large:'
" But in an alter'd sense."
                    I spake, and left him:
Left him to seek a tomb which three long years
Holds one I honour'd. Half-an-hour went by;
Then he rejoin'd me. With a knitted brow,
And clear vindictiveness of speech like him

Who, loving, hates the sin of whom he loves,
He spake against the men who, having won
By right or wrong the mastery of this isle,
(For in our annals he was versed, nor ran
In custom's blinkers, save on modern roads,)
Could make of it, seven hundred years gone by,
No more than this!—Then I:—" No country loved
  " they:
" Her least, the imperial realm !—'Tis late to mourn;
" Let past be past."   " The past," he said, " is
  " present;
" And o'er the future stretches far a hand
" Shadowy and minatory."   " Come what may,"
I said, " no suffering can to us be new;
" No shadow fail to dew some soul with grace.
" The history of a Soul holds in it more
" Than doth a nation's!   In its every chance
" Eternity lies hid; from every step
" Branch forth two paths piercing infinity.
" These things look noblest from their spiritual side:
" A statesman, from the secular point you see them,
" And doubt a future based on such a past.
" 'Tis true, with wrong dies not the effect of wrong,
" Or sense thereof :—'tis true stern Power with time
" Changes its modes, not instinct: true it is
" That hollow peace is war that wears a mask :
" Yet let us quell to-day unquiet thoughts.
" She rests who lies in yonder tomb: sore pains
" She suffer'd : yet within her there was peace:
" In God's high Will she rests, and why not we ?"

Thus we conversed till twilight, thickening, crept,
Compassionate, o'er a scene to which we said
Twilight seem'd native, day a garish vest
Worn by a slave.   Returning, oft my friend
Cast loose, in wrath, the arch-rebel Truth; I an-
    swer'd:
" She rests, and why not we?   O suffering land!
" Thee, too, God shields; and only for this cause
" Can they that love thee sleep."   Her tale at last
He sought with instance.   'Twas not marvellous,
I told him: yet to calm his thoughts perturb'd,
Thus, while the broad moon o'er the lonely moor
Rose, blanching as she soar'd, till pools, at first
With trembling light o'erlaid, gave back her face,
And all the woodland waves as eve advanced
Shone bright o'er sombre hollows, I recounted
The fragments of a noteless Irish life,
Not strange esteem'd among us.   Such a theme
I sought not.   Ill it were to forge for friend
A providence, or snare him though to peace.
Yet I was pleased he sought that tale.   'Twas sad:
But in its dusky glass (and this I hid not)
Shadow'd a phantom image of my country,
Vanquish'd yet victor, in her weal and woe.

The Father in the prime of manhood died;
The Mother follow'd soon; their children twain,
Margaret Mac Carthy, and her sister Mary,
The eldest scarcely ten years old, survived

To spread cold hands upon a close-seal'd grave,
And cry to those who answer'd not. The man
Who, in that narrow spot to them the world,
Stood up and seem'd as God;—that gentler one
Who overhung like Heaven their earliest thought,
And in the bosom of whose sleepless love
Reborn they seem'd each morning—both were dead.
In grief's bewilderment the orphans stood
Like one by fraud betray'd : nor moon, nor sun,
Nor trees, nor grass, nor herds, nor hills appear'd
To them what they had been. In sadden'd eyes,
Frighten'd yet dull, in voice subdued, and feet
That moved as though they fear'd to wake the dead,
Men saw that nowhere loneliness more lives
Than in the breasts of children. Time went by ;
The farm was lost ; and to her own small home
Their father's mother led them. 'Twas not far ;
They could behold the orchard they had loved ;
Behind the hedge could hear the robin sing,
And the bees murmur. Slowly, as the trance
Of grief dissolved, the present lived once more ;
The past became a dream !

                 I see them still !
Softly the beauty-making years on went,
And each one as he pass'd our planet's verge
Look'd back, and left a gift. A darker shade
Dropp'd on the deepening hair; a brighter gleam
Forth flash'd from violet eyes with darkness fringed.
Like, each to each, their stature growing kept
Unchanged gradation. To her grandmot

A quick eye, and a serviceable hand
Endear'd the elder most; she kept the house;
Hers was the rosier cheek, the livelier mind,
The smile of readier cheer.   In Mary lived
A visionary and pathetic grace
Through all her form diffused, from those small feet
Up to that beauteous-shaped and netted head,
Which from the slender shoulders and slight bust
Rose like a queen's.   Alone, not solitary,
Full often half an autumn day she sat
On the high grass-banks, foot with foot enclasped,
Now twisting osiers, watching cloud-shades now,
Or rushing vapours, through whose chasms there
      shone
Far off an alien race of clouds like Alps
O'er Courmayeur white-gleaming, and like them
To stillness frozen.   Well that orphan knew them,
Those marvellous clouds that roof our Irish wastes,
Spring's lightsome veil outblown, sad Autumn's bier,
And Winter's pillar of electric light
Slanted from heaven.   A spirit-world, so seem'd it,
In them was imaged forth to her.
                   With us
The childish heart betroths itself full oft
In vehement friendship.   Mary's was of these;
And thus her fancy found that counterweight
Which kept her feet on earth.   With her there
      walk'd
Two years a little maiden of the place,
Her comrade, as men call'd her.   Eve by eve

Homeward from school we saw them as they pass'd,
One arm of each about the other's neck,
Above both heads a single cloak.   She died,
To Mary leaving what she valued most,
A rosary strung with beads from Olivet.
Daily did Mary count those beads :—from each
The picture of some Christian truth ascending,
Till all the radiant Mysteries shone on high
Like constellations, and man's gloomy life
For her to music roll'd on poles of love
Through realms of glory.   Hope makes Love
          immortal !
That friend she ne'er forgot.   In later years
Working with other maidens equal-aged,
(A lady of the land instructed them,)
In circle on the grass, not them she saw,
Heard not the songs they sang: alone she sat,
And heard 'mid sighing pines and murmuring
          streams
The voice of the departed.
                    Smoothly flow'd
Till Margaret had attain'd her eighteenth year
The tenour of their lives ; and they became,
Those sisters twain, a name in all the vale
For beauty, kindness, truth, for modest grace,
And all that makes that fairest flower of all
Earth bears, heaven fosters—peasant nobleness :—
For industry the elder.   Mary fail'd
In this, a dreamer ; indolence her fault,
And self-indulgence, not that coarser sort

Which seeks delight, but that which shuns annoy.
And yet she did her best. The dull red morn
Shone, beamless, through the wintry hedge while
        pass'd
That pair with panniers, or, on whitest brows,
The balanced milk-pails. Margaret ruled serene
A wire-fenced empire smiling through soft glooms,
The pure, health-breathing dairy. Softer hand
Than Mary's ne'er let loose the wool; no eye
Finer pursued the on-flowing line : her wheel
Murmur'd complacent joy like kitten pleased.
With us such days abide not.
                        Sudden fell
Famine, the Terror never absent long,
Upon our land. It shrank—the daily dole ;
The oatmeal trickled from a tighter grasp ;
Hunger grew wild through panic ; infant cries
Madden'd at times the gentle into wrong :
Death's gentleness more oft for death made way ;
And like a lamb that openeth not its mouth
The sacrificial People, fillet-bound,
Stood up to die. Amid inviolate herds
Thousands the sacraments of death received,
Then waited God's decree. These things are
        known :
Strangers have witness'd to them ; strangers writ
The epitaph again and yet again.
The nettles and the weeds by the way-side
Men ate : from sharpening features and sunk eyes
Hunger glared forth, a wolf more lean each hour ;

Children seem'd pigmies shrivell'd to sudden age ;
And the deserted babe too weak to wail
But shook if hands, pitying or curious, raised
The rag across him thrown.   In England alms
From many a private hearth were largely sent,
As ofttimes they have been. 'Twas vain.   The land
Wept while her sons sank back into her graves
Like drowners 'mid still seas. Who could escaped :
And on a ghost-throng'd deck, amid such cries
As from the battle-field ascend at night
When stumbling widows grope o'er heaps of slain.
Amid such cries stood Mary, when the ship
Its cables slipp'd and, on the populous quays
Grating, without a wind, on the slow tide,
Dropp'd downward to the main.

                 For western shores
Those emigrants were bound.   At Liverpool,
Fann'd by the ocean breeze, the smouldering fire
Of fever burst into a sudden flame :
The stricken there were left ;—among them Mary.
How long she knew not in an hospital
She lay, a Babel of confused distress
Dinn'd with delirious strife.   But o'er her brow
God shook the dew of dreams wherein she trod
The shadow'd wood-walks of old days once more,
And dabbled in old streams.   Ere long, still weak,
Abroad she roam'd, a basket on her arm,
With violets heap'd.   The watchman of the city
Laid his strong hand upon her drooping head
Banning the impostor.   'Twas her rags, she thought,

Incensed him, and in meekness moved she on.
When one with lubrique smile toy'd with her flowers,
And spake of violet eyes and easier life,
She understood not, but misliked, and pass'd.
In Liverpool an aged priest she found,
A kinsman of her mother's.   Much to her
Of emigrants he spake. and of their trials,
Old ties annull'd, and 'mid temptations strange
Lacking full oft the Bread of Life.   She wept ;
Before the tabernacle's lamp she pray'd,
Freshly-absolved and heavenliest, with a prayer
That shower'd God's blessing o'er the wanderers
        down ;
But dead was her desire to cross the main.
Her strength restored, beyond the city bound
With others of her nation she abode,
Amid the gardens labouring.   A rough clan
Those outcasts seem'd ; not like their race at home :
Nor chapel theirs, nor school.   Their strength was
        prized ;
Themselves were so esteem'd as that sad tribe
Beside the Babylonian streams that wept,
By those that loved not Sion.
                        Weeks grew months ;
And, with the strength to suffer, sorrow came.
Hard by their nomad camp a youth there lived
Of wealthier sort, who look'd upon this maid :
Her country was his own : he loved it not ;
Had rooted quickly in the stranger's land ;
And versatile, cordial, specious, seeming-frank,

Contracting for himself a separate peace,
Had prosper'd, but had prosper'd in such sort
As they that starve within.   Her confidence
He gain'd.   To love unworthy, still he loved her:
Loved with the love of an unloving heart—
That love which either is in shallows lost,
Or in its black depth breeds the poison weed.
She knew him not; how could she?   He himself
Knew scantly.   Near her what was best within him
Her golden smile sunn'd forth ; but, dark and cold,
Like a benighted hemisphere abode
A moiety of his being which she saw not.
His was a superficial nature, vain,
And hard, to good impressions sensitive,
And most admiring virtues least his own ;
A mirror that took in a seeming world,
And yet remain'd blank surface.   He was crafty,
Follow'd the plough with diplomatic heart ;
His acts were still like the knight's move at chess.
Each a surprise ; not less, to nature's self
Who heard him still referr'd them.   " What !" men said,
        " Marry the portionless !"   Strange are fortune's
            freaks !
The wedding-day was fix'd, the ring brought home,
When from a distant uncle tidings came :
His latest son was dead.   " Take thou my farm,
" And share my house "—So spake the stern old
            man—
" And wed the wife whom I for thee have found."

He show'd the maid that letter.   Slowly the weeds
Made way adown the thick and stifled stream,
And others follow'd ; slowly sail'd the cloud
Through the dull sky, and others follow'd slowly :
At last he spake.   Low were his words and thin,
Many, but scarcely heard. He asked—her counsel !
Her cheek one moment burn'd.   Death-cold, once
        more,
A little while she sat ; then rose and said :—
" You would be free ; I free you ; go in peace."
'Twas the good angel in his heart that loved her ;
'Twas not the man himself ! He wept, but went.
The woman of the house that night was sure
The girl had loved him not.   She thought not so
When, four months past, she mark'd her mouth,
        aside,
Tremble, his name but utter'd.

                        Sharp the wrong !
Yet they on Life's bewilder'd book would force
A partial gloss it bears not who assume
The injured wholly free from blame.   The world
Is not a board in squares of black and white,
Or else the judgment-executing tongue
Would lack probation.   Wrong'd men are not
        angels ;—
Wrong's chiefest sin is this—it genders wrong ;
So stands the offender in his own esteem
Exculpate ; while the feebly-judging starve
The just cause, babbling " mutual was the offence ! "
—The man was weak ; not wholly vile.   'Twas well,

Doubtless, to free him ; yet in after years,
When early blight had struck his radiant head,
The girl bewail'd the pride that left thus tempted
The man she loved ; arraign'd the wrath that left
     him   .
Almost without farewell.   His letter too,
Unopen'd she return'd. 'Twas strange ! so sweet—
Not less there lived within her, down, far down,
A fire-spring seldom waken'd !   When a child
At times, by some strange jealousy disturb'd,
From her still dream she flash'd in passion quell'd
Ere from her staider sister's large blue eyes
The astonishment had pass'd.   Such mood remain'd,
Though rare—that wrath of tender hearts, which
     scorns
Revenge, which scarcely utters its complaint,
And yet forgives but slowly.
                    In those days
Within the maiden's bosom there arose
Sea-longings, and desire to sail away
She knew not whither ; and her arms she spread,
Weeping, to winds and waves, and shores unknown,
Lighted by other skies ; and inly thus
She reason'd, self-deceived.   " What keeps thee here?
" 'Twas for a farther bourne thou bad'st farewell
" To those at home, and here thou art as one
" That hangs between two callings."   In her heart
Tempests low-toned to ocean-tempests yearn'd,
And ever when she mark'd the shipmast forest
That on the smoky river sway'd far off

Her wish became a craving.   Soon once more
Alone 'mid hundreds on a rain-wash'd deck
She stood, and saw the billows heave around,
And all the passions of that headlong world.
Dark-visaged ocean frown'd with hoary brows
Against dark skies; huge, lumbering water-weights
Went shouldering through the abysses: streaming
        clouds
Ran on the lower levels of the wind;
And in the universe of things she seem'd
An atom random blown.   Full many a morn
Rose red through mists, like babe that weeps to rise;
Full many an evening died from wave to wave;—
Then gradual peace possess'd her.   Love may wound,
But 'tis self-love that wound exasperates;
A noble nature casts out bitterness,
And o'er the scar, like pine-tree incorrupt,
Weeps healing gums.   Heart-whole she gazed at last,
On the great city chiefest of that realm
Which wears the future's glory.   Landed, soon
Back to old duties with a mightier zest
Her heart, its weakening sadness pass'd, return'd;
Kindness made service easier; and the tasks
At first distasteful, smiled on her ere long.
There she was loved once more; there all went well;
And there in peace she might have lived and died;
Yet in that region she abode not long.
In part a wayward instinct drave her forth;
In part a will that from the accomplish'd end
Unstable swerved; in part a hope forlorn.

A site she sought, their sojourn who had left
Long since her village.   There old names, old
          voices,
Faces unknown, yet recognized, throng'd round her
In unconsummate union, (hearts still like,
Yet all beside so different,) not like Souls
Re-met in heaven—more like those Shades antique
That, 'mid the empurpled fields, of other airs
Mindful, in silence trod the lordly land,
Or flock'd around the latest guest of Death
With question sad of home.   Imperfect ties
Rub severance into soreness.   Mary pass'd,
Thus urged, ere long to lonelier climes.   She track'd
Companion'd sometimes, sometimes without friend,
The boundless prairie, sail'd the sea-like lake,
Descended the broad river as it rush'd
Through immemorial forests :—lastly stood
Sole, 'mid that city by the southern sea.

    There sickness fell upon her : there her hand
Dropt, heavier daily, on her task half done ;
Her feet wore chains unseen.   The end, she thought,
Was coming.   Ofttimes, in her happier days,
She wish'd to die and be with God : yet now,
Wearied by many griefs, to life she clung,
Upbraiding things foregone and inly sighing
" None loves to die."   Sorrow, earth-born, in some
Breeds first the Earth-infection ; in them works,
Like those pomegranate seeds that barr'd from light
For aye sad Ceres' child ! Alas ! how many,

The ill-honour'd ecstacies of youth surceased,
Exchange its clear spring for the mire! Hope sick,
How oft Faith dies! How few are they in whom
Virgin but yields to Vestal; casual pureness
Merged in essential; childhood's matin dew
Fix'd, ere exhaled, in the soul's adamant!
Mary with these had part: to her help came—
That help the proud despise. One eve it chanced
Upon the vast and dusking quays she stood
Alone and weeping. She that morn had sent
Her latest hoardings to her grandmother;
And half was sorry she had nought retain'd:
The warm rain wet her hair : she heard within
The silver ringing of its drops commingling
With that still mere beside her childhood's home,
And with the tawny sedge that girt it round,
And with its winter dogwood far away
Reddening the faint, still gleam. As thus she stood
Upon her shoulder sank a hand. She turn'd :
It was a noble lady, clothed in black,
And veil'd. That veil thrown back, she recognized
At once the luminous stillness and the calm
Ethereal which the sacred cloister breeds.
A voice as pure and sweet as if from heaven
Toned, as friend speaks to friend, address'd her
         thus :—
" You lack a home : our convent is hard by."

    The lady, Spanish half, and Irish half,
No answer sought; but with compulsion soft

Drew her, magnetic, as the tree hard by
Draws the poor creeper on the ground diffused,
And lifts it into light.   The child's cold hand
Lurk'd soon in hers : and in that home which seem'd
An isle of heaven the meek lay-sister lived,
(Ere long by healthier airs to strength restored,)
A rapturous life of Christian freedom, mask'd
In what but servitude had been to one
Lacking vocation true.   The Life Divine,
" Hidden with God," is hidden from the world,
Lest Virtue should be dimm'd by Virtue's praise.
With men heroic Virtue least is prized :
The hero in the saint the crowd can honour,
The saint at best forgive.   To this world's ken
Convents, of sanctity chief citadels,
(Though sanctity in every place is found,)
The snowy banners and bright oriflambs
Of that resplendent realm by Counsels ruled,
Not Precept only, spread in vain, despised,
Or for their accidental good revered,
Not for their claims celestial.   Different far
The lesson Mary learn'd.   The poor were fed,
The orphan nursed ; around the sick man's couch
Gentle as light hover'd the healing hand ;
And beautiful seem'd, on mountain-tops of truth,
The foot that brought good tidings : times of trial
Were changed to sabbaths ; and the rude, rough girl,
Waiting another service, found a home
Where that which years had marr'd return'd once
          more

Like infant flesh clothing the leprous limb.
Yet these things Mary found were blossoms only:
The tree's deep root was secret. From the vow
Which bound the Will's infinitude to God,
Upwell'd that peaceful strength whose fount was God:
From Him behind His sacramental veil
In holy passion, for long hours adored,
Came that great Love which made the bonds of earth
Needless, thence irksome. Wondering, there she
        learn'd
The creature was not for the creature made,
But for the sole Creator; that His kingdom,
Glorious hereafter, lies around us here,
Its visible radiance painfully suppressing,
And waiting its transfigurance. Was it strange,
If while those brides of Christ around her moved
Her heart sang hymns to God? Much had she
        suffer'd:
Much of her suffering gladly there she learn'd
Came of her fault; and much had kindliest ends
Not yet in her fulfill'd. A light o'ershone her
Which slays Illusion, that white snake which slimes
The labyrinth of self-love's more tender ways—
Virtue's most specious mimic. She was loosed:—
The actual by the seeming thraldom slain;
Her life was from within and from above;
And as, when Winter dies, and Spring new-born
Her whisper breathes o'er earth, the earlier flowers
(Unlike the wine-dark growths of Autumn, dipp'd
In the year's sunset,) rise in lightest hues,

An astral gleam, white, green, or delicate yellow,
More light than colour, so the maiden's thoughts
Flash'd with a radiance that permitted scarce
Human affections tragic.   Oft, she told me,
As faithless to old friends she blamed herself:—
One hand touch'd Calvary, one the Eternal Gates;
The present nothing seem'd.   The years pass'd on:
The honey-moon of this heart-bridal waned;
But nothing of its spousal truth was lost,
Nor of its serious joy.   If failures came—
And much she marvell'd at her slow advance;
And for the first time (pierced by that stern grace
Wherein no sin looks trivial) fear'd; what then?
Failures that deepen'd humbleness, but sank
Foundations deeper for a loftier pile
Of solid virtue: transports homeward summon'd
For more disinterested love made way,
More perfect made obedience.

                     If a Soul,
Half-way to heaven, death past, once more to earth
Were sent, it could but feel as Mary felt
When on the convent grates a letter smote
Loud, harsh, with summons from the outward world.
Her sister, such its tidings, was a wife,
(That matron whom you praised :—ay, comely is she,
And good; laborious, kindly, faithful, true;
Yet Time has done Time's work, her spiritual beauty
Transposing gently to a lower key ;)
Her grandmother bereft, and weak through age,
Needed her tendance sorely.   Would she come?

Alas ! what could she ? Duty from afar
An iron hand stretch'd on her mounting steps ;
The little novices alone said " stay ! "
Upon her neck the saintly sisterhood
Wept their last blessing ; then she turn'd and went.

And so once more she trod this rocky vale,
And scarcely older look'd at twenty-six
Than at sixteen. Before so gentle, now
A humbler gentleness was o'er her thrown ;
Nor ruffled was she ever as of yore
With gusts of flying spleen : nor fear'd she now
Hindrance unlovely, or the word that jarr'd.
The sadness hers at first dispersed ere long,
And such strange sweetness came to her men said
A mad dog would not bite her. Lowliest toils
Were by her hand ennobled : Labour's staff
Beneath it burst in blossom. In the garden,
'Mid earliest birds, and singing like a bird,
She moved, her grandmother asleep. She mix'd
The reverence due to years with tenderness
The infant's claim. 'Twas hers the crutch to bring,
Nor mark the lameness ; hers with question apt
To prompt, not task, the memory. Tales twice-told
Wearied not her, nor orders each with each
At odds, nor causeless blame. Wiles she had many
To anticipate harsh moods, lest one rash word
Might draw a cloud 'twixt helpless eld and heaven,
Blotting the Eternal Vision felt, not seen,
By those in grace. With works of gay caprice,

Needless—yet prized—she made the spectre Want
Seem farther off.   Thus love in narrow space
Built a great world.   The grandmother preferr'd
To her, that dreamful girl of old, the woman
Who from the mystic precinct first had learn'd
Humanity, yet seem'd a human creature
By some angelic guest o'er-ruled.   At heart
Ever a nun, she minister'd with looks
That heal'd the sick.   The newly-widow'd door
Its gloom remitted when she pass'd; stern foes
Down trod their legend of old wrongs.   To her
Sacred were those that grieved;—those not yet
          stricken
Sacred scarce less because they smiled, nor knew
The ambush'd fate before them.   When a child
Grey-hair'd companionship or solitude
Had pleased her more than childish ways; but now
All the long eves of summer in the porch
The children of her sister and the neighbours,
A spotless flock, sat round her.   From her smiles
The sluggish mind caught light, the timid heart
Courage and strength.   Unconscious thus, each
          day
Her soft and blithesome feet one letter traced
In God's great Book above.   So pass'd her life;—
Sorrow had o'er it hung a gentle cloud;
But, like an autumn-mocking day in Spring,
Dewy and dim, yet ending in pure gold,
The sweets were sweeter for the rain, the growth
Stronger for shadow.

                You have seen her tomb!
Upon the young and beautiful it closed.
Her grandmother yet lingers.　What is Time?
Shut out the sun, and all the summer long
The fruit-tree stands as barren as the rock;
May's offering March can bring us.　Of the twain
The younger doubtless in the eyes of God
Had inly lived the longest.　She had learn'd
From action much, from suffering more, far more,
For stern experience is a sword whose point
Makes way for Truth.　Her trials, great and little,
And trials ever keep proportion just
With high vocations, and the spirit's growth,
Had done their work till all her inner Being
Freed from asperities, in the light of God
Shone like the feet of some old crucifix
Kiss'd into smoothness.　Here I fain would end,
Leaving her harbour'd; but her stern, kind fates
Not thus forwent her.　Like her life her death,
Not negative or neutral; great in pains,
In consolations greater.　Many a week
Much ail'd her, and yet what remain'd in doubt;
When certainty had come she trembled not.
Fix'd was her heart.　Those pangs that shook her
    frame,
Like tempests roaring round a mountain church,
Shook not that peace within her! She was thank-
    ful;
" More pain if such Thy Will, and patience more,"
This was her prayer; or wiping from moist eyes

The trembling tear, she whisper'd, " Give me, Lord,
" On earth Thy cleansing fire that I may see
" Sooner Thy Face, death past ! "

                                Alleviations,
Many and great, God granted her.   Once more
Her sister was her sister !   Unlike fortunes
Had placed at angles those two lives that once
Lay side by side ; and love that could not die
Had seem'd to sleep.   It woke ; and, as from mist,
Once more shone out their childhood ! Laugh'd and flash'd
Once more the garden-beds whose bright accost
Had cheer'd them for their parents mourning.   Tears
Remember'd stay'd the course of later tears ;
The prosperous from the unprosperous sister sought
Heart-peace ; nor wealth nor care could part them more ;
And sometimes Margaret's children seem'd to her
As children of another !   Greetings sweet
Cheer'd her from distant regions. Once it chanced
The nuns a relic sent her ne'er before
Seen in our vales, a fragment of that Cross
Whereon the world's Redeemer hung three hours :—
The neighbours entering knelt and wept, and smote
Their breasts ; her hands she raised in prayer ; and straight
Such Love, such Reverence in her heart there rose
Her anguish, like a fiend exorcised, fled ;
And for an hour at peace she lay as one
Imparadised.   A solace too was hers

Known but to babes. Her body, not her mind
Was rack'd; the pang to come she little fear'd,
Nor lengthen'd out morose the pang foregone:
Once gone, to sleep she sank in thankful prayer.

A week ere Mary died all suffering left her;
And from the realms of glory beams, as though
Further restraint they brook'd not, fell on her
Yet militant below, as there she lay
In monumental whiteness, spirit-lit.
The anthems of her convent charm'd once more
Her dreams; and scents from woods where she had
        sat
In tears. Then spake she of her wandering days;
Herself she scarcely seem'd to see in them;
Plainly thus much I saw:—When all went well
Danger stood nigh; but soon as sorrow came
Within that darkness nearer by her side
Walk'd her good Angel. In that latest week
Some treasures hidden ever near her heart
She show'd me:—faded flowers; her mother's hair;
Gold pieces that have raised our chapel's cross;
A riband by her youthful comrade worn:—
Upon its cover some few words I found
There traced when first beyond the western main
She heard the homeless cuckoo's cry well-known:
" When will my People to their land return?"

From the first hour her grandchild sank, once more
She that for years bed-ridden lay had risen,

And, autumn past, put forth a wintry strength,
Ministering.   Her frame was stronger than her
       mind;
O'er that at times a dimness hung, like cloud
That creeps from pine to pine.   Inly she miss'd
Her wonted place of homage lost; she mused
Sadly upon the solitary future:
But in her there abode a rock-like will,
And from her tearless service night or day
No man might push her.   Seldom did she speak;
She call'd her grandchild by her daughter's name
(Her daughter buried thirty years and more)
And once she said in wrath, " Why toil they thus?
" Nora is dead."   She labour'd till the end:—
It came—that mortal close !   'Twas Christmas Eve;
Far, far away we heard the city bells :
The sufferer slept.   At midnight I went forth;
Along the ice-film'd road a dull gleam lay,
And a sepulchral wind in woods far off
Sang dirges deep.   Upon her crutches bent
The aged woman stood beside the door,
With that long gaze intense which is an act
Silently looking towards that hill of graves
We trod to-day;—a sinking moon shone o'er it—
Then whisper'd she at last: " Each Saturday,
" Of those that in that churchyard sleep three Souls,
" Their penance done, ascend, and are with God."

     Thus as she spake a cry was heard within,
And many voices raised the Litany

For a departing Soul.   Long time—too long—
Had seem'd that dying !   Now the hour was come,
And change ineffable announced that Death
At last was standing on the floor.   Oh, hour,
When in brief space our life is lived again ;
Down cast the latest stake ! when fiends ascend,
Beckoning the phantoms of sins forgotten
Conscience to scare, or launching as from slings
Temptations new ; while Angels hold before us
The Cross unshaken as the sun in heaven,
And whisper, " Christ."   Oh, hour, when prayer
        is all ;
And they that clasp the hand are thrown apart
By the world's breadth from that they love !   The act
Sin's dread bequest, that makes an end of sinning,
Long lasted, while the heartstrings snapt, and all
The elements of the wondrous sensuous world
Slid from the fading sense, and those poor fingers,
As the loose precipice of life down crumbled,
Pluck'd at the roots.   Storm-wing'd the hours
        rush'd by ;—
There lay she like some barque on midnight seas,
Now toiling through the windless vale, anon
Hurl'd on and up to meet the implacable blast
Upon the rolling ridge, when not a foot
Can tread the decks, and all the sobbing planks
Tremble o'erspent.   The morning dawn'd at last,
Whitening the frosty pane ; the lights removed,
(Save that tall candle in her hand sustain'd
By others) she beheld it : " Ah," she said,

" Thank God, another day!"   Then, noting one
Who near her knelt, she said, " The night is sped,
" And you have had no sleep; alas! I thought
" Ere midnight I should die."   Her eyelids closed;
Into a sleep as quiet as a babe's
Gradual she sank; and while the ascending sun
Shot 'gainst the western hill his earliest beam
In sleep, without a sigh, her spirit pass'd.

I would you could have seen her face in death!
I would you could have heard that last dread rite,
The mighty Mother's, o'er the stormy gulf
And all the moanings of the unknown abyss
Flinging victorious anthems, or the strength
Of piercing prayer: " O ye at least, my friends.
" Have pity on me; plead for me with God!"—
That rite complete, the dark procession wound
Interminably through the fields and farms,
While wailing, like a midnight wind, the *keen*,*
Expired o'er moor and heath.   At eve we reach'd
The graveyard; slowly, as to-day, the sun
Behind a tomb-like bank of leaden cloud
Dropt while the coffin sank, and died away
The latest Miserere——
                    More than once
I would have ceased; but he, my friend and guest,
Or touch'd or courteous, will'd me to proceed.
Perhaps that tale the wild scene harmonized
By sympathy occult; perhaps it touch'd him,

---

* The Irish funeral cry.

Contrasting with his recent life—with England;
With Oxford, long his home ; its order'd pomp ;
Its intermingled groves, and fields, and spires,
Its bridges spanning waters calm and clear ;
The frequentation of its courts ; its chimes ;
Its sunset towers, and strangely youthful gardens
That breathe the ardours of the budding year
On the hoar breadth of grove-like cloisters old,
Chapels, and libraries, and statued halls,—
England's still saintly city !   Time has there
A stone tradition built like that all round
Woven by the inviolate hedges, where the bird
Her nest has made and warbled to her young,
May after May secure, since the third Edward
Held his last tournament, and Chaucer sang
To Blanche and to Philippa lays of love—
Not like Iernian records.   Homeward walking,
Swiftly we trod the moonlight-spotted rocks :
My friend now spake once more, remark or question
Brimful with pregnant matter oft more just
In thought than application ; and his voice
Was softer than it used to be.   At last,
After our home attain'd, we turn'd, and lo !
With festal fires the hills were lit !   Thine eve,
Saint John, had come once more ; and for thy sake
As though but yesterday thy crown were won,
Amid their ruinous realm uncomforted
The Irish people triumph'd.   Gloomy lay
The intermediate space ;—thence brightlier burn'd
The circling fires beyond it.   " Lo !" said I,

" Man's life as view'd by Ireland's sons; a vale
" With many a pitfall throng'd, and shade, and briar,
" Yet overblown by angel-haunted airs,
" And by the Light Eternal girdled round."

Brief supper past, within the porch we sat
As fire by fire burn'd low. We spake ;—were mute ;
Resumed ; but our discourse was gently toned,
(Touch'd by a spirit from that wind-beaten grave,
Which breathed among its pauses) as of old
That converse Bede records, when by the sea,
'Twixt Tyne and Wear, facing toward Lindisfarne,
Saxon Ceolfrid and his Irish guest,
Evangelist from old Iona's isle,
'Mid the half Pagan land in cloisters dim
Discuss'd the Tonsure, and the Paschal time,
Sole themes whereon, in sacred doctrine one,
They differ'd : but discuss'd them in such sort
That mutual reverence deeper grew. We heard
The bridgeless brook that sang far off, and sang
Alone : for not among us builds that bird
Which changes light to music, haply ill-pleased
That Ireland bears not yet, in song's domain,
To Spenser worthy fruit. Our beds at last,
Wearied, yet glad, we sought. Ere long the wind,
Gathering its manifold voices and the might
Of all its wills in valleys far, and roll'd
From wood to wood o'er ridge and ravine, woke
A hundred peaks to me by sound well known,
That stood dark-cluster'd in the night, and hung

With rainy skirt o'er lake and prone morass,
Or by sea-bays lean'd out procumbent brows
Waiting the rising sun.
                    At morn we met
Once more, my friend and I.   The evening's glow
Had from his feelings pass'd : in their old channels
They flow'd, scarce tinged.   But still his thoughts
        retain'd
The trace of late impressions quaintly link'd
With kindred thought-notes earlier.   Half his mind
Scholastic was ; his fancy deep ; the age
Alone had stamp'd him modern.   Much he spake
Of England, wise and wealthy, now no more,
He said, " a haughty nation proud in arms,"
Nor, as in Saxon times, a crownèd child
Propp'd 'gainst the Church's knee ; but ocean's Queen,
Spanning the world with glittering zone twin-clasp'd
By Commerce and by Freedom !   But no less
Of pride and suffering spake he, and that frown
Sun-press'd on brows once pure.   Of Ireland next :—
" How strange a race, more apt to fly than walk ;
" Soaring yet slight : missing the good things round
        " them,
" Yet ever out of ashes raking gems ;
" In instincts loyal, yet respecting law
" Far less than usage : changeful, yet unchanged :
" Timid, yet enterprising : frank, yet secret :
" Untruthful oft in speech : yet living truth,
" And truth in things divine to life preferring :—
" Scarce men ;—yet possible angels !—' Isle of
        " Saints !'

" Such doubtless was your land—again it might be—
" Strong, prosperous, manly never ! ye are Greeks
" In intellect, and Hebrews in the soul :—
" The solid Roman heart, the corporate strength
" Is England's dower !"   " Unequally if so,"
I said, " in your esteem the isles are match'd :—
" They live in distant ages, alien climes ;
" Native they are to diverse elements :
" Our swan walks awkwardly upon dry land ;
" Your boasted strength in spiritual needs so helps
          " you
" As armour helps the knight who swims a flood."
He laugh'd.   " At least no siren streams for us,
" Nor holy wells. We love ' the fat of the land,'
" Meads such as Rubens painted ! Strange our fates !
" Our feast is still the feast of fox and stork,
" The platter broad, and amphora long-neck'd ;
" Ill sorted yoke-mates truly.   Strength, mean-
          " while,
" Lords it o'er weakness !"   " Never yet," I an-
          swer'd,
" Was husband vassal to an intricate wife
" But roar'd he ruled her ;" ere his smile had ceased
Continuing thus :—" Ay ! strength o'er weakness
          " rules !
" Strength hath in this no choice.   But what is
          " Strength ?
" Two strengths there are.   Club-lifting Hercules,
" A mountain'd mass of gnarl'd and knotted sinews,
" How shows he near the intense, Phœbean Might

" That, godlike, spurns the ostent of thews o'er-
      " grown ;
" That sees far off the victory fix'd and sure,
" And, without effort, wings the divine death
" Like light, into the Python's heart ?—My friend,
" Justice is strength ; union on justice built ;—
" Good-will is strength—kind words—silence—that
      " truth
" Which hurls no random charge.   Your scribes
      " long time
" Blow on our island like a scythèd wind :
" The good they see not, nor the cause of ill :
" They tear the bandage from the wound half-
      " heal'd :—
" Is not such onset weakness?   Were it better,
" Tell me, free-trader staunch, for sister nations
" To make exchange for aye of scorn for scorn,
" Or blend the nobler powers and aims of each,
" Diverse, and for that cause correlative,
" True commerce, noblest, holiest, frankest, best,
" And breed at last some destiny to God
" Glorious, and kind to man ?—The choice is yours."

Thus as we spake, the hall clock vast and old,
A waif from Spain's Armada, chimed eleven :
And from the stables drew a long-hair'd boy
Who led a horse as shaggy as a dog,
A splenetic child of thistles and hill blast,
Rock-ribb'd, and rich in craft of every race
From weasel to the beast that feigns to die.

Mourning—alas! that friends should ever part,—
My guest bade thus adieu:—" For good or ill
" Our lands are link'd."   And I rejoin'd, " For
        which ?—
" This shall you answer when, your pledge fulfill'd,
" Before the swallow you return. and meet
" The unblown Spring in our barbaric vale."

ODE TO THE DAFFODIL.

I.

O LOVE-STAR of the unbeloved March,
        When, cold and shrill,
Forth flows beneath a low, dim-lighted arch
    The wind that beats sharp crag and barren hill,
    And keeps unfilm'd the lately torpid rill!

II.

        A week or e'er
Thou com'st thy soul is round us everywhere;
    And many an auspice, many an omen,
    Whispers, scarce-noted, thou art coming.
Huge, cloud-like trees grow dense with sprays and
        buds,
    And cast a shapelier gloom o'er freshening grass,
And through the fringe of ragged woods
    More shrouded sunbeams pass.

Fresh shoots conceal the pollard's spike
 The driving rack outbraving ;
The hedge swells large by ditch and dike ;
And all the uncolour'd world is like
 A shadow-limn'd engraving.

III.

Herald and harbinger ! with thee
Begins the year's great jubilee !
 Of her solemnities sublime
(A sacristan whose gusty taper
Flashes through earliest morning vapour),
 Thou ring'st dark nocturns and dim prime.
 Birds that have yet no heart for song
 Gain strength with thee to twitter ;
And, warm at last, where hollies throng,
 The mirror'd sunbeams glitter.
With silk the osier plumes her tendrils thin :
 Sweet blasts, though keen as sweet, the blue lake
   wrinkle ;
And buds on leafless boughs begin
 Against grey skies to twinkle.

IV.

To thee belongs
A pathos drown'd in later scents and songs !
Thou com'st when first the Spring
 On Winter's verge encroaches ;
When gifts that speed on wounded wing
 Meet little save reproaches !

Thou com'st when blossoms blighted,
  Retracted sweets, and ditty,
From suppliants oft deceived and spited
  More anger draw than pity!
Thee the old shepherd, on the bleak hill-side,
  Far distant eyeing leans upon his staff
Till from his cheek the wind-brush'd tear is dried:
  In thee he spells his boyhood's epitaph.
To thee belongs the youngling of the flock,
  When first it lies, close-huddled from the cold,
Between the sheltering rock
  And gorse-bush slowly over-crept with gold.

v.

        Thou laugh'st, bold outcast bright as brave,
When the wood bellows, and the cave,
  And leagues inland is heard the wave!
  Hating the dainty and the fine
  As sings the blackbird thou dost shine!
Thou com'st while yet on mountain lawns high up
  Lurks the last snow-wreath:—by the berried
        breer
While yet the black spring in its craggy cup
  No music makes or charms no listening ear.
Thou com'st while from the oak stock or red beech
Dead Autumn scoffs young Spring with splenetic
        speech;—
When in her vidual chastity the Year
With frozen memories of the sacred past
  Her doors and heart makes fast,

And loves no flower save those that deck the bier :—
    Ere yet the blossom'd sycamore
    With golden surf is curdled o'er ;
    Ere yet the birch against the blue
    Her silken tissue weaves anew.
Thou com'st while, meteor-like 'mid fens, the weed
  Swims, wan in light ; while sleet-showers whiten-
    ing glare ;—
Weeks ere by river-brims, new furr'd, the reed
  Leans its green javelin level in the air.

VI.

    Child of the strong and strenuous East !
Now scatter'd wide o'er dusk hill bases,
Now mass'd in broad, illuminate spaces ;—
  Torch-bearer at a wedding feast
Whereof thou may'st not be partaker,
But mime, at most, and merry-maker ;—
Phosphor of an ungrateful sun
That rises but to bid thy lamp begone :—
    Farewell ! I saw
Writ large on woods and lawns to-day that Law
Which back remands thy race and thee
To hero-haunted shades of dark Persephoné.
To-day the Spring has pledged her marriage vow :
  Her voice, late tremulous, strong has grown and
    steady :
To-day the Spring is crown'd a queen : but thou
  Thy winter hast already !
Take my song's blessing, and depart,
  Type of true service—unrequited heart.

I.

ROUND me thy great woods sigh
    In their full-foliaged glory; but I die—
  Ah, blame me not; although,
Tired and o'er-spent, I never pray'd to go.
  In thine old towers I leave
A cradled pledge to take his mother's part;
  To vex thee not, nor grieve,
Yet lay, at times, my hand about thy heart.

II.

  Nearer, this dying past,
Bend nearer down that noble head at last;
  Lower and yet more low
Till o'er my brow a tear has leave to flow.
  Then the brief seizure quell;
And say that all is over, all is well:
  Say I lived—and died—
For this, and am in silence satisfied.

SONG.

LOVE laid down his golden head
　　On his mother's knee ;—
" The world runs round so fast," he said,
　" None has time for me."

Thought, a sage unhonour'd, turn'd
　　From the on-rushing crew ;
Song her starry legend spurn'd ;
　　Art her glass down threw.

Roll on, blind world, upon thy track
　　Until thy wheels catch fire !
For that is gone which comes not back
　　To seller nor to buyer !

LINES WRITTEN BESIDE THE LAGO VARESE.

(See Henry Taylor's Poem, entitled, " Lago Varese.")

I.

STILL rise around that lake well sung
　　New growths as boon and good
As when, by sunshine sadden'd, hung
　　Her Poet o'er that flood,
And sang, in Idyll-Elegy, a lay
Which praised things beauteous, mourning their
　　　　decay.

II.

As then great Nature, " kind to sloth,"
　　Lets drop o'er all the land
Her gifts, the fair and fruitful both,
　　Into the sleeper's hand :
On golden ground once more she paints as then
The cistus bower, and convent-brighten'd glen.

III.

Still o'er the flashing waters lean
　　The mulberry and the maize,
And roof of vines whose purple screen
　　Tempers those piercing rays,

Which here forego their fiercer shafts, and sleep,
Subdued, in crimson cells, and verdurous chambers
    deep.

IV.

    And still in many a sandy creek
      Light waves run on and up,
    While the foam-bubbles winking break
      Around their channell'd cup :
Against the rock they toss the bleeding gourd,
Or lap on marble stair and skiff unmoor'd.

V.

    Fulfill'd thus far the Poet's words :—
      And yet a truth that hour
    By him unsung upon his chords
      Descends, their ampler dower.
Of Nature's cyclic life he sang, nor knew
That frailer shape he mourn'd should bloom perpetual
    too.

VI.

    There still—not skilful to retract
      A glance as kind as keen—
    By the same southern sunset back'd
      There still that Maid is seen :
Through song's high grace there stands she ! from
    her eyes
Still beams the cordial mirth, the unshamed sur-
    prise !

VII.

Not yet those parted lips remit
    A smile that grows and grows:
The Titianic morning yet
    Breaks from that cheek of rose:
Still from her locks the breeze its sweetness takes:—
Around her white feet still the ripple fawns and
      rakes.

VIII.

And, bright'ning in the radiance cast
    By her on all around,
That shore lives on, while song may last,
    Love-consecrated ground ;
Lives like that isthmus, headland half half isle,
Which smiled to meet Catullus' homeward smile.

IX.

O Sirmio ! thou that shedd'st thy fame
    O'er old Verona's lake,
Henceforth Varese without blame
    Thine honours shall partake:
A Muse hath sung her, on whose front with awe
Thy nymphs had gazed as though great Virtue's self
      they saw !

X.

What Shape is that, though fair severe,
    Which fleets triumphant by
Imaged in yonder mirror clear,
    And seeks her native sky,

With locks succinct beneath a threat'ning crest—
Like Juno in the brow, like Pallas in the breast?

XI.

A Muse that flatters nothing base
    In man, nor aught infirm,
" Sows the slow olive for a race
    Unborn."   The destined germ,
The germ alone of Fame she plants, nor cares
What time that secular tree its shining fruitage
    bears ;

XII.

Pleased rather with her function sage—
    To interpret Nature's heart ;
The words on Wisdom's sacred page
    To wing, through metric art,
With life ; and in a chariot of sweet sound
Down-trodden Truth to lift, and waft, the world
    around.

XIII.

Hail Muse, whose crown, soon won or late,
    Is Virtue's not thine own !
Hail Verse, that tak'st thy strength and state
    From Thought's auguster throne !
Varese too would hail thee ! Hark that song—
Her almond bowers it thrills and rings her groves
    along !

Oct. 4, 1856.

SPRING SONG.

HOLD on, hold on, while yet ye can,
    Old oak-leaves red and sere ;
Hold on, and clasp in narrow span
    The sunset of last year !

Your boast is just ; yet, ancient friends,
    Forgive me if at times
On that green beech my glance descends,
    On that white thorn my rhymes.

The rookery from the wintry woods
    Clang'd like a cataract's roar :—
Each eve our closed eyes saw great floods
    O'er rocky barriers pour :

But now the linnet or the thrush
    So shakes with treble clear
Yon apple bloom—that alder bush,
    No meaner sound we hear !

'Tis true when Winter's furrow'd brow
    Through snow-drifts lower'd we praised
Those hollies, grim and threat'ning now,
    And dark though sunshine-glazed.

But constant who to such could be
    And this young Spring resist,
Who flings her arms round every tree,
    Nor leaves a bud unkiss'd?

Dusk cedar drest in rusty vest
    Through every season worn,
Thou stand'st the Mayday's wedding guest,
    Yet treat'st the bride with scorn.

Thy part I take:—yet be not vex'd
    If, here and there, I throw
A random glance to see where next
    You butterfly will go!

CREEP slowly up the willow-wand,
        Young leaves; and in your lightness
Teach us that spirits which despond
    May wear their own pure brightness!

Into new sweetness slowly dip,
    O May! advance, yet linger;
Nor let the ring too swiftly slip
    Down that new-plighted finger!

Thy bursting blooms, O Spring, retard:—
  While thus thy raptures press on
How many a joy is lost or marr'd,
  How many a lovely lesson !

For each new grace conceded, those
  The earlier-loved are taken ;
In death their eyes must violets close
  Before the rose can waken.

Ye woods with ice-threads tingling late,
  Where late we heard the robin,
Your chaunts that hour but antedate
  When autumn winds are sobbing.

Ye gummy buds, in silken sheath
  Hang back content to glisten !
Hold in, O Earth, thy charmed breath ;
  ' Thou air. be still, and listen !

LINES WRITTEN NEAR SHELLEY'S HOUSE AT LERICI.

DEDICATED TO J. W. FIELD, ESQ. IN MEMORY OF
A DAY PASSED WITH HIM AT LERICI.

I.

AND here he paced! These glimmering path-
    ways strewn
With faded leaves his light swift footsteps
    crush'd ;
The odour of yon pine was o'er him blown :
    Music went by him in each wind that brush'd
Those yielding stems of ilex ! Here, alone,
    He walk'd at noon, or silent stood and hush'd
When the ground-ivy flash'd the moonlight sheen
Back from the forest carpet always green.

II.

Poised as on air the lithe elastic bower
    Now bends, resilient now against the wind
Recoils, like Dryads that one moment cower
    And rise the next with loose locks unconfined.
Through the dim roof like gems the sunbeams
    shower ;
    Old cypress trunks the aspiring bay-trees bind,
And soon will have them wholly underneath :
Types eminent of glory conquering death.

III.

Far down upon the shelves and sands below
   The respirations of a southern sea
Beat with susurrent cadence, soft and slow:
   Round the grey cave's fantastic imagery,
In undulation eddying to and fro,
   The purple waves swell up or backward flee;
While, dew'd at each rebound with gentlest shock,
The myrtle leans her green breast on the rock.

IV.

And here he stood; upon his face that light,
   Stream'd from some furthest realm of luminous
      thought,
Which clothed his fragile beauty with the might
   Of suns for ever rising! Here he caught
Visions divine. He saw in fiery flight
   " The hound of Heaven," with heavenly ven-
      geance fraught,
" Run down the slanted sunlight of the morn"—*
Prometheus frown on Jove with scorn for scorn.

V.

He saw white Arethusa, leap on leap,
   Plunge from the Acroceraunian ledges bare
With all her torrent streams, while from the steep
   Alpheus bounded on her unaware:
Hellas he saw, a giant fresh from sleep,
   Break from the night of bondage and despair.

---

* " Prometheus Unbound."

Who but had sung as there he stood and smiled
" Justice and truth have found their wingèd child !"*

VI.

Through cloud and wave and star his insight keen
    Shone clear, and traced a God in each disguise,
Protean, boundless.   Like the buskinn'd scene
    All Nature rapt him into ecstasies :
In him, alas ! had Reverence equal been
    With Admiration, those resplendent eyes
Had wander'd not through all her range sublime
To miss the one great marvel of all time.

VII.

The winds sang loud ; from this Elysian nest
    He rose, and trod yon spine of mountains bleak,
While stormy suns descending in the west
    Stain'd as with blood yon promontory's beak.
That hour, responsive to his soul's unrest,
    Carrara's marble summits, peak to peak,
Sent forth their thunders like the battle-cry
Of nations arming for the victory.

VIII.

Visions that hour more fair more false he saw
    Than those the mythologic heaven that throng ;
Mankind he saw exempt from faith and law,
    Move godlike forth, with science wing'd and song ;

---

* " Revolt of Islam."

He saw the Peoples spurn religious awe,
   Yet tower aloft through inbred virtue strong.
Ah, Circe ! not for sensualists alone
Thy cup ! It dips full oft in Helicon !

IX.

Mankind he saw one equal brotherhood,
   All things in common held as light and air !—
" Vinum demonum ! "—Just, and wise, and good—
   Were man all this, such freedom man might bear !
The slave creates the tyrant ! In man's blood
   Sin lurks, a panther couchant in his lair.
Nature's confession came before the creed's ;—
Authority is still her first of needs.

X.

All things in common ; equal all ; all free !
   Not fancies these, but gifts reserved in trust.
A spiritual growth is Liberty ;
   Nature, unnatural made through hate and lust,
Yields it no more or chokes her progeny
   With weeds of foul desire or fell disgust.
Convents have all things common : but on grace
They rest. Inverted systems lack a base.

XI.

The more obedience to a law divine
   Tempers the chaos of man's heart, the less
Becomes his need of outward discipline
   The balance of injustice to redress.

" Wild Bacchanals of Truth's mysterious wine "*
  Must bear the Mænad's waking bitterness.
Anticipate not heaven.   Not great thy worth
Heaven without holiness, and heaven on earth !

XII.

Alas, the errors thus to truth so near
  That sovereign truths they are, though misapplied,
Errors to pure but passionate natures dear,
  Errors by aspirations glorified,
Errors with radiance crown'd like Lucifer
  Ere fall'n, like him to darkness changed through
      pride,
These of all errors are the heart and head ;—
The strength of life is theirs ; yet they are dead !

XIII.

That truth reveal'd, by thee in madness spurn'd,
  Plato, thy master in the walks of light,
Had knelt to worship ! For its day he yearn'd
  Through the long hungry watches of the night :
Its dawn in Thought's assumptions he discern'd
  Silvering hoar contemplation's star-loved height ;
The God-Man came !   Alas, thy phantasy,
A Man-God feigning, storm'd against his sky.

XIV.

Sorrowing for thee with sorrow joy is mix'd ;

---

* " Shelley's Ode to Liberty."

With triumph shame ! Our hopes themselves are
  sad ;
But fitful lustres break the shades betwixt ;
 So gleams yon olive bower, in mourning clad,
And yet at times with showery gleams transfix'd ;
 That opal among trees which grave or glad
Its furtive splendour half reveal'd or wholly
Shoots ever from a base of melancholy.

XV.

Our warfare is in darkness.   Friend for foe
 Blindly, and oft with swords exchanged, we strike.
Opinion guesses : Faith alone can know
 Where actual and illusive still are like.
Thine was that strength which fever doth bestow ;
 The madness thine of one that, fever-sick,
Beats a sad mother in distemper'd sleep—
Perhaps death woke thee, on her breast to weep !

XVI.

Thee from that Mother sins ancestral tore !—
 No heart hadst thou, from Faith's sole guide re-
  mote,
With statutable worship to adore,
 Or learn a nation-licensed creed by rote ;
No heart to snatch thy gloss of sacred lore
 From the blind prophet of the public vote.
Small help from such in life, or when thy pyre
Cast far o'er reddening waves its mirror'd fire !

XVII.

Hark ! She thou knew'st not mourns thee ! Slowly
     tolls,
  As sinks the sun, yon church-tower o'er the sea :
Abroad once more the peal funereal rolls,
  And Spezzia now responds to Lerici.
This day is sacred to Departed Souls ;
  This day the dead alone are great ; and we
Who live, or seem to live, but live to plead
For the departed myriads at their need.

XVIII.

Behold, the long procession scales the rock ;
  In the red glare dusk banners sadly wave !
Behold, the lambs of the immaculate flock
  Fling flowers on noted and on noteless grave !
Oh Cross ! sole Hope that dost not woo to mock !
  Some, some that knew thee not thou liv'st to save—
All spirits not wholly—by their own decree—
From infinite Love exiled, and lost to thee !

All Souls' Day, 1856.

VANITY.

SUGGESTED BY A PICTURE OF HERODIAS' DAUGHTER.

BY LUINI.

ALAS, Salome! Couldst thou know
     How great man is—how great thou art—
What destined worlds of weal or woe
     Lurk in the shallowest human heart,

From thee thy vanities would drop
     Like sins in noble anger spurn'd
By one who finds, beyond all hope,
     The passion of his youth return'd.

Ah, sunbright face whose brittle smile
     Is cold as sunbeams flash'd on ice!
Ah, lips how sweet yet hard the while!
     Ah, soul too barren even for vice!

Vanity's glittering mask! Those eyes
     No beam the less around them shed
Albeit in that red scarf there lies
     The dancer's meed—the prophet's head.

VANITY.

I.

FALSE and fair! Beware, beware!
    There is a tale that stabs at thee!
The Arab seer—he stripp'd thee bare,
    He told thy secret, Vanity!
By day a mincing foot is thine;
Thou runnest along the spider's line—
Ay! but heavy sounds thy tread
By night, among the uncoffin'd dead!

II.

Fair and foul! Thy mate, the ghoul,
    Beats, bat-like, on thy latticed gate;
Around the graves the night-winds howl;
    " Arise," they cry, " thy feast doth wait!"
Dainty fingers thine, and nice,
With thy bodkin picking rice!—
Ay! but when the night's o'erhead
Limb from limb they rend the dead!

CHAUCER.

ESCAPED from the city—its smoke, its glare—
   'Tis pleasant (showers over, and birds in
   chorus)
To sit in green alleys and breathe cool air
   Which the violet only has breathed before us!

Such healthful solace is ours, forsaking
   The glass-growths of modern and modish rhyme
For the music of days when the muse was breaking
   On Chaucer's pleasance in song's sweet prime.

Hands rubb'd together smell still of earth :—
   The hot-bed verse has a hot-bed taint :
'Tis sense turn'd sour, its cynical mirth :
   'Tis pride, its darkness : its blush, 'tis paint !

His song was a feast where thought and jest
   Like monk and franklin alike found place—
Good will's Round Table ! There sat as guest
   Shakespearian insight with Spenser's grace.

His England lay laughing in Faith's bright morn !
   Life in his eye look'd as rosy and round
As the cheek of the huntsman that blows on the horn
   When the stag leaps up, and loud bays the hound.

King Edward's tourney—fair Blanche's court—
    Their clarions, their lutes in his verse live on :
But he loved better the birds' consort
    Under oaks of Woodstock while rose the sun.

The cloister—the war-field tented and brave,
    The shout of the burghers in hostel or hall,
The embassy grave over ocean's wave,
    And Petrarch's converse—he loved them all.

In Spring, when the breast of the lime-grove gathers
    Its roseate cloud, when the flush'd streams sing,
And the mavis tricks her in gayer feathers ;
    Read Chaucer then ; for Chaucer is spring !

On lonely evenings in dull Novembers
    When streams run choked under skies of lead,
And on forest-hearths the year's last embers,
    Wind-heap'd and glowing, lie, yellow and red,

Read Chaucer still ! In his ivied beaker
    With knights, and wood-gods, and saints em-
        boss'd,
Spring hides her head till the wintry breaker
    Thunders no more on the far-off coast.

SONNET.

L OVE is historic ; rests upon the past ;
    Still lingers lovingly on old detail ;
  Still, like the holy bells, rings out a tale
For ever new, from earliest to last :
Love is prophetic ; climbing still the mast
    Discerns of distant hope the signal pale,
    And on the straining spar extends the sail
Withheld by colder counsels from the blast.
Mysterious delight in what is lost !
    Wild half fruition of what may be won
By struggling perseverance, tempest-toss'd !
Yet love in silence wrapt, and deep repose
    Whilst one short hour its hasty course can run,
May find more joy than many a lifetime knows !

S. E. S. R.

SONNET.

THINK not man's fallen nature can accept,
  Or, if accepting, value at their worth
Rites that lack splendour; slave of grief or mirth
By fleshly lusts he is in bondage kept.
Far less believe that splendid rites give birth
  To heartfelt sorrow, such as his, who " wept
  And smote upon his breast," for this man stept
With downcast eyes, not heeding aught on earth.
Man must employ in worship every power—
  Will, reason, understanding, heart, and sense;
  And should he on some dull or fond pretence
Neglect but one, then from devotion's flower
  He cuts a leaf that drank the heavenly dew,
  Or root, that purity from baseness drew.

S. E. S. R.

SONNET.

IF, task'd beyond my strength, I crave delay
    And weakly wish that to another hand
Had been committed what divine command
Has sent to mine; if on th' appointed way,
I pause, and, thoughtless of my purpose, stray;
    If wearied with the men, the clime, the land
    Which I call mine, I seek another strand,
That on the wings of chance I lightly may
Outstrip the homely cares which day by day
    Hum in my ears; if by myself I stand
Accused of all these faults, and cannot say
That I less subject am unto their sway
    Now than of old—you needs must understand
How rashly upon me new duties would you lay.

S. E. S. R.

SONNET.

SOFT sighing wind that comest to dispel
    The rigid bond that holds the buds so long
  As almost to provoke a sense of wrong
  In those who now have sadly watch'd them swell
Slowly, for weeks ; oh, would that I could tell
  How deep the joy thou bringest, and how strong !
  Oh, that I too could blossom into song,
And hail thee loosen'd from thy southern cell
Whilst all surrounding Nature seems to smile
  And bare her breast at thy sunbright approach.
Oh, wherefore hast thou tarried so long while ?
  Dear spirit ! tenderly must I reproach
Thee, dallying upon the Italian shore,
Or launching thence across the purple, smooth sea
    floor.

S. E. S. R.

ODE.

THE GOLDEN MEAN.

FORTUNE! unloved of whom are those
    On whom the Virtues smile,
Forbear the land I love, and choose,
    Choose still some meaner isle!
Thy best of gifts are gilded chains;
The gold wears off; the bond remains.

Thus much of good, nor more, is thine,
    That, clustering round the wand
Thou lift'st, with honey smear'd and wine,
    In that unqueenly hand,
Close-limed are trapp'd those sun-bred flies
Which else had swarm'd about the wise.

The vanities of fleeting time
    To powers that fleet belong;
They fear and hate the sons sublime
    Of science and of song,
And those that, scorn'd as weak, o'errule
The strong, and keep the world at school.

For how could Song her tenderer notes
    Elaborate for the ear
Of one on vulgar noise who doats,
    Of one through deserts drear
On rushing in that race distraught
Whose goad is hate, whose goal is nought?

And how could Science trust that line
    (Her labyrinth's sacred clue)
Of subtly-woven thought, more fine
    Than threads of morning dew,
To those unhallow'd hands and coarse,
The drudges base of greed or force?

Faith to the sensual and the proud
    Whom this world makes her prey,
But glimmers with the light allow'd
    To tapers at noonday;
When garish joys have ta'en their flight
Like stars she glorifies the night.

Nor less the Heroic Life extracts
    From circumstance adverse
Her food of sufferings and of acts;
    While pain, a rugged nurse,
On the rough breasts of wintry seas
Rocks it 'mid stormy lullabies.

Hail, Poor Estate! Through thee man's race
    Partake, by rules controll'd,

The praise of them dis-calced who pace,
　And them that kneel white-stoled ;
Where thou hast honours due, hard by
Obedience stands and chastity.

Hail, too, O bard, nor poor nor rich,
　Whom one blue gleam of sea
Binds to our British Cuma's beach ;—
　Our wealth we store in thee ;
To thee not wealth but worlds belong,
Like Delos raised ; such might hath song !

Through thee to him who treads that down
　Arch'd onward toward the west,
White cliff, green shore, and stubble brown
　In Idyll grace are dress'd ;
Beside low doors, a later Ruth,
Thy Dora sits—serene as truth.

O long with freedom's gale refresh'd,
　With mild sea-murmurs lull'd,
O long by thee, in cares unmesh'd,
　Those healthier flowers be cull'd
Rich Egypt knew not, nor the wain
That creak'd o'er deep Bœotian plain !

They lit Arcadian peaks: they breathed
　(Light soils have airs divine)
O'er Scio's rocks with ivy wreathed,
　Stern Parnes' brow, and thine,

Pentelicus, whose marble womb
With temples crown'd all-conqu'ring Rome.

Teach us in all that round us lies
 To see and feel, each hour,
More than Homeric majesties,
 And more than Phidian power:
Teach us the coasts of modern life
With lordlier tasks are daily rife

Than theirs who plunged the heroic oar
 Of old by Chersonese :—
But bid our Argo launch from shore
 Unbribed by golden Fleece.
Bid us Dædalean arts to scorn
Which prostituted ends suborn !

That science—slave of sense—which claims
 No commerce with the sky,
Is vainer yet than that which aims
 With waxen wing to fly !
To grovel, or self-doom'd to soar—
Mechanic age, be proud no more !

Lugano, Oct. 7, 1856.

WRITTEN IN ISCHIA.

HERE in this narrow island glen
 Between the dark hill and the sea,
Remote from books remote from men
 I sit; but O how near to thee!

I bend above thy broidery frame;
 I smell thy flowers; thy voice I hear:
Of Italy thou speak'st: that name
 Woke long thy wish—at last thy tear!

Hadst thou but watch'd that azure deep;
 Those rocks with myrtles mantled o'er;
Misenum's cape, yon mountains' sweep;
 The smile of that Circean shore!

But seen that crag's embattled crest,
 Whereon Colonna mourn'd alone,
An eagle widow'd in her nest—
 Heart strong and faithful to thine own!

This was not in thy fates. Thy life
 Lay circled in a narrower bound:
Child, sister, tenderest mother, wife—
 Love made that circle holy ground.

Love bless'd thy home—its trees, its earth,
    Its stones—that ofttimes trodden road,
Which link'd the region of thy birth
    With that till death thy still abode.

From the loud river's rocky beach,
    To that clear lake the woodlands shade,
Love stretch'd his arms.   In sight of each,
    The place of thy repose is made.

Feb. 1, 1859.

FROM terraced heights that rise in ranks,
    Thick set with almond, fig, and maize,
O'er waters blue as violet banks,
    I hear the songs of boyhood's days.

Up walnut slopes, at morn and eve,
    And downward o'er the pearly shore,
From Clarens on they creep ; nor leave
    Uncheer'd cold Chillon's dungeon-floor.

Fair girls that please a mother's pride—
    Bright boys from joy of heart that sing—
The voice of bridegroom and of bride—
    Through trellised vines how clear they ring !

For me they blot these southern bowers :
  The ghosts of years gone by they wake :
They send the drift of northern showers
  Low-whispering o'er a narrower lake.

Once more upon the couch he lies
  Who ruled his halls with stately cheer :
Waves slow the lifted hand ; with eyes
  And lips rewards the strains most dear.

And ah ! from yon empurpled slope
  What fragrance swells that arch beneath !
Geranium, jasmine, heliotrope—
  They stay my breath :—of her they breathe !

Flower-lover ! wheresoe'er thou art
  May flowers and sunshine greet thee still ;
And voices vocal to the heart—
  No sound approach of sad or ill !

Vevey, Sept. 15 1856.

ODE

TO IRELAND, AFTER ONE OF THE FAMINE YEARS.

I.

THE golden dome, the Tyrian dye,
  And all that yearning ocean
Yields from red caves to glorify
  Ambition, or devotion—
I leave them—leave the bank of Seine,
  And those high towers that shade it,
To tread my native fields again,
  And muse on glories faded.

II.

The monumental city stands
  Around me in its vastness,
Girdling the spoils of all the lands
  In war's imperial fastness.
That stony scroll of every clime
  Some record boasts or sample—
Cathedral piles of oldest time,
  Huge arch and pillar'd temple.

III.

They charge across the field of Mars ;—
    The earth beneath them shaking
As breaks a rocket into stars
    The column'd host is breaking.
It forms : it bursts :—new hosts succeed :
    They sweep, the Tuileries under :
The thunder from the Invalides
    Answers the people's thunder.

IV.

Behold ! my heart is otherwhere,
    My soul these pageants cheer not :
A cry from famish'd vales I hear,
    That cry which others hear not.
Sad eyes, as of a noontide ghost,
    Whose grief, not grace, first won me,
'Mid regal pomps ye haunt me most :—
    There most your power is on me !

V.

Last night, what time the convent shades,
    Far-stretch'd, the pavement darken'd
Where rose but late the barricades,
    Alone I stood, and hearken'd.
Thy dove-note, O my country, thine,
    In long-drawn modulation,
Went by me, link'd with words divine
    That stay'd all earthly passion !

VI.

A man entranced, and yet scarce sad,
    Since then I see in vision
The scenes whereof my boyhood had
    Possession, not fruition.
Dark shadows sweep the landscape o'er,
    Each other still pursuing;
And lights from sinking suns once more
    Grow golden on the ruin.

VII.

Dark violet hills extend their chains
    Athwart the saffron even,
Pure purple stains not distant plains:
    And earth is mix'd with heaven.
One cloud o'er half the sunset broods;
    And from its ragged edges
The wine-black shower descends like floods
    Down dash'd from diamond ledges.

VIII.

Through rifted fanes the damp wind sweeps,
    Chaunting a dreary psalter:
I smell the bones that rise in heaps
    Where rose of old the altar;
Once more beside the blessed well
    I see the cripple kneeling:
I hear the broken chapel bell,
    Where organs once were pealing.

IX.

I come, and bring not help, for God
    Withdraws not yet the chalice.
Still on your plains by martyrs trod
    And o'er your hills and valleys,
His name a suffering Saviour writes—
    Letters black-drawn, and graven
On lowly huts, and castled heights,
    Dim haunts of newt and raven.

X.

I come, and bring not song; for why
    Should grief from fancy borrow?
Why should a lute prolong a sigh,
    Sophisticating sorrow?
Dull opiates, down! To wind and wave,
    Lethean weeds, I fling you:
Anacreontics of the grave,
    Not mine the heart to sing you.

XI.

I come the breath of sighs to breathe,
    Yet add not unto sighing;
To kneel on graves, yet drop no wreath
    On those in darkness lying.
Sleep, chaste and true, a little while,
    The Saviour's flock, and Mary's:—
And guard their reliques well, O Isle,
    Thou chief of reliquaries!

XII.

Blessed are they that claim no part
  In this world's pomp and laughter:
Blessed the pure; the meek of heart:—
  Blest here; more blest hereafter.
' Blessed the mourners.' Earthly goods
  Are woes, the Master preaches:—
Embrace thy sad beatitudes,
  And recognize thy riches!

XIII.

And if, of every land the guest,
  Thine exile back returning
Finds still one land unlike the rest,
  Discrown'd, disgraced, and mourning;—
Give thanks! Thy flowers to yonder skies
  Transferr'd pure airs are tasting;
And, stone by stone, thy temples rise
  In regions everlasting.

XIV.

Sleep well, unsung by idle rhymes,
  Ye sufferers late and lowly;
Ye saints and seers of earlier times,
  Sleep well in cloisters holy!
Above your bed the bramble bends,
  The yew tree and the alder:—
Sleep well, O fathers, and O friends,
  And in your silence moulder!

SONNET.

ALONE, among thy books, once more I sit;
 No sound there stirs except the flapping fire:
Strange shadows of old times about me flit
As sinks the midnight lamp or flickers higher.
I see thee pace the room. With eye thought-lit
Back, back, thou com'st once more to my desire:
Low-toned thou read'st once more the verse new-
  writ,
Too deep, too pure for worldlings to admire.
That brow all honour, that all gracious hand,
That cordial smile, and clear voice musical,
That noble bearing, mien of high command,
Yet void of pride—to-night I have them all.
Ah, phantoms vain of thought! The Christmas air
Is white with flying flakes. Where art thou—
  where?

Christmas, 1860.

ODE TO IRELAND.

(AGAINST FALSE FREEDOM.)

I.

THE Nations have their parts assign'd:—
The deaf one watches for the blind:
The blind for him that hears not hears:
Harmonious as the heavenly spheres
Despite their outward fret and jar
Their mutual ministrations are.
Some shine on history's earlier page;
Some prop the world's declining age:—
One, one reserves her buried bloom
To flower perchance on Winter's tomb

II.

Greece, weak of will but strong in thought,
To Rome her arts and science brought.
Rome, strong yet barbarous, gain'd from her
A staff; but, like Saint Christopher,
Knew nor for whom his strength to use,
What yoke to bear, what master choose.
His neck the giant bent!—thereon
The Babe of Bethlehem sat! Anon
That staff his prop, that sacred freight
His guide, he waded through the strait,
And enter'd at a new world's gate

III.

On that new stage was play'd once more
The parts in Greece rehearsed before.
Round fame's Olympic stadium vast
Fiercely the emulous Nations raced ;
Now Spain, now France the headship won
(Unrisen the Russian Macedon):
But nought, O Ireland, like to thee
Hath been ! A Sphinx-like mystery,
At the world's feast thou sat'st death-pale ;
And blood-stains tinged thy widow'd veil.

IV.

Apostle, first, of worlds unseen !
For ages, then, deject and mean :—
Be sure, sad land, a concord lay
Between thy darkness and thy day.
Thy hand, had temporal gifts been thine,
Had lost, perchance, the things divine.
Truth's witness sole ! The insurgent North
Gave way when falsehood's flood went forth :
On the scarr'd coasts deform'd and cleft
Thou, like the church's rock, wert left.

V.

That Tudor tyranny which stood
'Mid wrecks of faith, was quench'd in blood
When Charles its child and victim lay
The Rebel-Prophet's bleeding prey.

Once more the unhappy wheel goes round!
Heads royal long are half discrown'd:
Ancestral rights decline and die:—
Thus Despotism and Anarchy
Alternate each the other chase,
Twin Bacchantes wreathed around one vase.

VI.

The future sleeps in night: but thou
O Island of the branded brow,
Her flatteries scorn who rear'd by Seine
Fraternity's ensanguined reign,
And for a sceptre twice abhorr'd
Twice welcome the Cesarian sword—
Thy past, thy hopes, are thine alone!
Though crush'd around thee and o'erthrown,
The majesty of civil might
The hierarchy of social right
Firm state in thee for ever hold!
Religion was their life and mould.

VII.

The vulgar dog-like eye can see
Only the ignobler traits in thee;
Quaint follies of a fleeting time;
Dark reliques of the oppressor's crime.
The seer marks in thee what the West
Has never yet elsewhere possess'd;
The childlike faith; the will like fate,
And that Theistic Instinct great

New worlds that summons from the abyss
" The balance to redress of this."

VIII.

Wait thou the end; and spurn the while
False Freedom's meretricious smile!
Stoop not thy front to anticipate
A triumph certain !   Watch and wait !
The schismatic, by blood akin
To Socialist and Jacobin,
Will claim, when shift the scales of power,
His natural place.   Be thine that hour
With good his evil to requite ;
To save him in his own despite ;
And backward scare the brood of night !

WINTER, that hung around us as a cloud,
    Rolls slowly backward; from her icy sleep
Th' awaken'd earth starts up and shouts aloud,
    The waters leap

From rock to rock with a tumultuous mirth,
    With Bacchanalian madness and loud song;
From the fond bosom of the teeming earth
    All young things throng;

And hopes rise bubbling from the deepest fountain
    Of man's half-frozen heart.   Faith trustingly
Rests its broad base on God, as doth a mountain
    Upon the sea.

Affections pure, and human sympathies
    The summer sun of charity relumes,
That fire divine that warms and vivifies,
    But not consumes.

Love, vernal music, charity, hope, faith,
    Warm the cold earth, fair visions from on high,
Teaching to scorn and trample fear of death;
    For nought can die.

S. E. de V.

STANZAS.

ALTHOUGH I know that all my love,
  My true love, is in vain; yet I
Must loose the strained cord that holds
My bursting heart within its folds,
    And love or die.

Dear is the breath of early Spring
  To the low-crouching violet;
The grateful river smiles upon
The glories of the sinking sun;
    But dearer yet

Than breath of Spring to the young flower,
  Or sun-burst to the clouded sea,
One glance of pity from thine eye,
The music of thy faintest sigh,
    Sweet love, to me.

This dreary world is very cold.
  A heavy sorrow presses down
My famish'd heart.   One tear-drop shed
In memory of the faithful dead,
    When I am gone.

S. E. de V.

ODE.

THE ASCENT OF THE APENNINES.

I.

I MOVE through a land like a land of dream,
  Where the things that are and that shall be seem
Woven into one by a hand of air,
And the Good looks piercingly down through the Fair!
No form material is here unmated;
  Here blows no bud, no scent can rise,
Nor a song ring forth, unconsecrated
  To some antetype in paradise!
Fall'n, like her lord, is elsewhere the earth;
Human, at best, in her sadness and mirth;
Or if she aspires after something greater,
  Uplifting her hands from her native dust,
  In God she beholds but the wise, the just;
The Saviour she sees not in the Creator:
But here, like children of saints who learn
  The things above ere the things below,
Who choirs angelic in clouds discern
  Ere the butterfly's wing from the moth's they
    know,
Great Nature as ashes all beauty reckons
  That claims not hereafter some happier birth;
She calls from the height to the depth; she beckons
  From the nomad waste to a heavenly hearth:

"The curse is cancell'd," she cries; "thou dreamer,
Earth felt the tread of the great Redeemer!"

II.

Ye who ascend with reverent foot
  The warm vale's rocky stairs
Forget not, though your lips be mute,
  Forget not in your prayers
The noble hands, now dust, that rear'd
  Long ages since on crag or sward
Those Stations that preach from their cells revered
  The Passion of the Lord!
Ah! unseductive here the breath
  Of the vine-bud that blows in the breast of morn;
Yon orange bower, that jasmine wreath
  Hide not the crown of thorn!
Here none can bend o'er the spring, and drink
  Of the waters that upward to meet him burst,
Nor see the sponge and the reed, and think
  Of the three hours' unquenched thirst.
The Tender, the Beauteous receives its comment
  From a truth transcendent, a life Divine;
And the coin flung loose of the passing moment
  Is stamp'd with Eternity's sign!

III.

Alas, for the wilder'd days of yore
When Nature lay vassal to pagan lore!
Baia—what was she? A sorceress still
To brute subduing the human will!

Nor pine could whisper nor breeze could move
　　But a breath infected ran o'er the blood
Like the gale that whitens the aspen grove
　　Or the gust that darkens the flood.
Along the ocean's gleaming level
In guise of wood-gods they held their revel;
Dances on the sea-sands knitting,
　　With shouts the sleeping shepherd scaring;
Like Oreads o'er the hill-side flitting,
　　Like Mænads thyrsus-bearing—
The Siren sang from the moonlit bay;
　　The Siren sang from the redd'ning lawn,
Until in the crystal cup of day
　　Had dissolved the pearl of dawn.
Unspiritual intelligence
Changed Nature's fane to a hall of sense,
That rings with the upstart spoiler's jest,
And the beakers clash'd by the drunken guest.

IV.

　　Hark to that convent bell!
　　False pagan world, farewell;
From cliff to cliff the challenge vaults rebounded!
　　Echo, her wanderings done,
　　Repose at last hath won,
The rest of love on Faith not Fancy founded;
" By the parch'd fountain let the pale flower blow,"
She sings, " the joy that fades, the illusive hope
　　　　forego!"

O hymns, O psalms, that sail
  Breeze-born adown thé gale,
From those still cloisters waft your peace below !
  Pure incense-wreaths that rise
  Like clouds into those skies,
O teach our hearts, so heavy faint and slow,
Released from flesh, at last toward regions stable
To mount above the fret of all things perishable !

V.

The plains recede ; the olives dwindle :
  The ilex and chestnut are left behind :
The skirts of the billowy pinewoods kindle
  In the evening lights and the wind.
Not here we sigh for the Alpine glory
  Of peak primeval and death-pale snow :
Not here for the cold green, and glacier hoary,
  Or the blue caves that yawn below.
The landscape here is mature and mellow ;
Fruit-like, not flower-like :—long hills embrown'd ;
Gradations of violet purple and yellow
  From flush'd stream to ridge church-crown'd :
'Tis a region of mystery, hush'd and sainted :
  As still as the dreams of those artists old
When the thoughts of Dante his Giotto painted :—
  The summit is reach'd ! Behold !
Like a sky condensed lies the lake far down ;
  Its curves like the orbit of some fair planet !
A fire-wreath falls on the cliffs that frown
  Above it—dark walls of granite !

Thick-set, like an almond tree newly budded,
  The hillsides with homesteads and hamlets glow :
With convent towers are the red rocks studded,
  With villages zoned below.
Down drops by the island's woody shores
The banner'd barge with its rhythmic oars.
No solitude here, no desert cheerless
  Is needed pure thoughts or pure hearts to guard :
'Tis a populous solitude, festal, fearless,
  For men of good will prepared.
The hermit may hide in the wood, but o'er it
  The chimes of a hundred bells are toll'd :
The black crag may woo the cloud, but before it
  The procession winds on white-stoled.
Farewell, O Nature ! None standeth here
But his heart goes up to a happier sphere !
The radiance around him spread forgetting,
  That city he sees on whose golden walls
No light of a rising sun, or setting,
  Of moon or of planet falls,
For the Lamb alone is the light thereof—
The City of Truth, the Kingdom of Love !

VI.

There shall the features worn and wasted
  Cast off the sullen mask of years :
There shall that fruit at last be tasted
  Whose seed was sown in tears.
There shall that amaranth bloom for ever
  Whose blighted blossom droop'd erewhile

In this dim valley of exile,
And by the Babylonian river.
The loved and lost once more shall meet us :
Delights that never were ours shall greet us :
Delights for the love of the Cross foregone
Fullfaced shall greet us, ashamed of none.
Heroes unnamed the storm that weather'd
    There, there, shall sceptred stand and crown'd :
Apostles the wilder'd flocks that gather'd
    Shall sit with the nations round.
There, heavenly sweets from the earthly bitter
    Shall rise like the odour of herbs down-trod :
There, tears of the past like gems shall glitter
    On the trees that gladden the mount of God.
The deeds of the righteous, on earth despised,
By the lightning of God immortalised
Shall crown like statues the walls sublime
    Of all the illuminate, mystic city,
Serenest emblems that conquer Time,
    Yet tell his tale.   That Pity
Which gave to the desolate strength to speak,
That Love its hand like an angel's stooping
On the grey old head, or the furrow'd cheek,
    Or the neck depress'd and drooping,
Shall live for ever, emboss'd or graven
On the chalcedon gates or the streets pearl-paven :
The Thoughts of the just, at a flash transferr'd
From the wastes of earth to the courts of the Word,
The hopes abortive, the frustrate schemes,

Shall lack not their place in the wond'rous session ;
The prayers of the Saints, their griefs, their dreams,
  Shall be manifest there in vision ;
For they live in the Mind Divine, their mould,
  That Mind Divine the unclouded mirror
Wherein the glorified spirits behold
  All worlds, undimm'd by error.

VII.

Fling fire on the earth, O God,
    Consuming all things base !
Fling fire upon man, his spirit and blood,
    The fire of Thy Love and Grace :
    That his heart once more to its natal place
Like a bondsman freed may rise,
    Ascending for ever before Thy face
From the altar of sacrifice !

    And thou, Love's comrade, Hope,
Without whom Virtue lacks her lordlier scope,
    Without whom man and nation
Perish, uncheer'd by spiritual aspiration ;
Van-courier of the ages ; Faith's strong guide,
That still the attain'd foregoest for the descried :—
On, Seraph, on, through night and tempest
        winging—
  On heavenward, on, across the void, vast hollow !
And be it ours, to thy wide skirts close clinging
  Blindly, like babes, thy rushing flight to follow.

What though the storm of Time roar on beside us?
  Though this world mock or chide us,
We shall not faint or fail until at last
The eternal shore is reach'd, all danger past!

May, 1859.

A MOTHER'S SONG.

I.

O TIME, whose silent foot down treads
  The kingly towers and groves,
Who lay'st on loftiest, loveliest heads,
  The hand that no man loves,
Take all things else beneath the skies,
But spare one infant's laughing eyes!

II.

O Time, who build'st the coral reef,
  Whom dried-up torrents fear,
And rocks like storm-ungarner'd sheaf
  Scatter'd o'er glaciers drear,
Waste all things else; but spare the while
The lovelight of one infant's smile!

III.

Where sunflowers late from Summer's mint
  Brought back the age of gold,

Through thee once more the sleet showers dint
   The black and flowerless mould:—
But harm not, Time, and guard, O Nature,
What is not yours—this living creature!

IV.

From God's great love a soul forth sprang
   That ne'er till then had being:
The courts of heaven with anthems rang:—
   He bless'd it, He the All-seeing!
Nor suns nor moons, nor heaven nor earth,
Can shape a soul or match in worth.

V.

No thought of thee when o'er the leas
   A child I raced delighted;
No thought when under garden trees
   A girlish troth I plighted:—
We knew not what the church bells said—
Of thee they babbled, pretty maid!

TO A BIBLE.

SHE read thee to the last, beloved Book !
    Her wasted fingers 'mid thy pages stray'd,
  Upon thy promises her heart was stay'd,
Upon thy letters linger'd her last look
Ere life and love those gentlest eyes forsook
    Upon thy gracious words she daily fed ;
    And by thy light her faltering feet were led
When loneliness her inmost being shook.
O Friend, O Saviour, O sustaining Word,
    Whose conquering feet the Spirit-land have trod,
Be near her where she is, incarnate Lord ;—
    In the mysterious silence of the tomb
    Where righteous spirits wait their final doom,
    Forsake her not—O Omnipresent God !

E.

SPENSER.

ONE peaceful spot in a storm-vex'd isle
  Shall wear for ever the past's calm smile :—
Kilcoleman Castle ! There Spenser sate ;
There sang, unweeting of coming fate.

The song he sang was a life-romance
Woven by Virtues in mystic dance
Where the gods and the heroes of Grecian story
Themselves were virtues in allegory.

True love was in it, but love sublimed,
Occult, high-reason'd, bewitch'd, be-rhymed !
The knight was the servant of ends trans-human,
The women were seraphs, the bard half woman.

Time and its tumults, stern shocks, hearts wrung,
To him were mad words to sweet music sung,
History to him an old missal quaint
Border'd round with gold angel and azure saint.

Creative indeed was that eye, sad Mary,
That hail'd in thy rival a queen of faery,
And in Raleigh, half statesman, half pirate, could see
But the shepherd of ocean's green Arcady.

Under groves of Penshurst his first notes rang :
As Sidney lived so his Spenser sang.
From the well-head of Chaucer one stream found
      birth,
Like an Arethusa, on Irish earth.

From the court he had fled, and the courtly lure :—
One virgin muse in an age not pure
Wore Florimel's girdle, and mourn'd in song
(Disguised as Irena's) Ierne's wrong.*

Roll onward, thou western Ilyssus, roll,
" Mulla," far kenn'd by " old mountain Mole ! "
With thy Shepherds a Calidore loved to dwell ;
And beside him an Irish Pastorel.

Dead are the wild-flowers she flung on thy tide,
Bending over thee, giftless—that well-sung bride :
The flowers have pass'd by, but abideth the river ;
And the genius that hallow'd it haunts it for ever.

---

* Fairy Queen, Book v. Canto i.

SCOTLAND reveres her great Montrose,
    Scotland bewails her brave Dundee!
With Alfred's memory England's glows:—
    What lethal hemlock freezes thee,

My country, that thy trophies rise
    To noteless men, or men ill-famed,
While they thy manlier destinies
    Who shaped, so long remain unnamed?

The Dutchman strides his steed new-gilt
    In thy chief city's stateliest way;
The Kings thy monarchy who built
    Or died to save it, where are they?

Clontarf! That Prince who smote the Dane
    On thee—who raised a realm laid low—
On thee what hath he? Benburb's plain
    No record bears of Owen Roe!

Forgotten now as Nial and Conn
    Are those twin stars of Yellow-Ford
Who freed Tirconnell and Tirone,
    Their country's altars who restored.

The man who fear'd no hireling's scoff,
  Thine Abdiel 'mid the apostate crew—
Grattan !—his statue stands far off;
  Sarsfield wins late his laurels due.

Thy quarries have a barren womb,
  My country, or a monster birth !
Belong they, statue, pillar, tomb,
  To vice alone or modern worth ?

Arise, and for thy proper weal
  Yield thy great Dead their honours late :
Those only understand who feel
  How self-disfranchised are the ingrate !

SONG.

THE FLOWER OF THE TREE.

I.

O THE flower of the tree is the flower for me,
　　That life out of life, high-hanging and free,
By the finger of God and the south wind's fan
Drawn from the broad bough, as Eve from Man!
From the rank red earth it never upgrew ;—
It was woo'd from the bark in the breezy blue.

II.

Hail, blossoms green 'mid the limes unseen,
That charm the bees to your honey'd screen,
As like to the green trees that gave you birth
As noble manners to inward worth!
We see you not ; but, we scarce know why,
We are glad when the air ye have breathed goes by.

III.

O flowers of the lime! 'twas a merry time
When under you first we read old rhyme,
And heard the wind roam over pale and park,
(*We* not I) 'mid the lime-grove dark !
Summer is heavy and sad.　Ye bring
With your tardy blossoms a second Spring.　.

COMPOSED AT RYDAL.

SEPT. 1860

THE last great man by manlier times bequeath'd
 To these our noisy and self-boasting days
In this green valley rested, trod these ways,
With deep calm breast this air inspiring breathed ;
True bard, because true man, his brow he wreathed
With wild-flowers only, singing Nature's praise ;
But Nature turn'd, and crown'd him with her bays,
And said, " Be thou *my* Laureate."   Wisdom
        sheath'd
In song love-humble ; contemplations high,
That built like larks their nests upon the ground ;
Insight and vision ; sympathies profound
That spann'd the total of humanity—
These were the gifts which God pour'd forth at large
On men through him ; and he was faithful to his
        charge.

TO WORDSWORTH.

ON VISITING THE DUDDON.*

I.

SO long as Duddon 'twixt his cloud-girt walls
   Thridding the woody chambers of the hills
Warbles from vaulted grot and pebbled halls
Welcome or farewell to the meadow rills ;
So long as linnets chant low madrigals
Near that brown nook the labourer whistling tills,
Or the late-reddening apple forms and falls
'Mid dewy brakes the autumnal redbreast thrills,
So long, last poet of the great old race,
Shall thy broad song through England's bosom roll,
A river singing anthems in its place,
And be to later England as a soul.
Glory to Him who made thee, and increase
To them that hear thy word, of love and peace !

---

* See Wordsworth's " Sonnet to the Poet Dyer."

II.

WHEN first that precinct sacrosanct I trod
    Autumn was there, but Autumn just begun:
Fronting the portals of a sinking sun
The queen of quietude in vapour stood,
Her sceptre o'er the dimly-crimson'd wood
Resting in light.   The year's great work was
      done;
Summer had vanish'd, and repinings none
Troubled the pulse of thoughtful gratitude.
Wordsworth! the autumn of our English song
Art thou:—'twas thine our vesper psalms to sing.
Chaucer sang matins;—sweet his note and strong;
His singing-robe the green, white garb of Spring.
Thou like the dying year art rightly stoled—
Pontific purple and dark harvest gold.

TRUE AND FALSE LOVE OF FREEDOM.

THEY that for freedom feel not love but lust,
   Irreverent, knowing not her spiritual claim,
And they, the votaries blind of windy fame,
And they who cry " I will because I must ; "
They too that launch, screen'd by her shield august,
A bandit's shaft some private mark their aim ;
And they that make her sacred cause their game
From restlessness or spleen or sheer disgust
At duteous days ;—all these, the brood of night,
Diverse, by one black note detected stand,
Their scorn of every barrier raised by right
To awe self-will.   Howe'er by virtue bann'd,
By reason spurn'd, that act the moment needs
Licensed they deem ;—holy whate'er succeeds.

ROMANS, that lift to Liberty, your God,
  Not vows but swords, suppliants self-deified,
Betwixt her altars and your rock of pride
A stream there rolls fiercer than Alpine flood,
A fatal stream of murder'd Rossi's blood !
For Liberty he lived ; and when he died,
Prisoner, that new Rienzi's corse beside,
The king, the pontiff, and the father stood !
What rite piacular from that impious deed
Hath cleansed your hands ? Accuse not adverse stars,
If guilt unwept achieve not virtue's meed.
Years heal not treason.   All his sands old Time
Shakes down to keep unblurr'd those characters
Wherein are traced the calendars of crime.

ON THE INVASION OF THE

PAPAL STATES,

SEPT. 1860.

O ITALY! the guilt but half is thine!
　Thy sons they are not; foes they are, not
　　friends,
Those ill-crown'd kings that brim, for ill-mask'd
　　ends,
Freedom's pure cup with blasphemy's false wine.
Thou of the hermit's cell, the martyr's shrine!
Thou, dew'd with beauty and the Aonian dream
Like Greece, but higher placed in God's great scheme,
His second Salem's second Palestine!—
The malison of freedom evermore
Cleave to his name who burst the eternal band
That with religion links her, hand in hand,
And hurl'd the child against the sire in war.
Religion spurn'd, there freedom hath no place:—
Freedom the pillar is—Virtue its base!

WRITTEN IN CUMBERLAND,

SEPT. 1860.

LAUREATES of Freedom o'er these hills sublime
That stride and ask, "What news? What tyrant's fall
Draws out to-day, in ruin musical,
The storm-stop of an else monotonous chime?"
The news is this—strange news in prose or rhyme—
They that redeem'd the north, then Satan's thrall.
To Christ, were Ireland's sons: Iona's call
Your fathers spurn'd not in Faith's happy prime!
To-day the sons of Ireland, far and near,
Amerced of altar priest and sacrifice,
Like the blind labouring horse or harness'd steer,
Sweat in your fields! I speak where none replies:—
Calm as a sceptic's smile still shines the sun:
The slowly sailing cloud sails slowly on!

TO FURNESS ABBEY.

I.

GOD, with a mighty and an outstretched hand,
    Stays thee from sinking, and ordains to be
His witness lifted 'twixt the Irish sea
And that still beauteous, once Faith-hallow'd land.
Stand as a sign, monastic prophet, stand!
Thee, thee the speechless, God hath stablish'd, thee,
To be His Baptist, crying ceaselessly
In spiritual deserts like that Syrian sand!
Man's little race around thee creep and crawl.
And dig, and delve, and roll their thousand wheels;
Thy work is done: henceforth sabbatical
Thou restest, while the world around thee reels;
But every scar of thine and stony rent
Cries to a proud, weak age, " Repent, repent!"

TO FURNESS ABBEY.

II.

VIRTUE goes forth from thee and sanctifies
    That once so peaceful shore whose peace is
        lost,
To-day doubt-dimm'd, and inly tempest-tost,
Virtue most healing when seal'd up it lies
In relics, like thy ruins.   Enmities
Thou hast not.   Thy grey towers sleep on 'mid dust :
But in the resurrection of the just
Thy works contemn'd to-day, once more shall rise.
Guard with thy dark compeer, cloud-veil'd Black
        Coombe,
Till then a land to Nature and to Grace
So dear.   Thy twin in greatness, clad with gloom,
Is grander than with sunshine on his face :
Thou 'mid abjection and the irreverent doom
Art holier—oh, how much—to hearts not base.

CHRISTMAS EVE, 1860.

THIS night, O earth, a Saviour germinate !
  Drop down, ye heavens, your sweetness from
    above !
This night is closed the iron book of fate ;
Open'd this night the book of endless love.
On from the Orient like a breeze doth move
The joy world-wide—a breeze that wafts a freight
Of vernal song o'er lands benumb'd but late,
Rivers ice-bound, and winter-wasted grove.
Onward from Bethlehem, onward o'er the Ægean.
Travels like night the starry Feast Divine.
All realms rejoice ; but loudest swells the pean
From that white basilic on the Esquiline
Beneath whose roof in sunlike radiance clad
The suffering Pontiff stands—to-night not sad.

HOLY CROSS ABBEY.

NOT dead but living still and militant,
　　With things death-doom'd wrestling in
　　　　conquering war,
　More free for chains, more fair for every scar,
How well, huge pile, that forehead grey and gaunt
Thou lift'st our world of fleeting shapes to daunt!
The past in thee surviveth petrified:
Like some dead tongue art thou, some tongue
　　　　that died
To live;—for prayer reserved, of flatteries scant.
The age of Sophists takes on thee no hold:
From thine ascetic breast the hollow jibe
Falls flat, and cavil of the blustering scribe:
Thine endless iron winter mocks the gold
Of our brief autumns.　God hath press'd on thee
The impress of His own eternity.

SELF-DECEPTION.

L IKE mist it tracks us wheresoe'er we go,
    Like air bends with us ever as we bend;
And, as the shades at noontide darkest grow,
With grace ascending it too can ascend:
Weakness with virtue skill'd it is to blend,
Breed baser life from buried sins laid low,
Empty our world of God and good, yet lend
The spirit's waste a paradisal glow.
O happy children simple even in wiles!
And ye of single eye thrice happy poor!
Practised self-love, that cheat which slays with
      smiles,
Weaves not for you the inevitable lure.
Men live a lie:—specious their latest breath:—
Welcome, delusion-slayer, truthful Death!

POETIC RESERVE.

NOT willingly the Muses sing of love:
But ere their Songs descend to man's do-
main
Through the dark chambers of the poet's brain
They pass, and passing take the stamp thereof:
And, as the wind that sweeps the linden grove
Wafts far its odour, so that sphere-born strain
Learns from its mortal mould to mourn and plain,
Though the strong Muses sit like Gods above.
True poetry is doubly-dower'd—a brightness
Lit from above yet fuell'd from below:
A moon that rolls through heaven in vestal whiteness,
Yet, earthward stooping, wears an earthly glow.
Mysteries the Muse would hide the Bards reveal:—
They love to wound: her mission is to heal.

ON A GREAT FUNERAL.

NO more than this?—The chief of nations bears
   Her chief of sons to his last resting-place :
Through the still city, sad and slow of pace
The sable pageant streams : and as it nears
That dome, to-day a vault funereal, tears
Run down the grey-hair'd veteran's wintry face :
Deep organs sob ; and flags their front abase ;
And the snapt wand the rite complete declares.
—Soul, that before thy Judge dost stand this day,
Disrobed of strength and puissance, pomp and
       power ;
O Soul defrauded at thine extreme hour
Of man's sole help from man, and latest stay,
Swells there for thee no prayer from all that host ?
And is this burial but a Nation's boast ?

TO CHARLES ELIOT NORTON.

On reading his " Vita Nuova" of Dante.

NORTON! I would that oft in years to come
    The destined bard of that brave land* of
      thine,
Sole-seated 'neath the tempest-roughen'd pine,
In boyhood's spring when genius first doth plume
Her wing, 'mid forest scents and insects' hum
And murmurs from the far sea crystalline
May smell *this* blossom from the Tuscan vine,
May hear *this* voice from antique Christendom!
For thus from love and purity and might
Shall he receive his armour, and forth fare
Worthy to range in song that country's knight
Who early burst the chains weak nations bear
Weeping. 'Mid trumpet-blasts and standards torn
To manhood, with loud cries, thy land was born!

March 28, 1860.

---

* America.

TO THE SAME.

" TO manhood with loud cries thy land was
          born"
Not then, but now ! Her trumpets peal this hour
The authentic voice of Nationhood and Power !
The iron in her soul indignant worn
This day she tramples out.   Her lips have sworn
To lift the dusky race in chains that cower ;
And if once more the tempests round her lour
Her smile goes through them like the smile of morn !
   Great Realm ! The men that in thy sunnier day
Look'd on thee dubious or with brow averse
Now thou hast put the evil thing away,
(Our sin and thine, Time's dread transmitted curse)
Send up their prayers to prop that lifted hand
Which gives to God a liberated Land !

June 12, 1861.

THE STATUE OF ST. CARLO BORROMEO
AT ARONA.

TRUE fame is this ;—through love, and love
    alone,
To stand thus honour'd where we first saw day :
True puissance this ;—the hand of lawful sway
In love alone to lift, that hand whereon
Dove-like, Eternal Peace hath fix'd her throne,
And whence her blessing wings o'er earth its way ;—
True rule to God belongs.   Who share it ? They
Through whom God's gifts on human kind are
    strewn.
  Bless thus thy natal place, great Priest, for ever !
And thou, Arona, by thy placid bay,
Second thy sleepless shepherd's mute endeavour.
The choice is thine, if that high Grace, like showers
Of sunbeams rain'd on all thy hearths and bowers,
Shall feed thy growth, or quicken thy decay !

ROBERT ISAAK WILBERFORCE.

" NO way but this." There where the pleasant
           shade
Dropp'd from the ledges of the Alban hill
Creeps to the vast Campagna and is still,
The mightier shadow reach'd him ! Prayer was
           made :—
But he to God his tribute just had paid,
And earn'd his rest. The deep recall'd the rill :
A long life's labour with a perfect will
He on the altar of the Church had laid.

  Child of the old English Learning sage and pure,
Authentic, manly, grave, without pretence,
From this poor stage of changeful time and sense
Released, sleep well, of thy reward secure :
Beside the Apostles' threshold thou dost lie,
Waiting, well-pleased, thy great eternity.

Rome, 1857.

COMPOSED NEAR THE RUINS OF COR-
NELIA'S HOUSE AT BAIA.

I TURN from ruins of imperial power,
  Tombs of corrupt delight, old walls the pride
Of statesmen pleased for respite brief to hide
Their laurell'd foreheads in the Muses' bower,
And seek Cornelia's home.   At sunset's hour
How oft her eyes, that wept no more, descried
Yon purpling hills !   How oft she heard that tide
Fretting as now low cave or hollow tower !
The mother of the Gracchi !   Scipio's child !—
'Twas virtue such as hers that built her Rome !
Never towards it she gazed !   Far off her home
She made, like her great father self-exiled.
Woe to the nations when the souls they bare,
Their best and bravest, choose their rest elsewhere !

INISFAIL;

OR,

IRELAND IN THE OLDEN TIME.

PART I.

The period of Irish history illustrated by the following
poems is that included between the latter part of the twelfth
century and the latter part of the eighteenth.

HISTORY.

AT my casement I sat by night while the wind
      far off in dark valleys
Voluminous gather'd and grew, and waxing
    swell'd to a gale :
An hour I heard it or more ere yet it sobb'd on my
    lattice—
    Far off, 'twas a People's moan ; hard by, but a
    widow's wail.

Atoms we are—we men : of the myriad sorrow
    around us
    Our littleness little grasps ; and the selfish in
    that have no part :
Yet time with the measureless chain of a world-wide
    mourning hath wound us ;
    History but counts the drops as they fall from a
    Nation's heart.

To God there is fragment none :—nothing single ;—
    no isolation :
    The atoms to Him are one ; round Him the woe
    and the wrong
Roll like a spiritual star, and the cry of the
    desolate Nation :—
    The Souls that are under the Altar respond in
    music " how long ? "

By the casement I sat alone till sign after sign had
    descended:
  The Hyads rejoin'd their sea, and the Pleiads by
    fate were down borne:
And then with that distant dirge a tenderer anthem
    was blended,
  And, glad to behold her young, the bird gave
    thanks to the morn.

THE WARNING.

A.D. 1170.

I.

IN the heaven were portents dire:
  On the earth were sign and omen:
Bleeding stars and falling fire
  Dearth and plague foretold their coming.
Causeless panics on the crowd
Fell, and strong men wept aloud:—
Ere the Northmen cross'd the seas,
Said the bards, were signs like these.

II.

Time was given us to repent:
  Prophets challeng'd plain and city:
But we scorn'd each warning sent,
  And outwrestled God's great pity.

'Twixt the blood-stain'd brother bands
Mitred Laurence raised his hands,
Raised Saint Patrick's cross on high :—
We despised him ; and we die.

I.

OUR Kings sat of old in Emania and Tara :—
Those new kings whence are they?   Their
names are unknown !
Our saints lie entomb'd in Ardmagh and Cilldara ;
Their relics are healing ; their graves are grass-
grown.
Our princes of old, when their warfare was over,
As pilgrims forth wander'd ; as hermits found
rest :—
Shall the hand of the stranger their ashes uncover
In Bennchor the holy, in Aran the blest ?

II.

Not so,* by the race our Dalriada planted !—
In Alba were children ; we sent her a man.
Battles won in Argyle in Dunedin they chaunted :
King Kenneth completed what Fergus began.
Our name is her name : she is Alba no longer :

---

* See Note.

Her kings are our blood, and she crowns them at
    Scone:
Strong-hearted they are; and strong-handed: but
    stronger
When throned on our Lia Fail, Destiny's stone!

THE HOUSE NORMAN.

I.

THE walls are black: but the floor is red!
    Blood!—there is blood on the convent floor!
Woe to the mighty: that blood they shed:
    Woe, woe, de Bohun! Woe, woe, le Poer!
Fitz-Walter, beware! the years are strong:
De Burgh, de Burgh! God rights the wrong.
Ye have murder'd priests: the hour draws nigh
When your sons unshriven, without priest, shall die.

II.

Toll for the mighty ones:—brethren, toll!
    They stand astonish'd!—what seek they here?
Through tower and through turret the loud winds roll
    But the yellow lights shake not around the bier.
They are here unbidden!—stand back, ye proud!
God shapes the empires as wind the cloud.
The offence must come: but the deed is sin:—
Toll the death-bell: the death-psalms begin.

III.

The happy dead with God find rest :
  For them no funeral bell we toll.
Fitz-Hugh ! Death sits upon thy crest !
  De Clare ! Death sits upon thy soul !
Toll, monks, the death-bell, toll for them
Who masque under helmet and diadem :—
Death's masque is sin. The living are they
Who live with God in eternal day !

IV.

Fitz-Maurice is sentenced ! Sound, monks, his knell !
  As Roderick fell must de Courcy fall.
Toll for Fitz-Gerald the funeral bell :
  The blood of O'Rourke is on Lacy's wall.
The lions are ye of the robber kind !
But when ye lie old in your dens and blind
The wolves and the jackals on you shall prey.
From the same shore sent. Beware that day !

V.

Toll for the conquerors :—theirs the doom !
  For the great House Norman :—its bud is nipt !
Ah, princely house, when your hour is come
  Your dirge shall be sung not in church but
    crypt !
We mourn you in time. A baser scourge
Than yours that day will forbid the dirge !
Two thousand years to the Gael God gave :—

Four hundred shall open the Norman's grave!

Thus with threne and with stern lament
    For their brethren dead the old monks made
       moan
In the convent of Kells, the first day of Lent,
    One thousand one hundred and seventy one.

THE MALISON.

I.

THE Curse of that land which in ban and in
      blessing
    Hath puissance, through prayer and through pe-
      nance alight
On the False One who whisper'd, the traitor's hand
      pressing,
    " I ride without guards in the morning,—good-
      night!"
O beautiful serpent! O woman fiend-hearted!
    Wife false to O'Ruark! queen base to thy trust!
The glory of ages for ever departed
    That hour from the isle of the saintly and just.

II.

The Curse of that land on the monarchs disloyal,
   Who welcomed the invader, and knelt at his
      knee !
False Dermod, false Donald—the chieftains once
   royal
Of the Deasies and Ossory, cursed let them be !
Their name and their shame make eternal. Engrave
   them
   On the cliffs which the great billows buffet and
      stain :
Like billows the nations, when tyrants enslave them,
   Swell up in their fury—not always in vain !

III.

But praise in the churches, and worship and honour
   To him who, betray'd and deserted, fought on !
All praise to king Roderick, the prince of Clan
   Connor,
   The king of all Erin, and Cathall his son !
May the million-voiced chaunt that in endless ex-
   pansion
   Sweeps onward through heaven his praises prolong;
May the heaven of heavens this night be the mansion
   Of the good king who died in the cloisters of
      Cong !

THE LEGENDS.

I.

THE woods rose slowly; the clouds sail'd on :
    Man trod not yet the island wide:
A ship drew near from the rising sun ;—
    Who ruled it ? the Scythian Parricide.
Battles were lost and battles were won ;
    New lakes burst open, old forests died ;
For ages once more in the land was none—
    God slew the race of the Parricide.

II.

There is nothing that lasts save the Pine and Bard,
    I, Fintan the bard, was living then !
Tall grows the pine upon Slieve-Clonard :
    It dies—in the loud harp it lives again.
Give praise to the bard and a huge reward !
    Give praise to the bard who gives praise to men !
My curse upon Aodh the priest of Skard
    Who jeers at the bard-songs of Ikerren !

HYMN,

ON THE FOUNDING OF THE ABBEY OF ST. THOMAS THE MARTYR (A BECKET), IN DUBLIN, A.D. 1177.

" The celebrated Abbey of St. Thomas the Martyr was
" founded in Dublin by Fitz-Adelm, by order of Henry Second.
" The site was the place now called Thomas' Court.   In the
" presence of Cardinal Vivian and St. Laurence O'Toole the
" deputy endowed it with a carucate of land called Donore."
                    HAVERTY's *Hist. of Ireland*, p. 222.

I.

REJOICE thou race of man, rejoice!
   To-day the Church renews her boast
Of England's Thomas; and her voice
   Is echoed by the heavenly host.
Rejoice, whoever loves the right;
   Rejoice, ye faithful men and true:
The Prince of Peace o'errules the fight;
   The many fall before the few.

II.

Behold a great high priest with rays
   Of martyrdom's red sunset crown'd!
No other like him in the days
   Wherein he trod the earth was found.

The swords of men unholy met
　　Above him clashing, and he bled:
But God, the God he served, hath set
　　A wreath unfading on his head.

III.

Great is the priestly charge, and great
　　The line to whom that charge is given!
It comes not, that pontificate,
　　Save from the great High Priest in heaven!
A frowning king no equal brook'd:—
　　" Obey," he cried, " my will, or die."
Thomas, like Stephen, heavenward look'd
　　And saw the Son of Man on high.

IV.

Blest is the People, blest and strong,
　　That 'mid its pontiffs counts a saint!
His virtuous memory lasting long
　　Shall keep its altars pure from taint.
The heathen plot, the tyrants rage;
　　But in their Saint the poor shall find
A shield, or after many an age
　　A light restored to guide the blind.

Thus with expiatory rite
　　The Roman priest and Laurence sang,
And loud the regal towers that night
　　With music and with feasting rang.

I.

DEAD is the Prince of the Silver Hand,
    And dead Eochy the son of Erc !
Ere lived Milesius they ruled the land
    Thou hast ruled and lost in turn, O'Ruark !
Two thousand years have pass'd since then,
    And clans and kingdoms in blind commotion
Have butted at heaven and sunk again
    As the great waves sink in the depths of ocean.

II.

Last King of the Gaels of Eire, be still !
    What God decrees must come to pass :
There is none that soundeth His Way or Will :
    His hand is iron, and earth is glass.
Where built the Firbolgs there shrieks the owl :
    The Tuatha bequeath'd but the name of Eire :—
Roderick, our last of kings, thy cowl
    Outweighs the crown of thy kingly sire !

THE FAITHFUL NORMAN.

I.

PRAISE to the valiant and faithful foe !
　Give us noble foes, not the friend who lies !
We dread the drugg'd cup, not the open blow ;—
　We dread the old hate in the new disguise.
To Ossory's King they had pledged their word :
　He stood in their camp, and their pledge they
　　　　broke ;
Then Maurice the Norman upraised his sword :
　The cross on its hilt he kiss'd, and spoke :—

II.

" So long as this sword or this arm hath might
　" I swear by the cross which is lord of all,
" By the faith and honour of noble and knight
　" Who touches yon Prince by this hand shall
　　　　" fall ! "
So side by side through the throng they pass'd ;
　And Eire gave praise to the just and true.
Brave foe ! Wrongs past truth heals at last ;—
　There is room in the great heart of Eire for you !

SONG.

I.

WILLOW-LIKE maid with the long loose
tresses,
  With locks like Diarba's, and fairy foot
That gatherest up from the streamlet its cresses
  Above the low caroller bending mute,
Those tresses black in a fillet bind,
Or beware of Manannan the god of the wind!

II.

No fear of the Stranger with feet like those;
  No fear of the robbers that couch in the glen:
But the wind-god blows on thy cheek a rose,
  Then back returns to kiss it again.
Manannan they say is the god in air—
So sing the Tuatha—Bind close thy hair!

III.

The rose on her cheek was crescent still;
  A smile ran o'er it and made reply
As she cast from the darkling and sparkling rill
  The flash of a darkling and sparkling eye;
Then over her shoulder her long locks flung
And homeward tripp'd with a mirthful song.

THE LEGENDS.

I.

THEY fought ere sunrise at Tor Conainn ;
　　All day they fought on the wild sea-shore :
The sun dropp'd downward ; they fought amain ;
　　The tide rose upward ; they fought the more.
The sands were cover'd ; the sea grew red ;
　　The warriors fought in the reddening wave ;
That night the sea was the sea-king's bed ;
　　The land-king drifted past cliff and cave.

II.

Great was the rage in those ancient days
　　(We were pagans then) in the land of Eire ;
Like eagles men vanquish'd the noontide blaze ;
　　Their bones were iron ; their nerves were wire.
We are hinds to-day ! The Nemedian kings
　　Like elk and bison of old stalk'd forth ;
Their name—the sea-kings'—for ever clings
　　To the " Giant Stepping Stones " round the North.

THE BARD ETHELL.

THIRTEENTH CENTURY.

I.

I AM Ethell, the son of Conn ;
   Here I live at the foot of the hill ;
I am clansman to Brian and servant to none ;
   Whom I hated I hate, whom I loved love still.
Blind am I. On milk I live,
   And meat (God sends it) on each Saint's Day,
Though Donald Mac Art—may he never thrive—
   Last Shrovetide drove half my kine away !

II.

At the brown hill's base, by the pale blue lake,
   I dwell, and see the things I saw ;
The heron flap heavily up from the brake,
   The crow fly homeward with twig or straw,
The wild duck, a silver line in wake,
   Cutting the still mere to far Bunaw.
And the things that I heard though deaf I hear ;
From the tower in the island the feastful cheer ;
The horn from the woodlands ; the plunge of the
     stag,

With the loud hounds after him, down from the crag.
Sweet is the chase; but the battle is sweeter;
More healthful, more joyous, for true men meeter!

III.

My hand is weak; it once was strong:
  My heart burns still with its ancient fire:—
If any man smites me he does me wrong
  For I was the Bard of Brian Mac Guire.
If any man slay me—not unaware,
  By no chance blow, nor in wine and revel,
I have stored beforehand a curse in my prayer
  For his kith and kin; for his deed is evil.

IV.

There never was king, and there never will be
In battle or banquet like Malachi!
The Seers his reign had predicted long;
He honour'd the bards, and gave gold for song.
If rebels arose he put out their eyes;
  If robbers plunder'd or burn'd the fanes
He hung them in chaplets, like rosaries,
  That others beholding might take more pains!
There was none to women more reverent-minded
  For he held his mother, and Mary, dear;
If any man wrong'd them that man he blinded
  Or straight amerced him of hand or ear.
There was none who founded more convents—none;
  In his palace the old and the poor were fed;
The orphan might walk, or the widow's son,

Without groom or page to his throne or bed.
In his council he mused with great brows divine
And eyes like the eyes of the musing kine,
Upholding a sceptre whereon there sate,
With her wings o'er empires a sleep-tranced Fate.
He drain'd ten lakes and he built ten bridges;
   He bought a gold book for a thousand cows;
He slew ten Princes who brake their pledges;
   With the bribed and the base he scorn'd to ca-
      rouse.
He was sweet and awful; through all his reign
God gave great harvests to vale and plain:
From his nurse's milk he was kind and brave:
And when he went down to his well-wept grave
Through the triumph of penance his soul uprose
To God and the saints. Not so his foes!

v.

The king that came after! ah woe, woe, woe!
He doubted his friend and he trusted his foe.
He bought and he sold: his kingdom old
   He pledged and he pawn'd to avenge a spite:
No bard or prophet his birth foretold:
   He was guarded and warded both day and night:
He counsell'd with fools and had boors at his feast;
He was cruel to Christian and kind to beast:
Men smiled when they talk'd of him far o'er the
      wave:
Well paid were the mourners that wept o'er his
      grave.

God plagued for his sake his people sore :—
    They sinn'd ; for the people should watch and
        pray
That their prayers, like angels at window and door,
May keep from the king the bad thought away !

VI.

The sun has risen : on lip and brow
    He greets me—I feel it—with golden wand.
Ah, bright-faced Norna ! I see thee now—
    Where first I saw thee I see thee stand !
From the trellis the girl look'd down on me :
Her maidens stood near :—it was late in spring :
The grey priests laugh'd as she cried in glee
    " Good bard, a song in my honour sing."
I sang her praise in a loud-voiced hymn
To God who had fashion'd her, face and limb,
For the praise of the clan and the land's behoof :
So she flung me a flower from the trellis roof.
Ere long I saw her the hill descending—
    O'er the lake the May morning rose moist and
        slow :
She pray'd me (her smile with the sweet voice
        blending)
    To teach her all that a woman should know.
Panting she stood : she was out of breath :
    The wave of her little breast was shaking :
From eyes still childish and dark as death
Came womanhood's dawn through a dew-cloud
        breaking.

Norna was never long time the same :
  By a spirit so strong was her slight form moulded
The curves swell'd out of the flower-like frame
  In joy ; in grief to a bud she folded :
As she listen'd her eyes grew bright and large
Like springs rain-fed that dilate their marge.

VII.

So I taught her the hymn of Patrick the apostle,
  And the marvels of Bridget and Columkille :
And ere long she sang like the lark or the throstle,
  Sang the deeds of the servants of God's high will :
I told her of Brendon who found afar
Another world 'neath the western star ;
Of our three great bishops in Lindisfarne isle ;
Of St. Fursey the wond'rous, Fiacre without guile ;
Of Sedulius, hymn-maker when hymns were rare ;
Of Scotus the subtle who clove a hair
Into sixty parts, and had marge to spare.
To her brother I spake of Oisin and Fionn,
And they wept at the death of great Oisin's son.
I taught the heart of the boy to revel
  In tales of old greatness that never tire,
And the Virgin's, up-springing from earth's low
     level,
  To wed with heaven like the altar fire.
I taught her all that a woman should know :
  And that none might teach her worse lore I gave
     her
A dagger keen, and I taught her the blow
  That subdues the knave to discreet behaviour.

A sand-stone there on my knee she set,
And sharpen'd its point—I can see her yet—
I held back her hair and she sharpen'd the edge
While the wind piped low through the reeds and
　　　　sedge.

VIII.

She died in the convent on Ina's height:—
　　I saw her the day that she took the veil:
As slender she stood as the Paschal light,
　　As tall and slender and bright and pale!
When I saw her I dropp'd as dead:—bereaven
Is earth when her holy ones leave her for heaven:—
Her brother fell in the fight at Beigh—
May they plead for me, both, on my dying day!

IX.

All praise to the man who brought us the Faith!
'Tis a staff by day and our pillow in death!
All praise, I say, to the holy youth
　　Who heard in a dream from Tyrawley's strand
　　That wail, " put forth o'er the sea thy hand;—
In the dark we die: give us hope and truth!"
But Patrick built not on Iorras' shore
　　That convent where now the Franciscans dwell:
Columba was mighty in prayer and war;
　　But the young monk preaches as loud as the bell,
That love must rule all and all wrongs be for-
　　　　given,
Or else, he is sure, we shall reach not heaven!

This doctrine I count right cruel and hard:
And when I am laid in the old churchyard
The habit of Francis I will not wear;
Nor wear I his cord, or the cloth of hair
In secret.   Men dwindle :—till psalm and prayer
Had soften'd the land no Dane dwelt there!

X.

I forgive old Cathbar who sank my boat:
   Must I pardon Feargal who slew my son ;—
Or the pirate, Strongbow, who burn'd Granote,
   They tell me, and in it nine priests, a nun,
And (worst) Saint Finian's old crosier staff?
At forgiveness like that I spit and laugh!
My chief, in his wine-cups, forgave twelve men:
And of these a dozen rebell'd again!
There never was chief more brave than he!
   The night he was born Loch Dool up-burst:
He was bard-loving, musical, loud of glee,
   The last to fly, to advance the first.
He was like the top spray upon Uladh's oak,
   He was like the tap-root of Argial's pine:
He was secret and sudden: as lightning his
     stroke:
   There was none that could fathom his veil'd
     design!
He slept not: if any man scorn'd his alliance
He struck the first blow for a frank defiance
With that look in his face, half night half light,
Like the lake gust-blacken'd yet ridged with white!

L

There were comely wonders before he died :
The eagle swoop'd, and the Banshee cried ;
The witch-elm wept with a blighted bud :
The spray of the torrent was red with blood :
The chief, return'd from the mountain's bound,
Forgat to ask after Bran, his hound.
We knew he would die : three days were o'er ;—
He died.   We waked him for three days more.
One by one, upon brow and breast
The whole clan kiss'd him.   In peace may he rest !

XI.

I sang his dirge.   I could sing that time
Four thousand staves of ancestral rhyme :
To-day I can scarcely sing the half :
Of old I was corn and now I am chaff !
My song to-day is a breeze that shakes
   Feebly the down on the cygnet's breast :
'Twas then a billow the beach that rakes
  Or a bright storm that buffets the mountain's
     crest.
Whatever I bit with a venomed song
  Grew sick—were it beast, or tree, or man :
The wrong'd one bade me avenge his wrong
  With the flail of the Satire and fierce Ode's fan.
I sang to the chieftains : each stock I traced
Lest rights should grow tangled through fraud or
     haste.
To princes I sang in a loftier tone
Of Moran the Just who refused a throne ;

Of Moran whose torque would close and choke
The wry-neck'd witness that falsely spoke.
I taught them how to win love and hate,
Not love from all, and to shun debate.
To maids in the bower I sang of love :
And of war at the feastings in hall or grove.

XII.

Great is our Order ; but greater far
   Were its pomp and its power in the days of old,
When the five chief bards in peace or war
   Had thirty bards each in his train enroll'd ;
When Ollave Fodhla in Tara's hall
   Fed bards and kings : when the boy, king Nial
Was train'd by Torna : when Britain and Gaul
   Their laurel crowns sent to Dallan Forgial.
To-day we can launch the clans into fight :
   That day we could freeze them in mid career !
Whatever man knows, was our realm by right :
   The lore without music no Gael would hear.
Old Cormac, the brave blind king, was bard
Ere fame rose yet of O'Daly and Ward.
The son of Milesius was bard—" Go back,
   " My People," he sang ; " ye have done a wrong !
" Nine waves go back o'er the green sea track :
" Let your foes their castles and coasts make strong.
" To the island ye came by stealth and at night :—
" She is ours if we win her in all men's sight ! "
'Tis past ! some think that we err'd through pride,
Though Columba the vengeance turn'd aside.

Too strong we were not: too rich we were:
Give wealth to knaves:—'tis the true man's snare!

XIII.

But now men lie: they are just no more:
   They forsake the old ways: they quest for new:
They pry and they snuff after strange false lore
   As dogs hunt vermin.　It never was true:—
I have scorn'd it for twenty years—this babble
That eastward and southward a Saxon rabble
Have won great battles, and rule large lands,
And plight with daughters of ours their hands.
We know the bold Norman o'erset their throne;—
Long since!　Our lands!　Let them guard their
      own!

XIV.

How long He leaves me—the great God—here!
   Have I sinn'd some sin. or has God forgotten?
This year I think is my hundredth year:
   I am like a bad apple unripe yet rotten!
They shall lift me ere long—they shall lay me—the
      clan—
By the strength of men on mount Cruachan!
God has much to think of!　How much he has
      seen!
And how much is gone by that once has been!
On sandy hills where the rabbits burrow
   Are Raths of kings men name not now:
On mountain tops I have track'd the furrow
   And found in forests the buried plough.

For one now living the strong land then
Gave kindly food and raiment to ten.
No doubt they wax'd proud and their God defied,
So with blight or a tyrant their bloom He gored;
Or He sent them plague or He sent the sword;
Or He sent them lightning; and so they died
Like Dathi, the king, on the dark Alp's side.

XV.

Ah me that man who is made of dust
Should have pride toward God!   'Tis an angel's
sin!
I have often fear'd lest God, the All-just,
Should bend from heaven and sweep earth clean,
Should sweep us all into corners and holes,
Like dust of the house-floor, both bodies and
souls :—
I have often fear'd He would send some wind
In wrath; and the nation wake up stone-blind!
In age or in youth we have all wrought ill :—
I say not our great king Nial did well
(Although he was Lord of the Pledges nine,)
When, beside subduing this land of Eire,
He raised in Armorica banner and sign,
And wasted the British coasts with fire.
Perhaps in his mercy the Lord will say,
" These men, these men!   'Twas a rough boy-
" play!"
He is certain—that young Franciscan Priest—
God sees great sin where men see least.

Yet this were to give unto God the eye
(Unmeet the thought) of the humming fly!
I trust there are small things He scorns to see
In the lowly who cry to Him piteously.
Our hope is Christ. I have wept full oft

   He came not to Eire in Oisin's time;
Though love, and those new monks, would make
     men soft

   If they were not harden'd by war and rhyme.
I have done my part: my end draws nigh:
I shall leave old Eire with a smile and sigh:
She will miss not me as I miss'd my son:
Yet for her, and her praise, were my best deeds
     done.
Man's deeds! man's deeds! they are shades that
     fleet,
Or ripples like those that break at my feet.
The deeds of my chief and the deeds of my king
Grow hazy, farseen, like the hills in spring.
Nothing is great save the death on the cross!

   But Pilate and Herod I hate, and know

   Had Fionn lived then he had laid them low
Though the world thereby had sustain'd great
     loss.
My blindness and deafness and aching back
With meekness I bear for that suff'ring's sake;
And the Lent-fast for Mary's sake I love,
And the honour of Him, the Man Above!
My songs are all over now:—so best!

They are laid in the heavenly Singer's breast
Who never sings but a star is born :
May we hear His song in the endless morn !
I give glory to God for our battles won
    By wood or river, on bay or creek :
For Norna, who died ; for my father, Conn :
    For feasts, and the chase on the mountains
        bleak :
I bewail my sins, both unknown and known,
    And of those I have injured forgiveness seek.
The men that were wicked to me and mine ;—
(Not quenching a wrong, nor in war nor wine),
I forgive and absolve them all, save three :—
May Christ in His mercy be kind to me !

A CHRISTMAS CAROL.

PRIMEVAL night had repossess'd
    Her empire in the fields of space;
Calm lay the kine on earth's dark breast,
    The earth lay calm in heaven's embrace.

That hour where shepherds kept their flocks
    From God a glory sudden fell;
The splendour smote the trees and rocks,
    And lay like dew along the dell.

God's Angel close beside them stood:
    " Fear naught," that angel said, and then,
" Behold, I bring you tidings good:
    " The Saviour Christ is born to men.

And straightway round him myriads sang
    Loud song again, and yet again,
Till all the hollow valley rang
    " Glory to God, and peace to men."

The shepherds went and wondering eyed,
    In Bethlehem born the heavenly Stranger:
Mary and Joseph knelt beside:
    The Babe was cradled in the manger!

ST. PATRICK AND THE BARD.

THE land is sad, and dark our days :
    Sing us a song of the days that were !—
Then sang the bard in his Order's praise
    This song of the chief bard of king Laeghaire.

I.

The King is wrath with a greater wrath
    Than the wrath of Nial or the wrath of Conn !
From his heart to his brow the blood makes path,
    And hangs there, a red cloud, beneath his crown.

II.

Is there any who knows not, from south to north,
    That Laeghaire to-morrow his birthday keeps?
No fire may be lit upon hill or hearth
'Till the King's strong fire in its kingly mirth
    Leaps upward from Tara's palace steeps !

III.

Yet Patrick has lighted his paschal fire
    At Slane,—it is holy Saturday,—
And bless'd his font 'mid the chaunting choir !
    From hill to hill the flame makes way :

While the King looks on it his eyes with ire
    Flash red, like Mars, under tresses grey.

IV.

The great King's captains with drawn swords
      rose;
    To avenge their Lord and the State they swore:
    The Druids rose and their garments tore;
" The strangers to us and our gods are foes!"
Then the King to Patrick a herald sent,
    Who said, " Come up at noon, and show
" Who lit thy fire, and with what intent?—
    " These things the great King Laeghaire would
      " know."

V.

But Laeghaire conceal'd twelve men in the way.
Who swore by the sun the saint to slay.

VI.

When the waters of Boyne began to bask,
    And the fields to flash, in the rising sun
The Apostle Evangelist kept his Pasch,
    And Erin her grace baptismal won:
Her birthday it was;—his font the rock
He bless'd the land, and he bless'd his flock.

VII.

Then forth to Tara he fared full lowly:
    The Staff of Jesus was in his hand;

Eight priests paced after him chaunting slowly,
  Printing their steps on the dewy land.
It was the Resurrection morn ;
The lark sang loud o'er the springing corn ;
The dove was heard, and the hunter's horn.

VIII.

The murderers stood close by on the way ;
Yet they saw nought save the lambs at play.

IX.

A trouble lurk'd in the King's strong eye
When the guest that he counted for dead drew nigh.
He sate in state at his palace gate ;
  His chiefs and his nobles were ranged around ;
The Druids like ravens smelt some far fate ;
  Their eyes were gloomily bent on the ground.
Then spake Laeghaire : " He comes—beware !
" Let none salute him, or rise from his chair !"

X.

Like some still vision men see by night,
  Mitred, with eyes of serene command,
Saint Patrick moved onward in ghostly white :
  The Staff of Jesus was in his hand.
His priests paced after him unafraid,
And the boy, Benignus, more like a maid,
Like a maid just wedded he walked and smiled,
To Christ new-plighted, that priestly child.

XI.

They enter'd the circle; their hymn they ceased;
  The Druids their eyes bent earthward still:
On Patrick's brow the glory increased,
  As a sunrise brightening some breathless hill.
The warriors sat silent: strange awe they felt;—
The chief bard, Dubtach, rose up, and knelt!

XII.

Then Patrick discoursed of the things to be
When time gives way to eternity,
Of kingdoms that cease, which are dreams not things,
And the Kingdom built by the King of kings.
Of Him he spake who reigns from the Cross;
Of the death which is life, and the life which is
        loss;
And how all things were made by the Infant Lord,
And the small hand the Magian kings adored.
His voice sounded on like a throbbing flood
That swells all night from some far-off wood,
And when it was ended—that wondrous strain—
Invisible myriads breathed low, "Amen!"

XIII.

While he spake, men say that the refluent tide
  On the shore beside Colpa ceased to sink;
And they say the white deer by Mulla's side
  O'er the green marge bending forbore to drink:
That the Brandon eagle forgat to soar;
  That no leaf stirr'd in the wood by Lee.—

Such stupor hung the island o'er,
  For none might guess what the end would be.

XIV.

Then whisper'd the King to a chief close by
" It were better for me to believe than die!"

XV.

Yet the King believed not; but ordinance gave
  That whoso would might believe that word:
So the meek believed, and the wise, and brave,
  And Mary's Son as their God adored.
Ethnea and Fethlimea, his daughters twain,
That day were in baptism born again;
And the Druids, because they could answer nought,
Bow'd down to the faith the stranger brought.
That day upon Erin God pour'd His Spirit,—
Yet none like the chief of the bards had merit,
Dubtach!—He rose and believed the first,
Ere the great light yet on the rest had burst.

It was thus that Erin, then blind but strong,
  To Christ through her chief bard paid homage due:
And this was a sign that in Erin Song
  Should from first to last to the cross be true!

I.

'TWAS a holy time when the king's long foemen
   Fought, side by side, to uplift the serf;
Never triumph'd in old time Greek or Roman
   As Brian and Malachi at Clontarf.
There was peace in Eire for long years after;
   Canute in England reign'd and Sweyn;
But Eire found rest, and the freeman's laughter
   Rang out the knell of the vanquish'd Dane.

II.

Praise to the king of ninety years
   Who rode round the battle-field, cross in hand!
But the blessing of Eire and grateful tears
   To him who fought under Brian's command!
A crown in heaven for the king who brake,
   To staunch old discords, his royal wand;
Who spurn'd his throne for his people's sake,
   Who served a rival and saved the land!

THE EPIPHANY.

THEY leave the land of gems and gold,
   The shining portals of the East;
For Him, " the Woman's Seed" foretold,
   They leave the revel and the feast.

To earth their sceptres they have cast,
   And crowns by kings ancestral worn;
They track the lonely Syrian waste;
   They kneel before the Babe new-born.

Oh happy eyes that saw Him first!
   Oh happy lips that kiss'd His feet!
Earth slakes at last her ancient thirst;
   With Eden's joy her pulses beat.

True kings are those who thus forsake
   Their kingdoms for the Eternal King;—
Serpent! her foot is on thy neck!
   Herod! thou writh'st, but canst not sting!

He, He is King, and He alone,
   Who lifts that Infant hand to bless;
Who makes His Mother's knee His throne,
   Yet rules the starry wilderness.

THUS sang to the princes the bard Maelmire;
    But the princes received not the words he
       said :
There was ever great feud and great hate in Eire :
    Yet O'Donnell wept when O'Neill was dead.

I.

" Thou son of Calphurn, in peace go forth !
    " This hand shall slay them whoe'er shall slay thee!
" The carles shall stand to their necks in earth
    " Till they die of thirst who mock or stay thee !

II.

" But my father, Nial, who is dead long since,
    " Permits not me to believe thy word ;
" For the servants of Jesus, thy heavenly Prince.
    " Once dead, lie flat as in sleep, interr'd ;
" But we are as men through dark floods that wade ;—
" We stand in our black graves undismay'd ;
" Our faces are turn'd to the race abhorr'd,
" And ready beside us stand spear and sword,
" Ready to strike at the last great day,
" Ready to trample them back into clay.

III.

" This is my realm and men call it Eire,
  " Wherein I have lived and live in hate
" (Like Nial before me and Ere his sire)
  " Of the race Lagenian, ill-named the Great !"

IV.

Thus spake Laeghaire, and his host rush'd on,
  A river of blood as yet unshed :—
At noon they fought : and at set of sun
  That king lay captive, that host lay dead !

V.

The brave foe loosed him, but bade him swear
  He would never demand of them Tribute more.
  So Laeghaire by the dread God-elements swore,
By the moon divine and the earth and air ;
He swore by the wind and the broad sunshine
  That circle for ever both land and sea,
By the long-back'd rivers, and mighty wine,
  By the cloud far-seeing, by herb and tree,
By the boon spring shower, and by autumn's fan,
By woman's breast, and the head of man,
By night and the noonday Demon he swore
He would claim the Boarian Tribute no more.

VI.

But with years wrath wax'd ; and he brake his faith ;—
Then the dread God-elements wrought his death ;

For the wind and sunshine by Cassi's side
Came down and smote on his head that he died.
Death-sick three days on his throne he sate:
Then he died, as his father died, great in hate.

VII.

They buried the king upon Tara's hill,
In his grave upright;—there stands he still.
Upright there stands he as men that wade
By night through a castle-moat, undismay'd;
On his head is the gold crown, the spear in his hand,
And he looks to the hated Lagenian land.

VIII.

Patrick the Apostle, the son of Calphurn,
　　These pagan interments endured no longer;
And Eire he commanded this song to learn,
　　" Though hate is strong yet love is stronger!"
To the Gaels of Eire he gave a Creed:
He bade them to fear not Fate, Demon, or Faery;
But to fast in Lent, and by no black deed
　　To insult God's Son, and His mother, Mary.

Thus sang to the princes the bard Machnire:—
　　O! when will it leave me, that widows' wail?
My heart is stone and my brain is fire
　　For the men that died in thy woods, Imayle!

PATRICK AND THE KNIGHT;

OR, THE INAUGURATION OF IRISH CHIVALRY.

I.

"THOU shalt not be a priest," he said ;
   "Christ hath for thee a lowlier task :
"Be thou His soldier! Wear with dread
   "His cross upon thy shield and casque!
"Put on God's armour, faithful knight!
   "Mercy with justice, love with law;
"Nor e'er except for truth and right
   "This sword cross-hilted dare to draw."

II.

He spake, and with his crosier pointed
   Graved on the broad shield's brazen boss
(That hour baptized, confirm'd, anointed
   Stood Erin's chivalry) the cross :
And there was heard a whisper low
   From one unseen,—Saint Michael, thine!—
"Thou Sword, keep pure thy virgin vow,
   "And trenchant shalt thou be as mine."

THE BIER THAT CONQUERED;

OR, O'DONNELL'S ANSWER.

A. D. 1257.

LAND which the Norman would make his own!
  (Thus sang the Bard 'mid a host o'erthrown
While their white cheeks some on the clench'd hand
      propp'd,
And from some the life-blood scarce heeded dropp'd)
There are men in thee that refuse to die,
And that scorn to live, while a foe stands nigh!

I.

O'Donnell lay sick with a grievous wound:
  The leech had left him; the priest had come;
The clan sat weeping upon the ground,
  Their banners furl'd and their minstrels dumb.

II.

Then spake O'Donnell, the king: "Although
" My hour draws nigh, and my dolours grow;
" And although my sins I have now confess'd,
" And desire in the land, my charge, to rest,
" Yet leave this realm, nor will I nor can,
" While a stranger treads on her, child or man.

III.

" I will languish no longer a sick man here:
" My bed is grievous; build up my Bier.
" The white robe a king wears over me throw;
" Bear me forth to the field where he camps—your
   " foe,
" With the yellow torches and dirges low.
" The heralds his challenge have brought and fled:
" The answer they bore not I bear instead.
" My people shall fight my pain in sight,
" And I shall sleep well when their wrong stands
   " right."

IV.

Then the clan to the words of their Chief gave ear,
And they fell'd great oak-trees and built a bier;
Its plumes from the eagle's wing were shed,
And the wine-black samite above it they spread
Inwoven with sad emblems and texts divine,
And the braided bud of Tireonnell's pine,
And all that is meet for the great and brave
When past are the measured years God gave,
And a voice cries " Come " from the waiting grave.

V.

When the Bier was ready they laid him thereon;
And the army forth bare him with wail and moan:
With wail by the sea-lakes and rock abysses;
With moan through the vapour-trail'd wildernesses;

And men sore wounded themselves drew nigh
And said, " We will go with our king and die ;"
And women wept as the pomp pass'd by.
The sad yellow torches far off were seen ;
No war-note peal'd through the gorges green ;
But the black pines echo'd the mourners' keen.

VI.

What said the Invader, that pomp in sight?
" They sue for the pity they shall not win."
But the sick king sat on the Bier upright,
And said, " So well! I shall sleep to-night :—
" Rest here my couch, and my peace begin."

VII.

Then the war-cry sounded—" Bataillah Aboo !"
  And the whole clan rush'd to the battle plain :
They were thrice driven back, but they form'd anew
    That an end might come to their king's great
        pain.
'Twas a people not army that onward rush'd ;
'Twas a nation's blood from their wounds that gush'd :
Bare-bosom'd they fought, and with joy were slain ;
Till evening their blood fell fast like rain ;
But a shout swell'd up o'er the setting sun,
And O'Donnell died for the field was won.

So they buried their king upon Aileach's shore ;
And in peace he slept ;—O'Donnell More.

PECCATUM PECCAVIT.

I.

WHERE is thy brother?   Heremon, speak !
    Heber, the son of Milesius, where ?
The orphans' wail and their mother's shriek
    For ever they ring upon Banba's air !
And whose, O whose was the sword, Heremon,
    That smote Amergin, thy brother and bard ?
'Twas the Fate of thy house or a mocking Demon
    That raised thy hand o'er his forehead scarr'd !

II.

Woe, woe to Banba ! That blood of brothers
    Wells up from her bosom renew'd each year ;
'Twas her's the shriek—that desolate mother's :—
    'Twas Banba wept o'er that first red bier !
The priest has warn'd, and the bard lamented :
    But warning and wailing her sons despised ;
The head was sage, and the heart half-sainted ;
    But the sword-hand was evermore unbaptized !

THE DAYS OF OUTLAWRY.

I.

A CRY comes up from wood and wold,
    A wail from fen and marish,
" Grant us your laws, and take our gold ;
    " Like beasts dog-chased we perish"—
The hunters of their kind reply,
    " Our sport we scorn to barter ;
" We rule ! the Irish enemy
    " Partakes not England's charter."

II.

A cry comes up for ever new,
    A wail of hopeless anguish,
" Your laws, your laws !—our laws ye slew :
    " In living death we languish"—
" Not so ! We keep our hunting ground ;
    " We chase the flying quarry.
" Hark, hark, that sound ! the horn and hound !
    " Away ! we may not tarry !"

III.

For Scotland England's king with glee
    Forsakes his court and palace.

O Erin, if that hour in thee
  A Bruce had risen—a Wallace!
For conquests new king Edward burns
  In Scotland's farthest highland;
The forest lord the offal spurns
  Of one subjected island!

IV.

Sad isle, thy laws are Norman lords
  That, dower'd by Henry's bounty,
On cities sup 'mid famish'd hordes,
  And dine on half a county!
A laughing Titan, Outlawry
  Strides drunk o'er hill and heather;
Justice to him is as a fly
  'Twixt mail'd hands clash'd together.

V.

O memory, memory, leave the graves
  Knee-deep in grass and darnel!
Wash from a kingdom, winds and waves,
  The odour of the charnel!
Be dumb, red graves in valleys deep,
  Black towers on plains blood-sloken:—
Dark fields, your thrilling secrets keep,
  Nor speak till God hath spoken!

THE DIRGE OF ATHUNREE.

A.D. 1316.

This great battle marked an epoch in Irish History. In it the Norman power at last triumphed over that of the Gael, which had long been enfeebled by the divisions in the royal house of O'Connor. From this period also the Norman Barons more rapidly than before became Irish Chiefs. As such they were accepted by Ireland. The power of the English Crown on the other hand gradually declined till it became unknown beyond the narrow limits of a part of the Pale. It rose again after the accession of Henry VII.

I.

ATHUNREE! Athunree!
Erin's heart, it broke on thee!
Ne'er till then in all its woe
Did that heart its hope forego.
Save a little child—but one—
The latest regal race is gone.
Roderick died again on thee,
　　　Athunree!

II.

Athunree! Athunree!
A hundred years and forty-three

Winter-wing'd and black as night
O'er the land had track'd their flight:
In Clonmacnoise from earthy bed
Roderick raised once more his head :—
Fedlim floodlike rush'd to thee,
    Athunree !

III.

Athunree ! Athunree !
The light that struggled sank on thee !
Ne'er since Cathall the red-handed
Such a host till then was banded.
Long-hair'd Kerne and Galloglass
Met the Norman face to face ;
The saffron standard floated far
O'er the on-rolling wave of war ;
Bards the onset sang o'er thee,
    Athunree !

IV.

Athunree ! Athunree !
The poison tree took root in thee !
What might naked breasts avail
'Gainst sharp spear and steel-ribb'd mail ?
Of our Princes twenty-nine,
Bulwarks fair of Connor's line,
Of our clansmen thousands ten
Slept on thy red ridges. Then—
Then the night, came down on thee,
    Athunree !

v.

Athunree !   Athunree !
Strangely shone that moon on thee !
Like the lamp of them that tread
Staggering o'er the heaps of dead,
Seeking that they fear to see.
Oh that widows' wailing sore !
On it rang to Oranmore ;
Died, they say, among the piles
That make holy Aran's isles ;—
It was Erin wept on thee,
    Athunree !

vi.

Athunree !   Athunree !
The heart of Erin burst on thee !
Since that hour some unseen hand
On her forehead stamps the brand.
Her children ate that hour the fruit
That slays manhood at the root ;
Our warriors are not what they were ;
Our maids no more are blithe and fair ;
Truth and Honour died with thee,
    Athunree !

vii.

Athunree !   Athunree !
Never harvest wave o'er thee !
Never sweetly-breathing kine
Pant o'er golden meads of thine !

Barren be thou as the tomb;
May the night-bird haunt thy gloom,
And the wailer from the sea,
    Athunree!

VIII.

Athunree!   Athunree!
All my heart is sore for thee,
It was Erin died on thee,
    Athunree!

LAMENT FOR EDWARD BRUCE.

A.D. 1318.

I.

HE is dead, dead, dead!—
    The man to Erin dear!
The king who gave our Isle a head—
    His kingdom is his bier.
He rode into our war;
    And we crown'd him chief and prince,
For his race to Alba's shore
    Sail'd from Erin, ages since.
Woe, woe, woe!
    Edward Bruce is cold to-day;
He that slew him lies as low,
    Sword to sword and clay to clay.

II.

King Robert came too late !—
    Long long may Erin mourn !
Famine's rage and dreadful Fate
    Forbade her Bannockburn !
As the galley touch'd the strand
    Came the messenger of woe ;
The king put back the herald's hand—
    " Peace," he said, " thy tale I know !
" His face was in the cloud ;
    " And his wraith was on the surge"—
Maids of Alba, weave his shroud !
    Maids of Erin, sing his dirge !

I.

BETWEEN two mountains' granite walls one
            star
    Shines in this sea-lake quiet as the grave ;
The ocean moans against its rocky bar ;
    That star no reflex finds in foam or wave.

II.

Saints of our country ! if, no more a nation,
    Vain are henceforth her struggles, from on high
Fix in the bosom of her desolation
    So much the more that hope which cannot die !

ODE.

I.

THE unvanquish'd land puts forth each year
   New growth of man and forest;
Her children vanish; but on her
   Stranger, in vain thou warrest!
She wrestles, strong through hope sublime,
   (Thick darkness round her pressing)
Wrestles with God's great Angel, Time—
   And wins, though maim'd, the blessing.

II.

As night draws in what day sent forth,
   As Spring is born of Winter,
As flowers that hide in parent earth
   Re-issue from the centre,
Our land takes back her wasted brood,
   Our land, in respiration,
Breathes from her deep heart unsubdued
   A renovated nation!

III.

Man's mortal frame, for heaven design'd,
   In caves of earth must wither;
Of all its myriad atoms join'd
   No twain may cleave together.

Our land is dead.   Upon the blast
  Far forth her dust is driven ;
But the glorified shape shall be hers at last,
  And the crown that descends from heaven !

IV.

Her children die ; the nation lives :—
  Through signs celestial ranging
The nation's Destiny still survives
  Unchanged, yet ever changing.
The many-centuried Wrath goes by :
  But while earth's tumult rages
" In Cælo quies."   Burst and die
  Thou storm of temporal ages !

V.

Burst, and thine utmost fury wreak
  On things that are but seeming !
First kill ; then die ; that God may speak,
  And man surcease from dreaming !
That Love and Justice strong as love
  May be the poles unshaken
Round which a world new-born may move ;
  And Truth that slept may waken !

THE WEDDING OF THE CLANS;

A GIRL'S BABBLE.

I GO to knit two clans together;
   Our clan and this new clan unseen of yore :—
Our clan fears nought! but I go, O whither?
   This day I go from my mother's door!

Thou redbreast sing'st the old song over
   Though many a time thou hast sung it before;
They never sent thee to some strange new lover :—
   I sing a new song by my mother's door.

I stepp'd from my little room down by the ladder,
   The ladder that never so shook before;
I was sad last night ;—to-day I am sadder,
   Because I go from my mother's door.

The last snow melts upon bush and bramble :
   The gold bars shine on the forest's floor;
Shake not, thou leaf! it is I must tremble
   Because I go from my mother's door.

From a Spanish sailor a dagger I bought me;
   I trail'd three rose-trees our grey bawn o'er;
The creed and my letters our old bard taught me;
   My days were sweet by my mother's door.

My little white goat that with raised feet huggest
  The oak stock, thy horns in the ivies frore,
Could I wrestle like thee—how the wreaths thou
      tuggest !—
  I never would move from my mother's door.

O weep no longer, my nurse and mother !
  My foster-sister, weep not so sore !
You cannot come with me, Ir, my brother—
  Alone I go from my mother's door.

Farewell, my wolf-hound, that slew Mac Owing
  As he caught me and far through the thickets
      bore ;—
My heifer, Alb, in the green vale lowing,
  My cygnet's nest upon Lorna's shore !

He has kill'd ten chiefs, this chief that plights me :
  His hand is like that of the giant Balor :
But I fear his kiss ; and his beard affrights me,
  And the great stone dragon above his door.

Had I daughters nine with me they should tarry ;
  They should sing old songs ; they should dance
      at my door ;
They should grind at the quern ;—no need to marry ;—
  O when will this marriage-day be o'er ?

Had I buried, like Moirin, three mates already
  I might say, "Three husbands ! then why not four?"
But my hand is cold and my foot unsteady
  Because I never was married before !

THE STATUTE OF KILKENNY.

A.D. 1367.

OF old ye warr'd on men : to-day
    On women and on babes ye war ;
The Noble's child his head must lay
    Beneath the peasant's roof no more !

I saw in sleep the Infant's hand
    His foster-brother's fiercely grasp ;
His warm arm, lithe as willow wand,
    Twines me each day with closer clasp !

O infant smiler ! grief beguiler !
    Between the oppressor and the oppress'd
O soft, unconscious reconciler,
    Smile on ! through thee the land is bless'd

Through thee the puissant love the poor ;
    His conqueror's hope the vanquish'd shares
For thy sake by a lowly door
    The clan made vassal stops and stares.

Our vales are healthy. On thy cheek
    There dawns, each day, a livelier red :
Smile on ! Before another week
    Thy feet our earthern floor will tread !

Thy foster-brothers twain for thee
　　Would face the wolves on snowy fell :
Smile on ! the Irish Enemy
　　Will fence their Norman nursling well.

The nursling as the child is dear ;—
　　Thy mother loves not like thy nurse !
That babbling Mandate steps not near
　　Thy cot but o'er her bleeding corse !

THE TRUE KING.

A.D. 1399.

I.

HE came in the night on a false pretence ;
　　As a friend he came ; as a lord remains :
His coming we noted not—when—or whence ;
　　We slept : we woke in chains.
Ere a year they had chased us to dens and caves ;
　　Our streets and our churches lay drown'd in blood ,
The race that had sold us their sons as slaves
　　In our land our conquerors stood !

II.

Who were they, those princes that gave away
　　What was theirs to keep not theirs to give ?

A king holds sway for a passing day;
　　The kingdoms for ever live !
The tanist succeeds when the king is dust :
　　The king rules all; yet the king hath nought.
They were traitors not kings who sold their trust;
　　They were traitors nót kings who bought !

III.

Brave Art Mac Murrough !—Arise, 'tis morn !
　　For a true king the nation waited long.
He is strong as the horn of the unicorn,
　　This true king who rights our wrong !
He rules in the fight by an inward right;
　　From the heart of the nation her king is grown;
He rules by right; he is might of her might;
　　Her flesh, and bone of her bone !

THE EVE OF THE PURIFICATION.

ON February's face once more
    What airs are softly playing?
By pale blue meers and forests hoar
    How goes the Church a-maying?

A Beam there rests on wold and wild
    And hoar-frost slowly dying,
With touch as light as Mary's Child
    On Simeon's bosom lying!

On yonder hill, half blue half brown,
    The spotty snows wind-sifted
Gleam like a flock of wild swans down
    From realms of azure drifted.

Loud sings the blackbird! well he knows
    The Spring is hurrying onward;
Our omens wait not for the rose;
    Our ensigns still fly vanward!

At morn the Church her lights shall lift
    To Simeon and to Anna;
The mother-maid shall bring her gift
    The temples ring, " Hosanna!"

Two turtle-doves !—their wings e'en now
  On Erin's air are beating !
Fresh odours launch'd from Carmel's brow
  O'er western wastes are fleeting !

St. Agnes' lamb again has stared
  Upon her flowery dressing,
And, wonderingly, with Christians shared
  The Pontiff's annual blessing :

St. Agnes' lamb that sends the Palls,
  In purity's devotion,
Beyond the snowy Alpine walls
  And foam-fields of the ocean !

COMPLINE.

HOW oft her cradled babe beside,
    Singing some mother kneeleth,
While, dimpling o'er the darkening tide,
    A ray from Hesper stealeth.

Thus, but with sweeter song, the Church
    While shades the dark hills cumber
Kneels in the twilight's starry porch,
    And sings her babes to slumber!

The earth is vext,—her love gives rest,
    Sole love which cannot vary;
And those Sabæan hymns thrice-blest
    The antiphons of Mary.

Die, quiet day in blight or bloom
    Sweet anthems round thee ringing!
The Bride of Heaven above thy tomb
    Her compline rite is singing!

QUEEN MARGARET'S FEASTING.

A.D. 1451.

I.

FAIR she stood—God's queenly creature!
  Wondrous joy was in her face;
Of her ladies none in stature
  Like to her, and none in grace.
On the church-roof stood they round her,
  Cloth of gold was her attire;
They in jewell'd circle wound her;—
  Beside her Ely's king her sire.

II.

Far and near the green fields glitter'd
  Like to poppy-beds in Spring,
Gay with companies loose-scatter'd
  Seated each in seemly ring
Under banners red or yellow:
  There all day the feast they kept
From chill dawn and noontide mellow,
  Till the hill-shades eastward crept.

III.

On a white steed at the gateway
　　Margaret's husband, Calwagh, sate:
Guest on guest, approaching, straightway
　　Welcomed he with love and state.
Each pass'd on with largess laden,
　　Chosen gifts of thought and work,
Now the red cloak of the maiden,
　　Now the minstrel's golden torque.

IV.

On the wind the tapestries shifted:
　　From the blue hills rang the horn;
Slowly toward the sunset drifted
　　Choral song and shout breeze-borne.
Like a sea the crowds unresting
　　Murmur'd round the grey church-tower;
Many a prayer, amid the feasting,
　　For Margaret's mother rose that hour!

V.

On the church-roof kerne and noble
　　At her bright face look'd half dazed;
Nought was hers of shame or trouble;—
　　On the crowds far off she gazed:
Once, on heaven her dark eyes bending,
　　Her hands in prayer she flung apart;
Unconsciously her arms extending
　　She bless'd her people in her heart.

VI.

Thus a Gaelic queen and nation
　At Imayn till set of sun
Kept with feast the Annunciation,
　Fourteen hundred fifty-one.
Time it was of solace tender;—
　'Twas a brave time, strong yet fair!
Blessing, O ye angels, send her
　From Salem's towers, and Inisglaaire!

O F things above we know the worth :—
　　What stamps a worth on things below?
Justice and Truth! Insurgent Earth
　No claim to reverence canst thou show

Save these.   What marvel then if Song
　Strike oft the plectrum with a sword!
Invoke the right, denounce the wrong,
　Muse, none of mine unless abhorr'd

By all who have not made a pact
　With Truth though trod to death, and sworn
Nor by inaction nor by act
　To side with them the Right who scorn!

Muse clad in mail ! by many a dint
  That cuirass and that helm I know :—
Go, set thy countenance like a flint
  Against the storm, and let it blow !

No part hast thou in courtly praise !
  Tyrannicides must strike and die :—
Ah, better die than dumbly gaze
  On prosperous Wrong with edgeless eye !

Thus sang thy mission'd Bard, O'Neill,
  At England's court a threatening guest,
In robes of state.   Round ranks of steel
  Ran the shrill whisper ill suppress'd.

INISFAIL;

OR,

IRELAND IN THE OLDEN TIME.

PART II.

A VOICE from the midnoon call'd, " Arise, be
        " alone, and remove thee ;
    " Descend into valleys of bale, and look on the
        " visions of night ;
  " From the stranger flee, and be strange to the men
        " and the women that love thee,
    " That thy wine may be tears, and that ashes may
        " mix with the meats of delight.

  " To few is the Vision shown, and to none for his
        " weal or from merit :
    " As lepers they live who see it ; as those that
        " men pity or hate ;
  " And to few the Voice is reveal'd ;—yet to them
        " who hear and can bear it
    " If bitterness cometh at first yet sweetness
        " cometh more late."

Then in vision I saw a corse—death-cold ; but the
        angels had draped it
    In light ; and the light it cast round the unseal'd
        death-cave was strewn ;
And an anthem rush'd o'er the worlds : but the
        tongue that moulded and shaped it
    Was a great storm through ruins borne ; and the
        lips that spake it were stone.

PLORANS PLORAVIT.

A.D. 1583.

SHE sits alone on the cold grave stone
      And only the dead are nigh her :
In the tongue of the Gael she makes her wail :—
   The night wind rushes by her.

" Few, O few are the leal and true,
   " And fewer shall be, and fewer :
" The land is a corse ;—no life, no force—
   " O wind with sere leaves strew her !

" Men ask what scope is left for hope
   " To one who has known her story :—
" I trust her dead ! Their graves are red :
   " But their souls are with God in glory."

ROISIN DUBH;

OR, THE BLEEDING HEART.

Roisin Dubh signifies literally the "Black little Rose,"
and was one of the mystical names under which the bards
celebrated Ireland.

I.

O WHO art thou with that queenly brow
And uncrown'd head?
And why is the vest that binds thy breast,
O'er the heart, blood-red?
Like a rose-bud in June was that spot at noon
A rose-bud weak;
But it deepens and grows like a July rose—
Death-pale thy cheek!

II.

" The babes I fed at my foot lay dead;
" I saw them die:
" In Ramah a blast went wailing past;
" It was Rachel's cry.
" But I stand sublime on the shores of Time,
" And I pour mine ode,

" As Myriam sang to the cymbals' clang,
  " On the wind to God.

III.

" Once more at my feasts my Bards and Priests
  " Shall sit and eat ;
" And the Shepherd whose sheep are on every steep
  " Shall bless my meat !
" Oh, sweet, men say, is the song by day,
  " And the feast by night ;
" But on poisons I thrive, and in death survive
  " Through ghostly might."

I.

BESIDE that Eastern sea—there first exalted
    Heaven-high—behold the Cross of Christ
      lies low !
Sad St. Sophia ! 'neath thy roofs gold-vaulted
  Who kneels this hour ? the blind and turban'd
      Foe !

II.

O Eire ! a sister hast thou in thy sorrow ;
  If thine the earlier, hers the bitterer moan ;—
She weeps to-day; great Rome may weep to-morrow !
  Claim not that o'er-proud boast to weep alone.

WAR-SONG OF MAC CARTHY.

I.

TWO lives of an eagle, the old song saith,
    Make the life of a black yew-tree;
For two lives of a yew-tree the furrough's path
    Men trace, grass-grown on the lea;
Two furroughs they last till the time is past
    God willeth the world to be;
For a furrough's life has Mac Carthy stood fast,
    Mac Carthy in Carbery.

II.

Up with the banner whose green shall live
    While lives the green on the oak!
And down with the axes that grind and rive
    Keen-edged as the thunder stroke!
And on with the battle-cry known of old,
    And the clan-rush like wind and wave;—
On, on! the Invader is bought and sold;
    His own hand has dug his grave!

FLORENCE MAC CARTHY'S FAREWELL
TO HIS ENGLISH LOVE.

I.

MY pensive-brow'd Evangeline!
  What says to thee old Windsor's pine
  Whose shadow o'er the pleasance sways?
It says, " Ere long the evening star
" Will pierce my darkness from afar :—
  " I grieve as one with grief who plays."

II.

Evangeline! Evangeline!
In that far distant land of mine
  There stands a yew-tree among tombs!
For ages there that tree has stood,
A black pall dash'd with drops of blood—
  O'er all my world it breathes its glooms.

III.

England's fair child, Evangeline!
Because my yew-tree is not thine,
  Because thy Gods on mine wage war,
Farewell! Back fall the gates of brass ;
The exile to his own must pass ;—
  I seek the land of tombs once more.

TO THE SAME.

WE seem to tread the self-same street,
    To pace the self-same courts or grass :
Parting, our hands appear to meet—
    O vanitatum vanitas !

Distant as earth from heaven or hell
    From thee the things to me most dear :
Ghost-throng'd Cocytus and thy will
    Between us rush.　We might be near.

Thy world is fair :—my thoughts refuse
    To dance its dance or drink its wine ;
Nor canst thou hear the reeds and yews
    That sigh to me from lands not thine.

WAR-SONG OF TIRCONNELL'S BARD AT THE BATTLE OF BLACKWATER,

A. D. 1597.

At this battle the Irish of Ulster were commanded by
" Red Hugh " O'Neill, Prince of Tirone, and by Hugh O'Donnell (called also " Red Hugh "), Prince of Tirconnell. Queen
Elizabeth's army was led by Marshal Bagnal, who fell in the
rout with 2,500 of the invading force. Twelve thousand
gold pieces, thirty-four standards, and all the artillery of the
vanquished army were taken.

I.

GLORY to God, and to the powers that fight ·
    For Freedom and the Right !
We have them then, the Invaders ! There they stand
    Once more on Oriel's land !
They have pass'd the gorge stream-cloven,
    And the mountain's purple bound ;
Now the toils are round them woven,
    Now the nets are spread around !
Give them time : their steeds are blown ;—
    Let them stand and round them stare
    Breathing blasts of Irish air.
    Our clouds are o'er them sailing ;
    Our woods are round them wailing ;
Our eagles know their own !

II.

Thrice we've met them—race and brood !
First at Clontibret they stood :—
How soon the giant son of Meath
Roll'd from his horse upon the heath !
Again we met them ; once again ;
Portmore and Banburb's plain know where ;
There fell de Burgh ; there fell Kildare :
(His valiant foster-brothers twain
Died at his feet, but died in vain ;)
There Waller, Turner, Vaughan fell,
Vanquish'd, though deem'd invincible !
We raised that hour a battle-axe
That dinn'd the iron on your backs !
Vengeance, that hour, a wide-wing'd Fury,
On drave you to the gates of Newry :
There rest ye found ; by rest restored,
Sang there your song of Battleford !

III.

Thou rising sun, fair fall
Thy greeting on Armagh's time-honour'd wall,
And on the willows hoar
That fringe thy silver waters, Avonmore !
See ! on that hill of drifted sand
The far-famed Marshal holds command,
Bagnal, their bravest :—to the right
That recreant neither chief nor knight
" The Queen's O'Reilly," he that sold
His country, clan and church for gold !

" Saint George for England !"—Rebel crew !
What are the Saints ye spurn to you ?
They charge ; they pass yon grassy swell ;
They reach our pitfall's hidden well.
On, warriors native to the sod,
Be on them in the power of God !

IV.

Twin stars ! Twin regents of our righteous war !
This day remember whose, and who ye are—
Thou that o'er green Tir-owen's tribes hast sway !
Thou whom Tir-connell's vales obey !
  The line of Nial, the line of Conn
  So oft at strife, to-day are one !
  Both Chiefs are dear to Eire ; to me
  Dearest he is and needs must be
  My Prince, my Chief, my child, on whom
  So early fell the dungeon's doom.
  O'Donnell ! hear this day thy Bard !
  By those young feet so maim'd and scarr'd,
  Bit by the winter's fangs when lost
  Thou wandered'st on through snows and frost,
Remember thou those years in chains thou worest,
  Snatch'd in false peace from unsuspecting halls,
And that one thought, of all thy pangs the sorest,
  Thy subjects groan'd the upstart alien's thralls !
    That thought on waft thee through the fight :
      On, on, for Erin's right !

V.

Seest thou yon stream whose tawny waters glide
Through weeds and yellow marsh lingeringly and
       slowly?
     Blest is that spot and holy!
There, ages past, Saint Berean stood and cried,
" This spot shall quell one day the Invaders' pride!"
     He saw in mystic trance
      The blood-stain flush yon rill :—
  On, hosts of God, advance ;
     Your country's fates fulfil !
  On, clansmen, leal and true,
  Lambdearg ! Bataillah-aboo !
  Be Truth this day your might !
  Truth lords it in the fight !

VI.

  O'Neill ! That day be with thee now
When, throned on Ulster's regal seat of stone,
  Thou satt'st and thou alone ;
While flock'd from far the Tribes, and to thy hand
  Was given the snow-white wand,
Erin's authentic sceptre of command !
Kingless a People stood around thee ! Thou
Didst dash the British bauble from thy brow,
  And for a coronet laid down
  That People's love became once more thy crown !
   True King alone is he
In whom summ'd up his People share the throne :—

Fair from the soil he rises like a tree :
　Rock-like the stranger presses on it, prone !
　　Strike for that People's cause !
　　For Tanistry ; for Brehon laws :
The sage traditions of civility ;
Pure hearths, and faith set free !

VII.

Hark ! the thunder of their meeting!
Hand meets hand, and rough the greeting !
Hark ! the crash of shield and brand ;
They mix, they mingle, band with band,
Intertwisted, intertangled,
Mangled forehead meeting mangled
Like two horn-commingling stags
Wrestling on the mountain crags !
Lo ! the wavering darkness through
I see the banner of Red Hugh ;
Close beside is thine, O'Neill !
Now they stoop and now they reel,
Rise once more and onward sail,
Like two falcons on one gale !—
O ye clansmen past me rushing
Like mountain torrents seaward gushing,
Tell the Chiefs that from this height
Their Chief of Bards beholds the fight ;
That on theirs he pours his spirit ;
Marks their deeds and chaunts their merit ;
While the Priesthood evermore

Like him that ruled God's host of yore
With arms outstretch'd that God implore!

VIII.

Mightiest of the line of Conn,
On to victory!   On, on, on!
It is Erin that in thee
Lives and works right wondrously!
Eva from the heavenly bourne
Upon thee her eyes doth turn,
She whose marriage couch was spread
'Twixt the dying and the dead!
Parcell'd kingdoms one by one
For a prey to traitors thrown;
Pledges forfeit, broken vows,
Roofless fane, and blazing house;
All the dreadful deeds of old
Rise resurgent from the mould
For their judgment peal is toll'd!
All our Future takes her stand
Hawk-like on thy lifted hand.
States that live not, vigil keeping
In the limbo of long weeping;
Palace-courts and minster-towers
That shall make this isle of ours
Fairer than the star of morn,
Wait thy mandate to be born!
Chief elect 'mid desolation
Wield thou well the inspiration
Thou drawest from a new-born nation!

IX.

Sleep no longer Bards that hold
Ranged beneath me harps of gold !
Smite them with a heavier hand
Than vengeance lays on axe or brand !
Pour upon the blast a song
Linking litanies of wrong,
Till, like poison-dews, the strain
Eat into the Invader's brain.
On the retributive harp
Catch that death-shriek shrill and sharp
Which she utter'd, she whose lord
Perish'd, Essex, at thy board !
Peerless chieftain ! peerless wife !
From his throat, and hers, the knife
Drain'd the mingled tide of life !
Sing the base assassin's steel
By Sussex hired to slay O'Neill !
Sing, fierce Bards, the plains sword-wasted,
Sing the cornfields burnt and blasted
That when raged the war no longer
Kernes dog-chased might pine with hunger !
Pour around their ears the groans
Of half-human skeletons
From wet cave or forest-cover
Foodless deserts peering over,
Or upon the roadside lying
Infant dead and mother dying
On their mouths the grassy stain
Of the wild weed gnaw'd in vain ;—

Look upon them hoary Head
Of the last of Desmonds dead;
His that drew—too late—his sword
Religion and his right to guard;
Head that evermore dost frown
From the tower of London down!
She that slew him from her barge
Makes that Head this hour the targe
Of her insults cold and keen,
England's caliph, not her queen!
—Portent terrible and dire
Whom thy country and thy sire
Branded with a bastard's name,
Thy birth was but thy lightest shame!
To honour recreant and thine oath;—
    Trampling that Faith whose borrow'd garb
    First gave thee sceptre crown and orb.
Thy flatterers scorn, thy lovers loathe
That idol with the blood-stain'd feet
Ill-throned on murder'd Mary's seat!

X.

Glory be to God on high!
That shout rang up into the sky!
The plain lies bare; the smoke drifts by;
Again that cry: they fly! they fly!
O'er them standards thirty-four
Waved at morn; they wave no more.
Glory be to Him alone who holds the nations in His
    hand,

And to them the heavenly guardians of our church
    and native land !
Sing, ye priests, your deep Te Deums ; bards, make
    answer loud and long,
In your rapture flinging heavenward censers of tri-
    umphant song.
Isle for centuries blind in bondage make once more
    thine ancient boast,
From the cliffs of Inishowen southward on to Car-
    bery's coast !
We have seen the right made perfect, seen the
    Hand that rules the spheres
Glance like lightning through the clouds, and back-
    ward roll the wrongful years.
Glory fadeth, but this triumph is no barren mundane
    glory ;
Rays of healing it shall scatter on the eyes that read
    our story :
Upon nations bound and torpid as they waken it shall
    shine
As on Peter in his chains the angel shone with light
    divine.
From the unheeding, from the unholy it may hide,
    like Truth, its ray ;
But when Truth and Justice conquer on their crowns
    its beam shall play.
O'er the ken of troubled tyrants it shall trail a me-
    teor's glare ;
For the blameless it shall glitter as the star of
    morning fair :

Whensoever Erin triumphs then its dawn it shall
    renew,—
Then O'Neill shall be remember'd, and Tirconnell's
    chief, Red Hugh !

WAR-SONG OF LEIX.

A.D. 1600.

I.

IS their isle so narrow that here they must come
    In search of the milk and grain?
Would they teach us the lesson they learn'd at home
    From Roman and Saxon and Dane?
Where'er they have march'd on the barren track
    Lies a plume from the raven's wing;
Where'er they have camp'd the land is black
    Whilst all around is Spring!

II.

Small love they have given, small love they have got
    Since first they darken'd our door;
The back of the hand and the sole of the foot
    From us they have had—no more!
They shall learn to-day 'twas an easier sport
    To catch the maid by the hair,
Or their captives to drown at the Golden Fort
    Than to beard O'More in his lair!

THE SUGANE EARL.

I.

'TWAS the White Knight that sold him,—his
flesh and his blood !
A Fitz-Gerald betray'd the Fitz-Gerald :
Death-pale the false friend in the 'mid forest stood ;—
Close by stood the conqueror's herald !
At the cave-mouth he lean'd on his sword pale and
dumb,
But the eye that was on him o'erbore him :
" Come forth," cried the White Knight ;—one
answer'd, " I come !"
And the Chief of his House stood before him !

II.

" Cut him down," said the Captive with cold smile
and stern,
" 'Twas a bold stake ; but Satan hath won it !"
In the days of thy father, Earl Desmond, no kerne
Had heard that command, and not done it !
The name of the White Knight shall cease, and his race !
His castle down fall, roof and rafter !—
This day is a day of rebuke ; but the base
Shall meet what he merits hereafter !

THE PHANTOM FUNERAL.

A.D. 1601.

James Fitz-Garret, son of the great Earl of Desmond, had been sent to England when a child as a hostage, and was for seventeen years kept a prisoner in the tower, and educated in the Queen's Religion. James Fitz-Thomas, the 'Sugane Earl,' having meantime assumed the title and prerogatives of Earl of Desmond, the Queen sent her captive to Ireland attended by persons devoted to her, and provided with a *conditional* patent for his restoration. Arriving at Kilmallock, on his way to Kerry, wheat and salt were showered on him by the people, in testimony of loyalty. The next day was Sunday. As the young earl walked to church, it was with difficulty that a guard of English soldiers could keep a path open for him. From street and window and housetop every voice urged him to fidelity to his ancestral faith. The youth, who did not even understand the language in which he was adjured, went on to the Queen's church, as it was called; and with loud cries his clan rushed away and abandoned his standard for ever. Shortly afterwards he returned to England, where, within a few months, he died. See LELAND's *History of Ireland*, Book IV, Cap. 5, and the *Pacata Hibernia*.

STREW the bed and strew the bier,
    (Who rests upon it was never man)
With all that a little child holds dear,
    With violets blue and violets wan.

Strew the bed and strew the bier
  With the berries that redden thy shores, Corann ;
His lip was the berry, his skin was clear
  As the waxen blossom.   He ne'er was man !

Far off he sleeps ; yet we mourn him here :
  Their tale is a falsehood ! he ne'er was man !
'Tis a phantom funeral ! Strew the bier
  With white lilies brush'd by the floating swan.

They lie who say that the false queen caught him
  A child asleep on the mountains wide ;
A captive rear'd him ; a strange faith taught him :—
  'Twas for no strange faith that his father died !

They lie who say that the child return'd
  A man unmann'd to his towers of pride ;
That his people with curses the false Earl spurn'd :—
  Woe, woe, Kilmallock ! they lie, and lied !

The clan was wroth at an ill report,
  But now the thunder-cloud melts in tears.
The child that was motherless play'd. 'Twas sport !
  A child must sport in his childish years !

Ululah ! Ululah ! Low, sing low !
  The women of Desmond loved well that child !
Our lamb was lost in the winter snow :—
  Long years we sought him in wood and wild.

How many a babe of Fitz-Gerald's blood
  In hut was foster'd though born in hall!
The old stock burgeon'd the fair new bud,
  The old land welcomed them, each and all!

Glynn weeps to-day by the Shannon's tide,
  And Shanid and she that frowns o'er Deal;
There is woe by the Laune and the Carra's side,
  And where the Knight dwells by the woody Feale.

In Dingle and Beara they chaunt his dirge;—
  Far off he faded—our child—sing low!
We have made him a bed by the ocean's surge;
  We have made him a bier on the mountain's brow.

The clan was bereft! the old walls they left;
  With cries they rush'd to the mountains drear!
But now great sorrow their heart has cleft;—
  See! one by one they are drawing near!

Ululah! Ululah! Low, sing low!
  The flakes fall fast on the little bier;—
The yew-branch and eagle-plume over them throw!
  The last of the Desmond Chiefs lies here.

THE MARCH TO KINSALE.

DECEMBER, A. D. 1601.

I.

O'ER many a river bridged with ice,
   Through many a vale with snow-drifts
      dumb,
Past quaking fen and precipice
   The Princes of the North are come!
Lo, these are they that year by year
   Roll'd back the tide of England's war ;—
Rejoice, Kinsale! thy hope is near!
   That wondrous winter march is o'er.
      And thus they sang, " To-morrow morn
        " Our eyes shall rest upon the foe :
        " Roll on, swift night, in silence borne,
        " And blow, thou breeze of sunrise, blow ! "

II.

Blithe as a boy on march'd the host
   With droning pipe and clear-voiced harp ;—
At last above that southern coast
   Rang out their war-steed's whinny sharp :
And up the sea-salt slopes they wound,
   And airs once more of ocean quaff'd ;—

Those frosty woods the rocks that crown'd
   As though May touch'd them waved and laugh'd.
   And thus they sang, " To-morrow morn
    " Our eyes shall rest upon our foe :
  " Roll on, swift night, in silence borne,
    " And blow, thou breeze of sunrise, blow !"

III.

Beside their watch-fires couch'd all night
   Some slept some laugh'd, at cards some play'd,
While, chaunting on a central height
   Of moonlit crag, the priesthood pray'd.
And some to sweetheart, some to wife
   Sent message kind ; while others told
Triumphant tales of recent fight,
   Or legends of their sires of old.
    And thus they sang, " To-morrow morn
     " Our eyes at last shall see the foe ;
    " Roll on, swift night, in silence borne,
     " And blow, thou breeze of sunrise, blow !"

A.D. 1602.

WHAT man can stand amid a place of tombs
    Nor yearn to that poor vanquish'd dust be-
        neath?—
Above a nation's grave no violet blooms;
    A vanquish'd nation lies in endless death.

'Tis past!—the dark is dense with ghost and vision!
    All lost!—the air is throng'd with moan and wail;
But one day more and hope had been fruition;—
    Oh Athunree, thy fate o'erhung Kinsale!

What Name is that which lays on every head
    A hand like fire, striking the strong locks grey?
What Name is named not save with shame and dread?
    Once let us name it,—then no more for aye!

Kinsale! accursed be he the first who bragg'd
    " A city stands where roam'd but late the flock;"
Accursed the day, when, from the mountain dragg'd,
    Thy corner-stone forsook the mother-rock!

I.

I AM black but fair, and the robe I wear
  Is dark as death;
My cheek is pale and I bind my veil
  With a cypress wreath.
Where the night-shades flower I build the bower
  Of my secret rest;—
O kind is sleep to the eyes that weep
  And the bleeding breast.

II.

My palace floor I tread no more;
  No throne is mine;
No sceptre I hold, nor drink from gold
  Spain's purple wine:
Yet I rule a queen in the worlds unseen
  By Saxon eye;
A realm I have in the hearts of the brave
  And an empery.

III.

In crypt, not aisle, of the ruin'd pile
  All day I lurk,
And in western caves when the ocean raves,
  Through the midnight murk.

But far o'er the sea there is one loves me
　'Neath the southern star :
The Fisherman's ring my help shall bring,
　And heal my scar.

SONG.

I.

HIS war-horse beats a distant bourne
　Till comes the glad new year ;
Therefore thy wheel in silence turn,
　And only dream him near.
He fights where native monarchs be,
　Where Moors no longer reign :
He strikes and cries, " My land, for thee !"
　Amid deliver'd Spain.

II.

O maiden of the moon-pale face
　And darkly lucid eye !
For knights wave-wash'd round Smerwick's base
　Fair Spanish maidens sigh !
The moss, till comes the glad new year,
　Alone may clothe the bough ;
Alone the raindrop deck the breer—
　It weeps, and so must thou !

THE IRISH EXILE AT FIESOLE.

I.

HERE to thine exile rest is sweet;
    Here, mother-land, thy breath is near him!
Thy pontiff, Donat, raised his seat
    On these fair hills that still revere him;
Like him that thrill'd the Helvetian vale,
    St. Gall's, with rock-resounded anthem:—
For their sakes honour'd is the Gael;
    The peace they gave to men God grant them!

II.

Far down in pomp the Arno winds
    By domes the boast of old religion;
The eternal azure shining blinds
    Serene Ausonia's balmiest region.
Assunta be her name! for bright
    She sits, assumed 'mid heavenly glories;
But ah! more dear, though dark like night,
    To me, my loved and lost Dolores!

III.

The mild Franciscans say—and sigh—
    " Weep not except for Christ's sweet Passion!"

They never saw their Florence lie,
   Like her I mourn, in desolation!
On this high crest they brood in rest,
   The pines their Saint and them embowering,
While centuries blossom round their nest
   Like those slow aloes seldom flowering.

IV.

" Salvete, flores martyrum!"
   Such is the Roman Philip's greeting
In banner'd streets with myrtles dumb
   The grave-eyed English college meeting.
There lives an older martyr-land!
   All lands once loved her—none would aid her;
Or reaching forth a tardy hand
   Enfeebled first, at last betray'd her!

V.

That land men named a younger Rome!
   She lit the north with radiance golden;
Alone survives the catacomb
   Of all that Roman greatness olden!
Her Cathall at Tarento sate:
   Virgilius! Saltzburgh was thy mission!
Who sow'd the faith fasts long, feasts late;
   Who reap'd retains unvex'd fruition.

VI.

Peace settles on the whitening hair;
   The heart that burned grows cold and colder;

My resurrection spot is there,
  Where yon Etrurian ruins moulder.
Foot-sore by yonder pillar's base
  My rest I make, unknown and lowly;
And teach the legend-loving race
  To weep a Troy than theirs more holy.

TO NUALA IN ROME.

Nuala was the sister of Red Hugh, and of Roderick O'Donnell. The former died an exile in Spain; the latter in Rome,
A. D. 1608. It was on finding her weeping at her brother's
grave in St. Pietro Montorio, that O'Donnell's Bard addressed
to her the ode well-known through Clarence Mangan's trans-
lation.

THY shining eyes are vague with tears,
  Though seldom and unseen they flow;
The playmate of thy childish years—
  My friend—at last lies low.

If I thus late thy love might win,
  Withheld for his sake, brief the gain;
I live in battle's ceaseless din:
  Thou liv'st in silent pain.

Nuala! exile, and the bread
  By strangers doled thy cheek make pale;
On blue Loch Eirne that cheek was red,
  In western Ruaidh's gale!

The branching stag looks down no more
From sunset cliffs upon thy path
In Doire.   Thou tread'st not now the shore
By Aileach's royal Rath.

No more thou hear'st the sea-wind sing
O'er cairns where Ulster monarchs sleep;
The linnets of the Latian spring
They only make thee weep.

To thee no joy from domes enskied,
Or ruins of Imperial Rome;
Thou look'st beyond them, hungry-eyed,
T'ward thy far Irish home.

On green Tirconnell, now a waste,
The sighs of myriads feed thine own;
Nuala! soon my clarion's blast
Those sighs and thine shall drown!

In Spain they call us king and prince,
And plight alliance, and betray;
In Rome through clouds of frankincense
Slow dawns our better day.

To king or kaiser, prince or pope,
I sue not, nor to magic spell;—
Nuala! on this sword my Hope
Stands like a God.   Farewell!

WINTER SONG.

THE high-piled cloud drifts on as in scorn,
   Like a ghost, half pining, half stately,
Or a white ice-island in silence borne
   O'er seas congeal'd but lately.

With nose to the ground, like a wilder'd hound,
   O'er the wood-leaves yellow and sodden
On races the wind but cannot find
   One sweet track where Spring hath trodden.

The moor is black; with frosty rime
   The wither'd brier is beaded;
The sluggard Spring hath o'erslept her time,
   The Spring that was never more needed.

What says the oak-leaf in the night-cold noon,
   And the beech-stock scoffing and surly?
" Who comes too soon is a witless loon
   " Like the clown that is up too early."

But the moss grows fair when the trees are bare,
Long torpid Spring finds a pillow there;
And beside it the fern with its green crown saith
" Best bloometh the Hope that is rooted in death."

THE SUPPRESSION OF THE FAITH IN ULSTER.

BARDIC ODE, A.D. 1623.

Throughout Ulster, and indeed in most parts of Ireland, it had been found impossible to carry the penal laws against the Roman Catholic Faith fully into effect until the reign of James I. The accession of that prince was hailed as the beginning of an era of liberty and peace. James had ever boasted himself a descendant of the ancient Milesian princes, had had frequent dealings with the Irish Chiefs in their wars against Elizabeth, and was believed by them to be, at least in heart, devoted to the religion of his mother. In the earlier part of his reign, though he refused to grant a legal toleration, he engaged that the " penal laws should not be executed.' In the year 1605 a proclamation was issued commanding all catholic priests to quit Ireland under the penalty of death. Next came the imputed plot and compulsory flight of Tirconnell and Tyrone, the Plantation of Ulster, and the swamping of the Irish Parliament by the creation of fictitious boroughs. In 1622 Archbishop Ussher preached before the new Lord Deputy, Lord Faulkland, his celebrated sermon with the text, " He beareth not the sword in vain." The next year a new proclamation was published commanding the departure of all the catholic clergy, regular and secular, within forty days. The victory of James over Ulster was the loss of Ireland to his son and grandson.

I.

NOW we know that they are dead!
   They, the Chiefs that kept from scaith
The northern land,—the sentenced Faith,—
Now we know that they are dead!

II.

Wrong, with rapine in her leash,
Walk'd her ancient rounds afresh !
Law—late come—with leaden mace
Smites religion in the face ;—
But the spoiler first had place !

III.

Axes and hammers, hot work and hard !
    From niche and from turret the saints they cast ;
The church stands naked as the church-yard ;
    The craftsman-army toils fiercely and fast :
They pluck from the altars the precious stones,
    As vultures pluck at a dead-man's eyes ;
Like wolves down-dragging the flesh from the bones
    They strip the gold from the canopies.
The tombs they rifle ; they melt the bells ;
The foundry furnace bubbles and swells !—
Spoiler, for once thou hast err'd ; what ho !
This shaft thou hast loosed from an ill-strung bow !
In the Faith thou wouldst strangle thy mother died !
Who slew her ? The false queen, our chiefs defied !
Thy heart was with Rome in those days of old ;
Thy counsel was ours ; thy counsel and gold !

IV.

A ban went forth from the regal chambers,
    From the prince that courted us once with lies,
From the secular synods where he who clambers,
    Not he that walks upright, receives the prize :—

" Go back to thy Judah, sad Prophet, go ;
" There break thy bread and denounce thy woe ;
" But no longer in Bethel thy prophecy sing,
" 'Tis the chapel and court of Samaria's king !"
—Let England renounce her church at will,
The children of Ireland are faithful still.
For a thousand years has that church been theirs ;—
They are God's, not Cæsar's, the creeds and prayers !

v.

Thou that art haughty and full of bread,
The crown falls soon from the unwise head !
The nations that rear strange altars up
With glory may feast, but with ruin sup ;
In the deserts of penance they peak and pine
'Till fulfill'd are the days of the wrath divine.
Thy covenant make with the cave and brier
For shelter by day and by night for fire ;
When the bolt is launch'd at the craggy crest,
And the cedars flame round the eagle's nest !

vi.

A voice from the ocean waves,
   And a voice from the forest glooms,
And a voice from old temples and kingly graves,
   And a voice from the catacombs :—
It cries, the king that warreth
   On religion and freedom entwined in one
Down drags in his blindness the fane, nor spareth
   The noble's hall, nor the throne !

I saw in my visions the walls give way
  Of the mystic Babylon;
I saw the gold Idol whose feet are clay
  On his forehead lying prone;
I saw a sea-eagle defaced with gore
  Flag wearily over the main;
But her nest on the cliff she reach'd no more,
  For the shaft was in her brain.
As when some strong man a stone uplifteth
  And flingeth into floods far down,
So God when the balance of justice shifteth
  Down dasheth the despot's crown,
Down dasheth the realm that abused its trust,
  And the nation that knew not pity,
And maketh the image of power unjust
  To vanish from out the city!

VII.

Wait, my country, and be wise;—
  Thou art gall'd in head and breast,
  Rest thou needest, sleep and rest:
Rest and sleep, and thou shalt rise
And tread down thine enemies.
That which God ordains is best;
That which God permits is good,
Though by man least understood.
Now His sword He gives to those
Who have wisdom won from woes;
In them fighting ends the strife:
At other times the impious priest

Q

Slipping on his victim's blood
Falls in death on his own knife,—
God is hard to 'scape! His ire
Strikes the son if not the sire!
In a time, to God not long,
Thou shalt reckon with this wrong!

SONG.

I.

A MARCH-WIND sang in a frosty wood,
  'Twas in Oriel's land on a mountain brown,
While the woodsman stared at the hard black bud,
  And the sun through mist went down:
" Not always," it sang, " shall triumph the wrong,
  " For God is stronger than man, they say :"—
(Let no man tell of the March-wind's song
  Till comes the appointed day.)

II.

" Sheaf after sheaf upon Moira's plain,
  " And snow upon snow on the hills of Mourne!
" Full many a harvest-moon must wane,
  " Full many a Spring return!
" The right shall triumph at last o'er wrong ;
  " Yet none knows how, and none knows the day :"—

The March-wind sang;—and bit 'mid the song
  The little black bud away.

III.

" Blow south-wind on through my vineyard, blow!"
  So pray'd that land of the palm and vine;
O Eire, 'tis the north-wind and wintry snow
  That strengthen thine oak and pine!
The storm breaks oft upon Uladh's hills;
  Oft falls the wave on the stones by Saul;
In God's time cometh the thing God wills,
  For God is the Lord of all!

EVA.

BY the light in thy sweet face that tells us ever
  Of a music as dulcet whose fount is thy
    heart;
By that pure life benign as a crystalline river,
  May the good saints protect thee wherever thou
    art!

Good tidings leap forth with thine eyes' swift
    glances;
  Good will finds rest in their skyey blue;
The man that has seen thee thenceforth advances
  In knowledge and love of the good and true.

When thy beauty draws near the old heart brightens;
  The cottager gladdens, thy foot on her floor;
The blind face clears like a sea that lightens :—
  Farewell! We have met: we shall meet no
    more.

I fight for Erin :—thine eyes flash o'er her!
  The land thou tread'st should be glad and free!
Who hates not the tyrants that spurn and gore her—
  Who loves not his country, he ill loves thee!

KING CHARLES' "GRACES."

A.D. 1626.

I.

THUS babble the strong ones, " The chain is
    " slacken'd!
  " Ye can turn half round on your side to sleep!
" With the thunder-cloud still your isle is blacken'd ;
  " But it hurls no bolt upon tower or steep.
" Ye are slaves in name: old laws proscribe you ;
  " But the king is kindly, the queen is fair ;
" They are knaves or fools who would goad or bribe
    " you
  " A legal freedom to claim! Beware !"

II.

We answer thus: our country's honour
　To us is dear as our country's life!
That stigma the bad law casts upon her
　Is the brand on the fame of a blameless wife.
Once more we answer: from honour never
　Can safety long time be found apart;
The bondsman that vows not his bond to sever,
　Is a slave by right, and a slave in heart!

I.

I DREAM'D.　Great bells around me peal'd;
　　The world in that sad chime was drown'd;
Sharp cries as from a battle-field
　Were strangled in the wondrous sound:
Had all the kings of earth lain dead;
Had nations borne them lapp'd in lead
To torch-lit vaults with plume and pall,
Such bells had served for funeral.

II.

'Twas phantasy's dark work!　I slept
　Where black Baltard o'erlooks the deep;
Plunging all night the billows kept
　Their ghostly vigil round my sleep.

But I had fed on tragic lore
That day—your annals, " Masters Four !"
And every moan of wind and sea
Was as a funeral chime to me.

I.

I WOKE.   In vain the skylark sang
   Above the breezy cliff: in vain
The golden iris flash'd and swang
   In hollows of the sea-pink plain.
As ocean shakes—no longer near—
The listening heart, and haunts the ear.
The sibyl and that volume's spells
Pursued me with those funeral bells !

II.

The Irish sibyl whispers slow
   To one who pass'd her tardy Lent
In purple and fine linen, " Lo !
   " Thou wouldst amend, but not repent !
" —Beware ! Long prospers fearless crime :
" Half courses bring the perilous time !
" His way who changes, not his will,
" Is strong no more, but guilty still."

THE INTERCESSION.

ULSTER, A.D. 1641.

IRIEL the Priest arose and said :—
  " The just cause never shall prosper by
        wrong !
" The ill cause battens on blood ill shed ;
  " 'Tis Virtue only makes Justice strong.

" I have hidden the Saxon's wife and child
  " Beneath the altar—behind the porch ;
" O'er them that believe not these hands have piled
  " The stoles and the vestments of holy Church !

" I have hid three men in a hollow oak ;
  " I have hid three maids in an ocean cave"—
As though he were lord of the thunder stroke,
  The old Priest lifted his hand—to save.

But the people loved not the words he spake ;
  And their face was changed for their heart was
        sore :
They answer'd nought ; but their brows grew black,
  And the hoarse halls roar'd like a torrent's roar.

" Has the Stranger robb'd you of house and land ?
  " In battle meet him and smite him down !
" Has he sharpen'd the dagger ? Lift ye the brand !
  " Has he trapp'd your princes ? Set free the
    " clown !

" Has the Stranger his country and knighthood
    " shamed ?
  " Though he 'scape God's vengeance so shall not
    " ye !
" His own God chastens ! Be never named
  " With the Mullaghmast slaughter ! Be just,
    " and free !"

But the people received not the words he spake,
  For the wrong on their heart had made it sore ;
And their brows grew black like the stormy rack,
  And the hoarse halls roar'd like the wave-wash'd
    shore.

Then Iriel the Priest put forth a curse ;
  And horror crept o'er them from vein to vein ;—
A curse upon man and a curse upon horse,
  As forth they rode to the battle plain.

Iriel the Priest sent forth a curse ;
  Like a centipede crept it through heart and brain
(Slow is thy footstep, but sure, Remorse !)
  As forth they rode to the battle plain.

And there never came to them luck or grace,
  In the battle-field no saint help'd them more,
Till O'Neill who hated the warfare base
  Had landed at Doe on Tirconnell's shore.

True Knight, true Christian, true Prince was he !
  He lived for Erin ; for Erin died :—
Had Charles proved true and the faith set free,
  O'Neill had triumph'd at Charles's side.

DIRGE OF RORY O'MORE.

A.D. 1642.

U P the sea-sadden'd valley at evening's decline
    A heifer walks lowing ;—" the silk of the
        " kine ;" *
From the deep to the mountains she roams, and again
From the mountains' green urn to the purple-rimm'd
    main.

Whom seek'st thou, sad Mother ! Thine own is not
    thine !
He dropp'd from the headland ; he sank in the brine !

---

* One of the mystical names for Ireland used by the
bards.

'Twas a dream!—but in dream at thy foot did he
    follow
Through the meadow-sweet on by the marish and
    mallow!

Was he thine? Have they slain him? Thou seek'st
    him not knowing
Thyself too art theirs, thy sweet breath and sad
    lowing!
Thy gold horn is theirs; thy dark eye, and thy silk!
And that which torments thee, thy milk, is their
    milk!

'Twas no dream, Mother Land! 'Twas no dream,
    Inisfail!
Hope dreams, but grief dreams not—the grief of
    the Gael!
From Leix and Ikerren to Donegal's shore
Rolls the dirge of thy last and thy bravest—O'More!

THE BATTLE OF BENBURB.

A BARDIC ODE.

This battle was won by Owen Roe O'Neill over the Parlia-
mentarian forces, A.D. 1646.

I.

AT even I mused on the wrong of the Gael ;—
    A storm-blast went by me with wolf-like
      wail,
And the leaves of the forest, plague-spotted and dead,
Like a multitude broken before it fled ;
Then I saw in my visions a host back driven
(Ye clansmen be true) by a chief from heaven !

II.

At midnight I gazed on the moonless skies ;—
There glisten'd, 'mid other star-blazonries,
A Sword all stars ; then heaven, I knew,
Hath holy work for a sword to do—
Be true, ye clansmen of Nial ! Be true !

III.

At morning I look'd as the sun uprose
On the fair hills of Antrim late white with snows ;
Was it morning only that dyed them red !—
Martyr'd hosts, methought, had bled

On their sanguine ridges for years not few !—
Ye clansmen of Conn, this day be true !

IV.

There is felt once more on the earth
  The step of a kingly man—
Like a dead man hidden he lay from his birth,
  Exiled from his country and clan :
This day his standard he flingeth forth ;
  He tramples the bond and ban ;—
Let them look in his face who usurp'd his hearth ;
  Let them vanquish him, they who can !
    Owen Roe, our own O'Neill !
    . He treads once more our land !
    The sword in his hand is of Spanish steel,
    But the hand is an Irish hand !

V.

I saw in old time with these eyes that fail
  The ship drop down Loch Swilly ;
Lessening 'mid billows the snowy sail
  Bent down like a storm-rock'd lily.
Far far it bore them, those Sceptres old
That had ruled o'er Ulster for ages untold,
The sceptre of Nial and the sceptre of Conn,
Thy Princes, Tirconnell and green Tyrone !—
No freight like that since the mountain-pine
Left first the hills for the salt sea-brine !
Down sank on the ocean a blood-red sun
As westward they drifted when hope was none,

With their priests and their children o'er oceans' foam
And every archive of house and home—
Amid the sea-surges their bards sang dirges:
God rest their bones in their graves at Rome!
  Owen Roe, our own O'Neill!
   He treads once more our land!
  The sword in his hand is of Spanish steel,
   But the hand is an Irish hand!

VI.

I saw in old time through the drifts of the snow
A shepherdless people dash'd to and fro,
With hands toss'd up in the wintry air,
With the laughter of madness or shriek of despair.
Dispersed is the flock when the shepherd lies low:—
The sword was of parchment: a lie was the blow:
Their crime? That with Christendom still to the
   death
They clung to that church which gave England her
   faith!
What is Time? I can see the rain beat the white hair,
And the sleet that defaces the face that was fair,
As onward they stagger o'er mountain and moor
From the cliffs of Slieve Donnard to Corrib's bleak
   shore:
I can hear the babe weep in the pause of the wind:
" To Connaught!" The bloodhounds are baying
   behind!
—Who dwell in their homesteads? That rabble
   accurst

Broad-cast by the false king that daintily trod
In the steps of the Tudor tigress whose thirst
Was quench'd in his mother's blood!
He was false to his mother; they lie to his son :—
Avengers of honour and Ireland, on, on !
　　　Owen Roe, our own O'Neill !
　　　　He treads once more our land !
　　The sword in his hand is of Spanish steel,
　　　　But the hand is an Irish hand !

VII.

Visions no more of the dreadful past !
The things that I long'd for are mine at last !
I see them and hold them with heart and eyes ;
On Irish ground, under Irish skies,
An Irish army, clan by clan,
The standard of Ulster on leading the van !
Each prince with his clansmen, tried men like steel ;
Unvanquish'd Maolmora, Cormac the leal !
And the host that meets them right well I know,
The psalm-singing boors of that Scot Munro !
—We hated you, Barons of the Pale !
But now half friends are Norman and Gael ;
For both the old foes are of lineage old,
And both the old faith and old manners hold.
Last came the Saxon ; first the Dane ;—
The latest pirate the worst of the twain !
Rebels against their English king,
O'er us their chains they dare to fling !
Forgers of creeds till now unknown,

To us they scorn to leave our own!
This night they shall sup with the Queen's O'Con-
      nor,
Like him in fate as like in dishonour.
Montgomery, Conway! base-born crew!
This day ye shall learn an old lesson anew!
Thou art red with sunset this hour, Blackwater;
But twice ere now thou wert red with slaughter!
Another O'Neill by the ford they met;
And " the bloody loaming " men name it yet!
     Owen Roe, our own O'Neill!
      He treads once more our land!
     The sword in his hand is of Spanish steel,
      But the hand is an Irish hand!

VIII.

The storm of the battle rings out! On! on!
Shine well in their faces thou setting sun!
The smoke grows crimson: from left to right
Swift flashes the spleenful and racing light!
The horses stretch onward with belly to ground.
Like the hawk when it swoops, or the arrow-swift
      hound!
Through the clangour of brands rolls the laughter
      of cannon :—
Wind-borne it shall reach thine old walls, Dun-
      gannon!
Our widow'd Cathedrals an ancient strain
To-morrow triumphant shall chaunt again!
On, on! This night on thy banks, Loch Neagh,

Men born in bondage shall couch them free !
Ye were slaves: no longer this Irish air
Consents to be vital breath to such ;
This soil of Ireland no more will bear
The feet that taint her with their touch.
On, warriors launch'd by a warrior's hand !
Four years ye were leash'd in a brazen band ;
He counted your bones, and he meted your might,
This hour he dashes you into the fight !
Strong sun of the battle, great chief whose eye
Wherever it gazes makes victory,
This hour thou shalt see them do or die !
  Owen Roe, our own O'Neill !
   He treads once more our land !
  The sword in his hand is of Spanish steel,
   But the hand is an Irish hand !

IX.

O my people ! O my chief !
 We live : we have not lived in vain :
Four hundred years of shame and grief
 Die ; and Erin lives again !
Priests that at her altars bled,
 Help us with your prayers this hour !
Help us ye of tonsured head
 That sank beneath the stony shower !
Let Connor's martyr'd pontiff raise
In heaven the might of prayer and praise ;
And earlier Cashel's—he who stood
'Mid the death-fires praising God !

Erin no martyrs had of old,
So swiftly flower'd her faith ! Behold,
That debt is paid a hundred fold !
   Owen Roe, our own O'Neill !
     He treads once more our land !
     The sword in his hand is of Spanish steel,
      But the hand is an Irish hand !

x.

Through the dust and the mist of the golden West
   New hosts draw nigh:—is it friend or foe?
They come ! They are ours ! Like a cloud their
      vanguard lours !
No help from thy brother this day, Munro !
They form : there stand they one moment, still !
   Now, now they charge under banner and sign :
They breast unbroken the slope of the hill,
   It breaks before them, the Invader's line !
Their horse and their foot are crush'd together
Like ships in a harbour 'mid stormy weather,
Each dash'd upon each, the churn'd wave strewing
With wreck upon wreck, and ruin on ruin.
The spine of their battle gives way with a yell :
Down drop their standards : that cry was their
      knell !
Some on the bank and some in the river
Struggling they lie that shall rally never.
'Twas God fought for us ! with hands of might
From on high He kneaded and shaped the fight !

R

To Him be the praise ! What He wills must be :—
With Him is the future : for blind are we !
Let Ormond at will make terms or refuse them !
Let Charles the Confederates win or lose them :
Uplift the old faith and annul the old strife,
Or cheat us, and forfeit his kingdom and life !
Come hereafter what must or may
Ulster, thy cause is avenged to-day :
What fraud took from us and force, the sword
That strikes in daylight makes ours, restored !

 Owen Roe, our own O'Neill !
  He treads once more our land !
 The sword in his hand is of Spanish steel,
  But the hand is an Irish hand !

THE WAIL OF THOMOND.

A.D. 1647.

Murrough O'Brien, Lord Inchiquin, is still known by an Irish name which means " Murrough of the Burnings," given to him after the massacre in the cathedral of Cashell.   In his case, as in that of Count Julian of Spain, the incentive to action appears to have been revenge.   He deserted the cause of Charles for that of the Parliamentarians, A. D. 1643, in consequence of having been refused the Presidency of Munster, and returned to it a short time after his own success had ruined it irrevocably—at least in the South.   Eventually he returned to the Catholic Church likewise;—for, like Ormond, he had been educated in a religion opposed to that of his father, under the celebrated " Court of Wards."

I.

CAN it be ?   Can it be ?   Can O'Brien be
   traitor ?
Can the great House Dalcassian be faithless to Eire ?
The sons of the stranger have wrong'd—let them
   hate her !
 Old Thomond well knows them ; they hate her
   for hire !
Can our Murrough be leagued with the rebels and
   ranters
 'Gainst his faith and his country his king and
   his race ?

Can he bear the low wailings the curses the banters?
    There's a scourge worse than these—the applause
        of the base !

II.

Was the hand that set fire to the churches descended
    From the hand of the king that up-rear'd them,
        Boroimhe ?
When the blood of the priests and the people ran
        blended
    Who was it cried " spare them not ?"—Inchiquin,
        who ?
Some Fury o'er-ruled thee ! Some root hadst thou
        eaten !
    'Twas a Demon that stalk'd in thy shape ! 'Twas
        not thou !
Oh, Murrough ! not tears of the angels can sweeten
    That blood-stain ; that Cain-mark erase from thy
        brow !

THE BISHOP OF ROSS.

A.D. 1650.

THEY led him to the peopled wall :—
   "Thy sons!" they said, "are those within !
" If at thy word their standards fall
   "Thy life and freedom thou shalt win!"

Then spake that warrior Bishop old ;
   " Remove these chains that I may bear
" My crosier staff and stole of gold :
   " My judgment then will I declare."

They robed him in his robes of state :
   They set the mitre on his head :
On tower and gate was silence great:
   The hearts that loved him froze with dread.

He spake: " Right holy is your strife !
   " Fight for your country, king,* and faith :
" I taught you to be true in life:
   " I teach you to be true in death.

---

* Charles the First.

" A priest apart by God is set
     " To offer prayer and sacrifice :
" And he is sacrificial yet
     " The pontiff for his flock who dies."

Ere yet he fell his hand on high
     He raised, and benediction gave ;
Then sank in death content to die :—
     Thy great heart, Erin, was his grave.

DIRGE.

A.D. 1652.

I.

WHOSE were they those voices? What foot-
          steps came near me?
  Can the dead to the living draw nigh and be
     heard?
I wept in my sleep ; but ere morning to cheer me
  Came a breeze from the woodland, a song from
     the bird.
O sons of my heart ! the long-hair'd the strong
     handed !
  Your phantoms rush by me with war-cry and
     wail :—
Ye too for your faith and your country late banded,
  My sons by adoption, mail'd knights of the Pale !

II.

Is there sorrow, O ye that pass by, like my sorrow?
　Of the kings I brought forth there remaineth not
　　one!
Each day is dishonour'd; disastrous each morrow :—
　In the yew-wood I couch till the day-light is
　　done.
At midnight I lean from the cliff o'er the waters,
　And hear, as the thunder comes up from the sea,
Your voices, my sons, and your wailings, my
　　daughters :
　With the sea-dirge they mix not: they clamour
　　to me!

THE THREE WOES.

THE Angel whose charge is Eire sang thus o'er
    the dark isle winging :—
By a virgin his song was heard at a tempest's
    ruinous close :
" Three golden ages God gave while your tender
    " green blade was springing :
" Faith's earliest harvest is reap'd. To-day God
    " sends you three Woes.

" For ages three, without Laws ye shall flee as beasts
    " in the forest :
" For an age, and a half age, Faith shall bring
    " not peace but a sword :
" Then Laws shall rend you, like eagles, sharp-
    " fang'd, of your scourges the sorest :—
" When these three Woes are past look up, for
    " your Hope is restored.

" The times of your woe shall be twice the time of
    " your foregone glory :
" But fourfold at last shall lie the grain on your
    " granary floor"—
—The seas in vapour shall fleet, and in ashes the
    mountains hoary :
Let God do that which He wills. Let His servants
    endure and adore !

INISFAIL;

OR,

IRELAND IN THE OLDEN TIME.

PART III.

PARVULI EJUS.

IN the night, in the night, O my country, the
    stream calls out from afar :
  So swells thy voice through the ages, sonorous
    and vast :
In the night, in the night, O my country, clear
    flashes the star :
  So flashes on me thy face through the gloom of
    the past.

I sleep not ; I watch : in blows the wind ice-wing'd,
    and ice-finger'd :
  My forehead it cools and slakes the fire in my
    breast ;
Though it sighs o'er the plains where oft thine exiles
    look'd back, and long linger'd,
  And the graves where thy famish'd lie dumb and
    thine outcasts find rest.

For up from those vales wherein thy brave and thy
    beautiful moulder,
  And on through the homesteads waste and the
    temples defiled,

A voice goes forth on that wind, as old as the Islands
and older,
  "God reigns: at His feet earth's Destiny sleeps
  "like a child."

THE LADY TURNED BEGGAR.

I.

"DROP an alms on shrunken fingers," faintly,
with a smile, she said;
But the smile was not of pleasure, and unroselike
was the red:—
"Fasts wear thin the pride fantastic;—one I left
"at home lacks bread."

II.

Lady! Hard is the beginning—so they say—of
shameless sinning:
Ay but (loss disguised in winning) easier grows it
day by day:—
May thy shamefaced, sinless pleading to the unhear-
ing or the unheeding
Lacerate less an inly bleeding bosom ere those locks
grow grey;
Locks whose midnight once was lighted with the
diamond's changeful ray!

III.

Silks worn bare with work's abusing; check made
wan with hailstorm's bruising;
Eye its splendour slowly losing; state less stately in
decay;—
Chaunting ballad or old ditty year by year she
roam'd the city:
Love at first is kin to pity; pity to contempt, men
say:—
Wonder lessen'd reverence slacken'd as the raven
locks grew grey.

IV.

What is that makes sadness sadder? What is that
makes madness madder?
Shame, a sharper-venom'd adder, gnaws when looks
once kind betray!
" She is poor:—the poor are common! 'Twas a
" countess:—'tis a woman:
" Looks she has at times scarce human!—England!
" there should be her stay:
" 'Twas for Charles the old lord battled—Charles
" and England—so men say."

V.

Charles! Whitehall! the wine, the revel! No, she
sinks not to *that* level!
Mime or pander;—King or devil! She will die on
Ireland's shore!

Ne'er, till Portsmouth's brazen forehead grows with
    virtuous blushes florid
Will she pass that gate abhorred, climb that stair-
    case, tread that floor:
Let *that* forehead wear the diamond which Lord
    Roche's widow wore!

VI.

Critic guest through Ireland wending, praise or cavil
    homeward sending,
Wonder not in old man bending or in beggar boys
    at play
Wonder not at aspect regal, princely front or eye
    of eagle :—
Common these where baying beagle, or the wire-
    hair'd wolf-hound grey
Chased old nobles once through woodlands which the
    ignoble made their prey.
That new-boasted art—*subsoiling*—old in Ireland
    is, men say :—
Old in Ireland—so men say.

ARCHBISHOP PLUNKET.

A. D. 1681.

(THE LAST VICTIM OF THE "POPISH PLOT.")

"The Earl of Essex went to the King (Charles II.) to apply for a pardon, and told his Majesty 'the witnesses must needs be perjured, as what they swore could not possibly be true;' but his Majesty answered in a passion, 'Why did you not declare this then at the trial? I dare pardon nobody— his blood be upon your head, and not mine!'"—HAVERTY'S *Hist.* See also Dr. Moran's Life of Archbishop Plunket.

WHY crowd ye windows thus, and doors?
    Why climb ye tower and steeple?
What lures you forth, O senators?
    What brings you here, O people?

Here there is nothing worth your note—
    'Tis but an old man dying:
The noblest stag this season caught,
    And in the old nets lying!

Sirs, there are marvels, but not here:—
    Here's but the thread-bare fable
Whose sense nor sage discerns, nor seer;—
    Unwilling is unable!

That prince who lurk'd in bush and brake
　　While blood-hounds bay'd behind him
Now, to his father's throne brought back,
　　In pleasure's wreaths doth wind him.

The primate of that race, whose sword
　　Stream'd last to save that father,
To-day is reaping such reward
　　As Irish virtues gather.

Back to your councils, courts, feasts !
　　'Tis but a new " Intruder "
Conjoin'd with those incivic priests
　　That dyed the blocks of Tudor !

A BALLAD OF SARSFIELD;

OR, THE BURSTING OF THE GUNS.

A. D. 1690.

SARSFIELD went out the Dutch to rout.
　　And to take and break their cannon ;
To mass went he at half-past three,
　　And at four he cross'd the Shannon.

Tirconnel slept.　In dream his thoughts
　　Old fields of victory ran on ;
And the chieftains of Thomond in Limerick's towers
　　Slept well by the banks of Shannon.

He rode ten miles and he cross'd the ford,
    And couch'd in the wood and waited ;
Till, left and right, on march'd in sight
    That host which the true men hated.

" Charge !" Sarsfield cried ; and the green hill-side
    As they charged replied in thunder ;
They rode o'er the plain and they rode o'er the slain,
    And the rebel rout lay under !

He burn'd the gear the knaves held dear,—
    For his king he fought, not plunder ;
With powder he cramm'd the guns and ramm'd
    Their mouths the red soil under.

The spark flash'd out—like a nation's shout
    The sound into heaven ascended ;
The hosts of the sky made to earth reply,
    And the thunders twain were blended !

Sarsfield went out the Dutch to rout,
    And to take and break their cannon ;—
A century after, Sarsfield's laughter
    Was echoed from Dungannon.*

---

* It was in the parish church of Dungannon that the
volunteers of 1782 proclaimed the constitutional independence
of the Irish Parliament.

A SONG OF THE BRIGADE.

RIVER that through this purple plain
　　Toilest (once redder) to the main,
Go, kiss for me the banks of Seine!

Tell him I loved, and love for aye,
That his I am though far away,—
More his than on the marriage-day.

Tell him thy flowers for him I twine
When first the slow sad mornings shine
In thy dim glass—for he is mine.

Tell him when evening's tearful light
Bathes those dark towers on Aughrim's height
There where he fought in heart I fight.

A freeman's banner o'er him waves!
So be it! I but kiss the graves
Where freemen sleep whose sons are slaves.

Tell him I nurse his noble race,
Nor weep save o'er one sleeping face
Wherein those looks of his I trace.

For him my beads I count when falls
Moonbeam or shower at intervals
Upon our burn'd and blacken'd walls:

And bless him! bless the bold Brigade,—
May God go with them, horse and blade,
For Faith's defence, and Ireland's aid!

SONG.

I.

NOT always the winter! not always the wail!
    The heart heals perforce where the spirit is
        pure!
The apple-tree blooms in the glens of Imayle;
    The blackbird sings loud by the Slane and the Suir!
There are princes no more in Kincora and Tara,
But the gold-flower laughs out from the Maigue at
       Athdara;
And the Spring-tide that wakens the leaf in the bud,
(Sad mother, forgive us) shoots joy through our blood!

II.

Not always the winter! not always the moan!
    Our fathers they tell us in old time were free;—

Free to-day is the stag in the woods of Idrone,
  And the eagle that fleets from Loch Lein o'er the
      Lee!
The blue-bells rush up where the young May hath
      trod;
The souls of our martyrs are reigning with God!
Sad mother, forgive us! yon skylark no choice
Permits us. From heaven he is crying, "Rejoice!"

GOOD-HEARTED.

I.

THE young lord betray'd an orphan maid,
  The young lord soft-natured and easy:
The man was " good-hearted," the neighbours said;
Flung meat to his dogs; to the poor flung bread;
His father stood laughing when Drogheda bled:
  He hated a conscience queasy!

II.

A widow met him, dark trees o'erhead,
  Her child and the man just parted;—
When home she walk'd her knife it was red:
Swiftly she walk'd, and mutter'd, and said,
" The blood rush'd fast from a full fount fed,—
  " Ay, the young lord was right ' good-hearted.'"

III.

When morning wan its first beam shed
    It fell on a corse yet wanner;
The great-hearted dogs the young lord had fed
Watch'd, one at the feet, and one at the head,—
But their mouths with a blood-pool hard-by were red:
    They loved—in the young lord's manner.

THE NEW RACE.

I.

O YE who have vanquish'd the land and retain it,
    How little ye know what ye miss of delight!
There are worlds in her heart—could ye seek it or
        gain it—
    That would clothe a true noble with glory and might.
What is she, this isle which ye trample and ravage,
    Which ye plough with oppression and reap with
        the sword,
But a harp never strung in the hall of a savage,
    Or a fair wife embraced by a husband abhorr'd?

II.

The chiefs of the Gael were the people embodied;
    The chiefs were the blossom, the people the root!

Their conquerors, the Normans, high-soul'd, and
    high-blooded,
  Grew Irish at last from the scalp to the foot.
And ye!—ye are hirelings and satraps, not nobles!
  Your slaves, they detest you; your masters, they
    scorn!
The river lives on—but its sun-painted bubbles
  Pass quick, to the rapids insensibly borne.

THE LAST MAC CARTHYMORE.

The last great chief of the Mac Carthy family, which had
reigned in South Desmond ever since the second century, went
into exile with James II. He spent the last years of his life
on a wild island strewn with wrecks in the mouth of the
Elbe.

ON thy woody heaths, Muskerry—Carbery, on
    thy famish'd shore,
Hands hurl'd upwards, wordless wailings, clamour
    for Mac Carthymore!
He is gone; and never, never shall return to wild
    or wood
Till the sun burns out in blackness and the moon
    descends in blood.

He, of lineage older, nobler, at the latest Stuart's
    side

Once again had drawn the sword for Charles in
    blood of traitors dyed;
Once again the stranger fattens where Mac Carthys
    ruled of old,
For a later Cromwell triumphs in the Dutchman's
    muddier mould.

Broken boat and barge around him, sea-gulls piping
    loud and shrill,
Sits the chief where bursts the breaker, and laments
    the sea-wind chill;
In a barren, northern island dinn'd by ocean's end-
    less roar,
Where the Elbe with all his waters streams between
    the willows hoar.

Earth is wide in hill and valley;—palace courts and
    convent piles
Centuries since received thine outcasts, Ireland, oft
    with tears and smiles;
Wherefore builds this grey-hair'd exile on a rock-
    isle's weedy neck?—
Ocean unto ocean calleth; inly yearneth wreck to
    wreck!

He and his, his church and country, king and kins-
    men, house and home,
Wrecks they are like broken galleys strangled by
    the yeasty foam;

Nations past and nations present are or shall be
    soon as these—
Words of peace to him come only from the breast of
    roaring seas.

Clouds and sea-birds inland drifting o'er the sea-bar
    and sand-plain ;
Belts of mists for weeks unshifting ; plunge of de-
    vastating rain ;
Icebergs as they pass uplifting agueish gleams
    through vapours frore,
These, long years, were thy companions, O thou
    last Mac Carthymore !

When a rising tide at midnight rush'd against the
    downward stream
Rush'd not then the clans embattled, meeting in
    the chieftain's dream ?
When once more that tide exhausted died in murmurs
    toward the main
Died not then once more his slogan ebbing far o'er
    hosts of slain ?

Pious river ! let us rather hope the low monotonies
Of thy broad stream seaward toiling and the willow-
    bending breeze
Charm'd at times a midday slumber, tranquillized
    tempestuous breath—
Music last when harp was broken, requiem sad and
    sole in death.

GAIETY IN PENAL DAYS.

BEATI IMMACULATI.

" THE storm has roar'd by; and the flowers
    " reappear:
" Like a babe on the battle-field born, the new year
" Through wrecks of the forest looks up on clear
      " skies
" With a smile like the windflower's, and violet eyes.

" There's warmth in the sunshine; there's song in
      " the wood:
" There's faith in the spirit, and life in the blood;
" We'll dance though the stranger inherits the soil:
" We'll sow though we reap not! For God be the
      " toil!"

O Earth that renewest thy beautiful youth!
The meek shall possess thee! Unchangeable Truth!
A childhood thou giv'st us 'mid grey hairs reborn
As the gates we approach of perpetual morn!

In the halls of their fathers the stranger held feast;
Their church was a cave and an outlaw their priest;
The birds have their nests and the foxes have holes—
What had these? Like a sunrise God shone in
      their souls!

HYMN FOR THE FEAST OF ST. STEPHEN.

I.

PRINCES sat and spake against me;
  Sinners held me in their net;
Thou, O Lord, shalt save thy servant,
  For on thee his heart is set.
Strong is he whose strength Thou art;
Plain his speech and strong his heart.

II.

Blessed Stephen stood discoursing
  In the bud of spotless youth
With his judges. Love, not malice,
  Edged his words and arm'd with truth.
They that heard him gnash'd their teeth;
Heard him speak, and vow'd his death.

III.

Gather'd on a thousand foreheads
  Dark and darker grew the frown,
Broad'ning like the pinewood's shadow
  While a wintry sun goes down.
On the Saint that darkness fell:—
At last they spake: it was his knell.

IV.

As a maid her face uplifteth
  Brightening with an inward light
When the voice of her beloved
  Calls her from some neighbouring height,
So his face he raised on high,
And saw his Saviour in the sky !

V.

Dimm'd a moment was that vision :—
  O'er him burst the stony shower;
Stephen with his arms extended
  For his murderers pray'd that hour.
To his prayer Saint Paul was given :
Then he slept, and woke in heaven.

VI.

Faithful deacon, still at Christmas
  Decking tables for the poor !
Martyr, at the bridal banquet
  Guest of God for evermore !
In the realms of endless day
For thine earthly clients pray !

UNA.

I.

TO the knee she stood 'mid rushes,
    And the broad, dark stream swept by her:
Smiles went o'er her, smiles and blushes,
    As the stranger's barque drew nigh her.
Near to Clonmacnoise she stood;
Shannon past her roll'd in flood.

II.

At her feet a wolf-hound wrestled
    With a bright boy bold as Mars;
On her breast an infant nestled,
    Like to her, but none of her's;
A golden iris graced her hand—
All her gold was in that wand.

III.

O'er the misty, moorish margin
    Frown'd a ruin'd tower afar;
Some one said, " This peasant virgin
    " Comes from chieftains great in war!
" Princes once had bow'd before her:
" Now the reeds alone adore her!"

IV.

Refluent dropt (that barque on gliding)
    The wave it heaved along the bank :
Like worldlings still with fortune siding
    The rushes with it backward sank.
Farewell to her ! The rushing river
Must have its way.   Farewell for ever !

ADDUXIT IN TENEBRIS.

THEY wish thee strong : they wish thee great !
    Thy royalty is in thy heart !
Thy children mourn thy widow'd state
    In funeral groves.   Be what thou art !

Across the world's vainglorious waste,
    As o'er Egyptian sands, in thee
God's hieroglyph, His shade is cast—
    A bar of black from Calvary.

Around thee many a land and race
    Have wealth or sway or name in story :
But on that brow discrown'd we trace
    The crown expiatory.

EGYPT'S LAST DAY.

THE fruitful river slides along;
   The Conqueror's city glitters nigh :
The palm-groves ring with dance and song :
   Earth trembles, crimson'd from the sky.

Far down the sunset lonely stands
   Some temple of a bygone age,
Slow-settling into sea-like sands,
   Long served with prayer and pilgrimage.

Here ruled the shepherd kings, and they
   That race from sun and moon which drew
The unending lines of priestly sway :
   Here Alexander's standard flew.

Here last the great Cæsarian star
   Through Egypt's sunset flash'd its beam,
While peal'd the Roman trump afar.
   And earth's first empire like a dream

Dissolved.   But who are they—the Three
   That pierce, thus late, yon desert wide ?
The Babe is on His Mother's knee ;
   Low-bent an old man walks beside.

What say'st thou, Egypt?—" Let them come !
  " Of such as little note I keep
" As of the least of flies that hum
  " Above my deserts, or my deep ! "

THE EVE OF THE ANNUNCIATION.

Cum Angelis, et Pueris, fideles inveniamur.

THE wild dove coos in the distant wood ;
  The gnat goes wailing by ;
The goldfinch sings from her golden perch
  On the aspen up in the sky.

Two seasons mix with a discord raw :—
  The sheathless east blows still ;
The vapour it bears is pierced with beams :
  Yet we scarce can see the hill.

All parch'd and dimm'd the daffodil droops,
  But the violet is unborn :
And the March buds sigh for the milky breath
  That plays with the sweet May morn.

The grass is brown ; the trees are grey ;.
  The wood-flowers winter-bound ;
But the little birds soon with silver notes
  Will draw them from the ground.

From God the Angel ere long will drop
　　With tidings of good to men :—
On hills—in valleys—the " Full of Grace,
　　" All hail," be heard again !

RELIGIO NOVISSIMA.

THERE is an Order by a northern sea,
　　Far in the West, of rule and life more
　　　　strict
Than that which Basil rear'd in Galilee,
　　In Egypt Paul, in Umbria Benedict.

Discalced it walks ;—a stony land of tombs,
　　A strange Petræa of late days, it treads !
Within its courts no high-toss'd censer fumes :
　　The night-rain beats its cells, the wind its beds.

Before its eyes no brass-bound, blazon'd tome
　　Reflects the splendour of a lamp high-hung :
Knowledge is banish'd from her earliest home
　　Like wealth :—it whispers psalms that once it
　　　　sung.

It is not bound by the vow celibate,
　　Lest through its ceasing anguish too might cease :

In sorrow it brings forth ; and Death and Fate
  Watch at Life's gate, and tithe the unripe in-
    crease.

It wears not the Franciscan's sheltering gown ;
  The cord that binds it is the Stranger's chain :
Scarce seen for scorn, in fields of old renown
  It breaks the clod ; another reaps the grain.

Year after year it fasts ; each third or fourth
  So fasts that common fasts to it are feast ;
Then of its brethren many in the earth
  Are laid unrequiem'd like the mountain beast.

Where are its cloisters ? Where the felon sleeps :
  Where its novitiate ? Where the last wolf died :
From sea to sea its vigil long it keeps—
  Stern Foundress ! is its Rule not mortified ?

Thou that hast laid so many an Order waste,
  A nation is thine Order ! It was thine
Wide as a realm that Order's seed to cast,
  And undispensed sustain its discipline !

T

I.

DESCEND, O Sun, o'er yonder waste,
    O'er moors and meads and meadows ;
Make gold a world but late o'ercast,
    With purple tinge the shadows !
Thou goest to bless some happier clime
    Than ours ; but sinking slowly
To us thou leav'st a Hope sublime
    Disguised in melancholy.

II.

A Love there is that shall restore
    What dreadful Death takes from us ;
A secret Love whose gift is more
    Than Faith's authentic promise :
A Love that says, " I hide a while,
    " For sense, that blinds, is round you : "—
O well-loved dead ! ere now the smile
    Of that great Love has found you !

OMENS OF THE EIGHTEENTH CENTURY.

SOOTHSAYER of the Imperial State,
  What saw'st thou in the skies of late?
  I saw a white cloud like a hand:
  It held aloft a harp, not brand.

Soothsayer of the Imperial State,
What saw'st thou in the streams of late?
  A pale hand rising from a brook:
  It raised a seal'd yet bleeding book.

Soothsayer of the Imperial State,
What saw'st thou on the seas of late?
  I saw ascending Liberty:
  Knowledge makes strong, and Commerce free.

Soothsayer of the Imperial State,
What saw'st thou 'mid the graves of late?
  I saw Religion upward burst,
  Her last crown lordlier than her first.

Soothsayer of the Imperial State,
What saw'st thou in the streets of late?

I saw old foes shake hands and say,
" One country have we—ours to-day."

Then up with the banner, and on with the steed!
By the red streets of Wexford—
    (*Soothsayer*)   My master, no need!
We conquer'd them never: our arms they defied:—
Here's money:—seduce them! here's falsehood:—
    divide!

IN the Cambrian valleys with sea-murmurs
    haunted
  The grave-yards at noontide are fresh with dawn-
    dew;
On the virginal bosom white lilies are planted
  'Mid the monotone whisper of pine-tree and yew.

In the dells of Etruria, where all day long warbles
  The night-bird, the faithful 'mid cloisters repose :
And the long cypress shadow falls black upon mar-
    bles
  That cool aching hearts like the Apennines'
    snows.

In Ireland, in Ireland the wind ever sighing
  Sings alone the death-dirge o'er the just and the
    good;
In the abbeys of Ireland the bones are round lying
  Like blocks where the hewer stands hewing the
    wood.

Be the Stranger content with soft glebe and text-
    seesaws!
  He wars with the dead who usurps the church-
    yard!
On the voice which is Jacob's, the hand which is
    Esau's,
  The ban of the priesthood and people lies hard.

THE CAUSE.

I.

THE kings are dead that raised their swords
  In Erin's right of old;
The bards that dash'd from fearless chords
  Her name and praise lie cold:
But fix'd as fate her altars stand;
  Unchanged, like God, her faith;
Her Church still holds in equal hand
  The keys of life and death.

II.

As well call up the sunken reefs
  Atlantic waves rush o'er
As that old time of native chiefs
  And Gaelic kings restore!
Things heavenly rise: things earthly sink:—
  God works through Nature's laws:
Sad Isle. 'tis He that bids thee link
  Thine Action with thy Cause!

" THEY are past. the old days:—let the past
    " be forgotten:
" Let them die. the old wrongs and old woes that
    " were ours.
" Like the leaves of the winter, down-trampled and
    " rotten.
" That light in the spring-time the forest with
    " flowers."

Well sing'st thou. sweet voice!—But the sad voice
    replieth:
" Unstaunch'd is the wound while the insult
    " remains :

" The Tudor's black banner above us still flieth :
  " The faith of our fathers is scorn'd in their fanes !

" Distrust the repentance that clings to its booty ;
  " Give the people their church, and the priest-
    " hood its right :—
" Till then to remember the past is a duty,
  " For the past is our Cause. and our Cause is our
    " might."

TO ETHNEA READING HOMER.

AH happy he who shaped the words
  Which bind thee in their magic net :
Who draws from those old Grecian chords
  The harmonies that charm thee yet !

Who waves from that illumined brow
  The dark locks back. upon that cheek
Pallid erewhile as Pindan snow
  Makes thus the Pindan morning break !

'Tis he that fringes lids depress'd
  With lashes heavier for a tear,
And shakes that inexperienced breast
  With womanhood. Upon the bier

Lies cold in death the hope of Troy;
   Thou hear'st the elders sob around,
The widow'd wife, the orphan'd boy,
   The old grey king, the realm discrown'd.

Hadst thou but lived that hour, by thee
   Well wept had been the heroic dead;
The heroic hands well kiss'd; thy knee
   Had propp'd the pallid, princely head!

From thee Andromache had caught
   Dirges more sweet; and she who burn'd
With anguish born of shame, a note
   Of holier woe from thee had learn'd!

Ah child, thy Troy in ruin lies
   Like theirs! Her princes too are cold:
Again Cassandra prophecies,
   Vainly prophetic as of old.

Brandon to Ida's cloudy verge
   Responds.   Iorras' son-less shore
Wails like the Lycian when its marge
   Saintly Sarpedon trod no more.

Not Gods benign, like Sleep and Death
   Who bore that shepherd-monarch home,
But famine's tooth and fever's breath
   Our victims hunt o'er ocean's foam.

Peace reigns in heaven.   The Fates each hour
    Roll round earth's wheel through darkness vast ;—
Abides alone the poet's power,
    A manlike Art that from the past

Draws forth that line whose sanguine track
    The wicked fear, the weak desert—
That clue through centuries leading back
    The patriot to his country's heart.

THE dying tree no pang sustains ;
        But, by degrees relinquishing
Companionship of beams and rains,
        Forgets the balmy breath of Spring.

From off th' enringed trunk that keeps
        His annual count of ages gone,
Th' embrace of Summer slowly slips ;—
        Still stands the giant in the sun.

His myriad lips that suck'd of old
        The dewy breasts of heaven, are dry ;
His roots remit the crag and mould ;
        Yet painless is his latest sigh.

He falls ; the forests round him roar ;—
    Ere long on quiet bank and copse
Untrembling moonbeams rest ; once more
    The startled babe his head down-drops.

But ah for one who never drew
    From age to age a painless breath !
And ah the old wrong ever new !
    And ah the many-centuried death !

I.

I THOUGHT it was thy voice I heard ;—
    Ah no ! the ripple burst and died ;
Among cold reeds the night-wind stirr'd ;
The yew-tree sigh'd ; the earliest bird
    Answer'd the white dawn far descried.

II.

I thought it was a tress of thine
    That grazed my cheek, and touch'd my brow ;—
Ah no ! in sad but calm decline
'Twas but my ever grapeless vine
    Slow-waving from the blighted bough.

III.

Ah known too late ! ah loved too soon !
    Thy sacred flower renews its bud ;

In sunless quarries still unhewn
Thy statue sleeps ; thy sunken moon
  Shall light once more the autumnal flood.

IV.

Memory for me her hands but warms
  O'er embers of thy greatness gone :
Or lifts to heaven phantasmal arms,
Muttering of talismans and charms
  And grappling after glories flown.

V.

Sleep, sleep, thou worn out palimpsest !
  She lives ! man's troubles soon are o'er :—
When in dark crypts my ashes rest
Star-high shall shine my country's crest,
  Where birds of darkness cannot soar !

G REY Harper, rest !—O maid, the Fates
    On those sad lips have press'd their seal !
Thy song's sweet rage but indicates
  That mystery it can ne'er reveal.

Take comfort ! Vales and lakes and skies,
  Blue seas, and sunset-girdled shore,
Love-beaming brows, love-lighted eyes,
  Contend like thee. What can they more ?

FRESH eve, that hang'st in yon blue sky
    On breeze-like pinions swaying,
And leav'st our earth reluctantly—
    Ah, hang there, long delaying !

Along the beach the ripples rake ;—
    Dew-drench'd the thicket flushes ;
And last year's leaves in bower and brake
    Are dying 'mid their blushes.

Is this the world we knew of yore,
    Long bound in wintry whiteness,
Which here consummates more and more
    This talismanic brightness ?

To music wedded, well-known lines
    Let forth a hidden glory :—
Thus, bathed in sunset, swells and shines,
    Lake, wood, or promontory.

New Edens pure from Adam's crime
    Invite the just to enter ;
The spheres of wrongful Life and Time
    Grow lustrous to their centre.

Rejoice, glad planet! Sin and Woe,
　　The void, the incompleteness,
Shall cease at last ; and thou shalt know
　　The mystery of thy greatness !

CARO REQUIESCET.

LOOK forth, O Sun, with beam oblique
　　O'er crags and lowlands mellow ;
The dusky beech-grove fire, and strike
　　The sea-green larch-wood yellow.

All round the deep, new-flooded meads
　　Send thy broad glories straying ;
Each herd that feeds 'mid flowers and weeds
　　In golden spoils arraying.

Flash from the river to the bridge :—
　　Red glance with glance pursuing,
Fleet from low sedge to mountain ridge,
　　Whatever thou dost undoing !

Kiss with moist lip those vapoury bands
　　That swathe yon slopes of tillage ;
Clasp with a hundred sudden hands
　　The gables of yon village.

But oh, thus sharpening to a point,
    Oh, brightening thus while dying,
Ere yet thou diest the graves anoint
    Where my beloved are lying !

Ye shades that mount the moorland dells,
    Ascend, the tree-tops dimming ;
But leave those amethystine hills
    Awhile in glory swimming !

DARK, dark that grove at the Attic gate
    By the sad Eumenides haunted,
Where the Theban King in his blindness sat,
    While the nightingales round him chaunted :

In a grove as dark of cypress and bay
    Upgrown to a forest's stature,
In vision I saw at the close of day
    A woman of God-like feature.

She stood like a queen, and her vesture green
    Shone out as a laurel sun-lighted ;
And she sang a wild song like a mourner's keen
    With an angel's triumph united.

She sang like one whose grief is done ;
  Who has solved Life's dread enigma ;—
A beam from the sun on her brow was thrown,
  And I saw there the conquering Stigma.

OH that the pines which crown yon steep
  Their fires might ne'er surrender !
Oh that yon fervid knoll might keep,
  While lasts the world, its splendour !

Pale poplars on the breeze that lean,
  And in the sunset shiver,
Oh that your golden stems might screen
  For aye yon glassy river !

That yon white bird on homeward wing
  Soft-sliding without motion,
And now in blue air vanishing
  Like snow-flake lost in ocean,

Beyond our sight might never flee,
  Yet forward still be flying ;
And all the dying day might be
  Immortal in its dying.

Pellucid thus in saintly trance,
  Thus mute in expectation,
What waits the earth? Deliverance?
  Ah no! Transfiguration!

She dreams of that new earth divine,
  Conceived of seed immortal;
She sings " Not mine the holier shrine,
  " Yet mine the steps and portal!"

ARBOR NOBILIS.

I.

LIKE a cedar our greatness arose from the
    earth;
Or a plane by some broad-flowing river;
Like arms that give blessing its boughs it put
    forth :—
We thought it would bless us for ever.
The birds of the air in its branches found rest;
  The old lions couch'd in its shadow;
Like a cloud o'er the sea hung its pendulous
    crest;
  It murmur'd for leagues o'er the meadow.

II.

Was a worm at its root ? Was it lightning that
 charr'd
 What age after age had created ?
Not so ! 'Twas the merchant its glory that marr'd,
 And the malice that, fearing it, hated.
Its branches lie splinter'd ; the hollow trunk groans
 Like a church that survives profanations ;
But the leaves, scatter'd far when the hurricane
 moans,
 For the healing are sent of the nations !

I.

All kindly and sweet, we must love thee perforce !
 The disloyal, the coward alone would not
 love thee :
Ah mother of heroes—strong mother ! soft nurse !
 We are thine while the large cloud swims onward
 above thee !
By thine hills ever-blue that draw heaven so near ;
 By thy cliffs, by thy lakes, and thine ocean-lull'd
 highlands ;
And more—by thy records disastrous and dear,
 The shrines on thy headlands, the cells on thine
 islands !

II.

Ah, well sings the thrush by Lixnau and Traigh-li!
  Ah, well breaks the wave upon Umbhall and
        Brandon!
Thy breeze o'er the upland blows element and free,
And o'er fields, once his own, which the hind must
        abandon.
A caitiff the noble who draws from thy plains
  His all, yet reveres not the source of his great-
        ness ;
A clown and a serf 'mid his boundless domains
  His spirit consumes in the prison of its straightness!

III.

Through the cloud of its pathos thy face is more
        fair :—
  In old time thou wert sun-clad ; the gold robe
        thou worest.
To thee the heart turns as thy deer to her lair,
  Ere she dies,—her first bed in the gloom of the
        forest.
Our glory, our sorrow, our mother! Thy God
  In thy worst dereliction forsook but to prove
        thee :—
Blind, blind as the blindworm ; cold, cold as the
        clod
  Who, seeing thee, see not, possess but not love
        thee !

GRATTAN.

I.

GOD works through man, not hills or snows!
   In man, not men, is the God-like power;
The man, God's potentate, God foreknows;
   He sends him strength at the destined hour.
His Spirit He breathes into one deep heart;
His cloud He bids from one mind depart,
A Saint!—and a race is to God re-born!
A Man! One man makes a nation's morn!

II.

A man, and the blind land by slow degrees
   Gains sight! A man, and the deaf land hears!
A man, and the dumb land, like wakening seas
   Thunders low dirges in proud, dull ears!
One man, and the People a three days' corse,
Stands up, and the grave-bands fall off perforce;
One man, and the Nation in height a span
To the measure ascends of the perfect man.

III.

Thus wept unto God the land of Eire:
   Yet there rose no man and her hope was dead:

In the ashes she sat of a burn'd-out fire ;
    And sackcloth was over her queenly head.
But a man in her latter days arose ;
Her deliverer stepp'd from the camp of her foes :—
He spake ;—the great and the proud gave way,
And the dawn began which shall end in day !

OH blithesome at times is life perforce
    When Death is the gate of Hope not Fear :
Rich streams lie dumb :—over rough stones course
    The runlets that charm the ear.

" Her heart is hard—she can laugh," they say,
    " That light one can jest who has cause to sigh !"—
Her conscience is light ; and with God are they
    She loves :—they are safe and nigh.

God's light shines brightest on cheeks grief-pale :
    The song of the darkling is sad and dark ;
That proud one boasts of her nightingale !
    Oh Eire, keep thou thy lark !

SHARP lie the shades on the sward close-bitten
  Which the affluent meadows receive but half;
Truth lies clear-edged on the soul grief-smitten,
  Congeal'd there in epitaph.

A Vision is thine by the haughty lost;
  An Insight reserved for the sad and pure:—
On the mountain cold in the grey hoar frost
  Thy Shepherd's track lies sure!

THE little Black Rose shall be red at last;—
  What made it black but the March wind
      dry,
And the tear of the widow that fell on it fast?—
  It shall redden the hills when June is nigh!

The Silk of the Kine shall rest at last;—
  What drave her forth but the dragon-fly?
In the golden vale she shall feed full fast
  With her mild gold horn, and her slow, dark eye.

The wounded wood-dove lies dead at last!
  The pine long-bleeding, it shall not die!
—This song is secret. Mine ear it pass'd
  In a wind o'er the stone plain of Athenry.

TO one in dungeons bound there came
   The last long night before he died
An Angel garlanded with flame
   Who raised his hand and prophesied:—

" Thy life hath been a dream: but lo !
   " This night thine eye shall see the truth :
" That which thou thoughtest weal was woe;
   " And that was joy thou thoughtest ruth.

" Thy land hath conquer'd through her loss ;
   " With her God's chief of creatures plain'd,
" The same who scaled of old the Cross
   " When Mary's self beneath remain'd.*

" Well fought'st thou on the righteous side :
   " Yet, being dust, thou wroughtest sin :—
" Once—twice—thy hand was raised in pride :
   " The promised land thou may'st not win ;

" But they, thy children shall."   Next morn
   Around the Patriot-martyr press'd
A throng that cursed him.   He in turn,
   The sentenced, bless'd them—and was bless'd.

---

* Dante's description of Holy Poverty.

ALL-HALLOWS;

OR, THE MONK'S DREAM.

A PROPHECY.

I.

I TROD once more the place of tombs :
  Death-rooted elder, full in flower,
Oppress'd me with its sad perfumes,
  Pathetic breath of arch and tower.
The ivy on the cloister wall
  Waved, gusty, with a silver gleam :
The moon sank low : the billows' fall
  In moulds of music shaped my dream.

II.

In sleep a funeral chaunt I heard,
  A " de profundis " far below ;
On the long grass the rain-drops stirr'd
  As when the distant tempests blow.
Then slowly, like a heaving sea,
  The graves were troubled all around ;
And two by two, and three by three,
  The monks ascended from the ground.

III.

From sin absolved, redeem'd from tears,
    There stood they, beautiful and calm,
The brethren of a thousand years,
    With lifted brows and palm to palm!
On heaven they gazed in holy trance;
    Low stream'd their aged tresses hoar:
And each transfigured countenance
    The Benedictine impress bore.

IV.

By angels borne the Holy Rood
    Encircled thrice the church-yard bound:
They paced behind it, paced in blood,
    With bleeding feet but foreheads crown'd;
And thrice they sang that hymn benign
    Which angels sang when Christ was born,
And thrice I wept ere yet the brine
    Shook with the first white flakes of morn.

V.

Down on the earth my brows I laid;
    In these, His saints, I worshipp'd God:
And then return'd that grief which made
    My heart since youth a frozen clod.
" O ye," I wept, " whose woes are past,
    " Behold these prostrate shrines and stones!
" To these can Life return at last?
    " Can Spirit lift once more these bones?"

VI.

The smile of him the end who knows
    Went luminous o'er them as I spake;
Their white locks shone like mountain snows
    O'er which the orient mornings break.
They stood: they pointed to the west:
    And lo! where darkness late had lain
Rose many a kingdom's citied crest
    Heaven-girt, and imaged in the main!

VII.

" Not only these, the fanes o'erthrown,
    " Shall rise," they said, " but myriads more;
" The seed—far hence by tempests blown—
    " Still sleeps on yon expectant shore.
" Send forth, sad Isle, thy reaper bands!
    " Assert and pass thine old renown:
" Not here alone—in farthest lands
    " For thee thy sons shall weave the crown."

VIII.

They spake; and like a cloud down sank
    The just and filial grief of years;
And I that peace celestial drank
    Which shines but o'er the seas of tears.
Thy mission flash'd before me plain,
    O thou by many woes anneal'd!
And I discern'd how axe and chain
    Had thy great destinies sign'd and seal'd!

IX.

That seed which grows must seem to die;—
　　In thee, when earthly hope was none,
The heaven-born faith of days gone by,
　　By martyrdom matured, lived on;
Conceal'd, like limbs of royal mould
　　'Neath some Egyptian pyramid,
Or statued shapes in cities old
　　Beneath Vesuvian ashes hid.

X.

For this cause by a power divine
　　Each temporal aid was frustrated:
Tirone, Tirconnell, Geraldine—
　　In vain they fought: in vain they bled.
Successive, 'neath th' usurping hand
　　Sank ill-starr'd Mary, erring James:—
Nor Spain nor France might wield the brand
　　Which for her own Religion claims.

XI.

Arise, long stricken! mightier far
　　Are they that fight for God and thee
Than those who head the adverse war!
　　Sad prophet! raise thy face and see!
Behold, with eyes no longer wrong'd
　　By mists the sense exterior breeds,
The hills of heaven all round thee throng'd
　　With fiery chariots and with steeds!

XII.

The years baptized in blood are thine ;
  The exile's prayer from many a strand ;
The wrongs of those this hour who pine
  Poor outcasts on their native land :
Angels and saints from heaven down-bent
  Watch thy long conflict without pause ;
And the most Holy Sacrament
  From all thine altars pleads thy cause !

XIII.

O great through Suffering, rise at last
  Through kindred Action tenfold great !
Thy future calls on thee thy past
  (Its soul survives) to consummate.
Let women weep ; let children moan :
  Rise, men and brethren, to the fight :
One cause hath Earth, and one alone :
  For it, the cause of God, unite !

XIV.

Hope of my country ! House of God !
  All-Hallows ! Blessed feet are those
By which thy courts shall yet be trod
  Once more as ere the spoiler rose !
Blessed the winds that waft them forth
  To victory o'er the rough sea foam ;
That race to God which conquers earth—
  Can God forget that race at home ?

HYMN.

I.

WHO is she that stands triumphant
  A rock in strength upon the Rock,
Like some city crown'd with turrets
  Braving storm and earthquake shock?
Who is she her arms extending
  In blessing o'er a world restored,
All the anthems of creation
  Lifting to creation's Lord?
    Hers the Kingdom, hers the Sceptre!
      Fall ye nations at her feet!
    Hers that truth whose fruit is freedom;
      Light her yoke; her burden sweet!

II.

As the moon its splendour borrows
  From a sun unseen all night
So from Christ, the Sun of Justice,
  Draws His Church her vestal light.
Touch'd by His her hands have healing,
  The Bread of Life, the absolving Key:—
The Word Incarnate is her Bridegroom;
  The Spirit hers; His Temple she.

Hers the Kingdom; hers the Sceptre!
  Fall ye nations at her feet!
Hers that truth whose fruit is freedom;
  Light her yoke; her burden sweet!

III.

Empires rise and sink like billows;
  Their place knoweth them no more;
Glorious as the star of morning
  She o'erlooks their wild uproar.
Hers the household all-embracing,
  Hers the vine that shadows earth;
Blest thy children, mighty mother!
  Safe the stranger at thy hearth!
    Hers the Kingdom, hers the Sceptre!
      Fall ye nations at her feet!
    Hers that truth whose fruit is freedom;
      Light her yoke; her burden sweet!

IV.

Like her Bridegroom, heavenly, human,
  Crown'd and militant in one,
Chaunting Nature's great Assumption
  And the abasement of the Son;
Her magnificats, her dirges
  Harmonize the jarring years;
Hands that fling to heaven the censer
  Wipe away the orphan's tears.
    Hers the Kingdom, hers the Sceptre!
      Fall ye nations at her feet!
    Hers that truth whose fruit is freedom;
      Light her yoke; her burden sweet!

I.

W AS it Truth; was it Vision? The old year
        was dying;
Clear rang the last chime from the turret of stone;
The mountain hung black o'er the village low-
        lying;
    O'er the moon, rushing onward, loose vapours
        were blown;
When I saw an angelical choir with bow'd faces
    Wafting on, like a bier, upon pinions outspread
An angel-like Form that of death wore no traces;
    Without pain she had died in her sleep;—but
        was dead.

II.

Was it Truth; was it Vision? The darkness was
        riven;
    Once more through the infinite breast of pure
        night
From heaven there look'd downward, more beauteous
        than heaven,
    A visage whose pathos was lost in its light.
" Why seek'st thou, my son, 'mid the dead for
        " the living?
    " Thy Country is risen, and lives on in thy Faith;
" I died but to live; and now, Life and Life-giving,
    " Where'er the Cross triumphs I conquer in
        death."

SEMPER EADEM.

I.

THE moon, freshly risen from the bosom of
    ocean,
  Hangs o'er it suspended, all mournful yet bright ;
And a yellow sea-circle with yearning emotion
  Swells up as to meet it, and clings to its light.
The orb unabiding grows whiter, mounts higher ;—
  The pathos of darkness descends on the brine—
O Erin ! The North drew its light from thy pyre ;
  Thy light woke the nations; the embers were
    thine.

II.

'Tis sunrise ! The mountains flash forth, and, new-
    redden'd,
  The billows grow lustrous, so lately forlorn ;
From the orient with vapours long darken'd and
    deaden'd
  The trumpets of Godhead are pealing the morn :
He rises—the Sun—in his might re-ascending ;
  Like an altar beneath him lies blazing the sea !
O Erin ! Who proved thee returns to thee, blending
  The future and past in one garland for thee !

WITH spices and urns they come :—ah me
　　how sorrow can babble !
Nothing abides save Love ; and to Love comes
　　gladness at last.
Sad was the Legend and sweet ; but its truth was
　　mingled with fable :
Dire was the Conflict and long ; but the rage of
　　the conflict is past.

They are past, the three great Woes ; and the days
　　of the dread desolation :
To amethyst changed are the stones blood-stain'd
　　of the temple-floor ;
A spiritual power she lives who seem'd to die as a
　　nation ;
Her story is that of a Soul ; and the story of
　　earth is no more.

Endurance it was that won—Suffering, than Action
　　thrice greater ;—
For Suffering humbly acts.　Away with sigh and
　　with tear !
She has gone before you and waits.　She has gifts
　　for the blinded who hate her ;
And that bright Shape by the death-cave in music
　　answers, " Not here."

NOTES.

NOTES.

Page 17.

THOUSANDS the sacraments of death received.

This is recorded of a southern parish in the famine of 1822.

P. 38. *Which changes light to music.*

The nightingale is said to feed on the glow-worm.

P. 50. *Which smiled to meet Catullus' homeward smile.*

" Peninsularum, Sirmio, insularumque ocelle."—CATULLUS.

P. 51. *Sow the slow olive for a race unborn.*

Quoted from Landor's *Gebir*.

P. 58. *Vinum demonum.*

This expression, used by one of the Fathers in speaking of poetry, is perhaps most applicable to that seductive species of poetry which embodies great aspirations at war with great truths:—poetry which enters the region of the spiritual, but yet does not acknowledge, and therefore sets itself up as a rival to, religion. The plea of " invincible ignorance," that is, of an ignorance relating to Revealed Truths, and not connected with the Will, *may* be applicable even in the case of errors the most deplorable. The ordinary latitudinarian theory is obliged to abandon such cases as beyond its pale, notwithstanding the violence which it is also compelled to offer to any fixed standard of faith.

P. 75. *Whereon Colonna mourn'd alone,*
An eagle widow'd in her nest.

Vittoria Colonna, the widow of the Marquis of Pescara, to whom Michael Angelo addressed his most remarkable poems.

P. 100. *Bending over thee, giftless, that well-sung bride.*

" Song made in lieu of many ornaments."—SPENSER's *Epithalamion.*

P. 104. *That built like larks their nest upon the ground.*

I am told by a friend that this image occurs in Burns or in some other poet. Probably it has been unconsciously borrowed by me.

P. 110.   *Iona's call*
Your fathers spurn'd not in faith's happy prime.

The testimony of the Venerable Bede respecting the Irish missions in England and Scotland, especially those of the monks from Iona, is not only interesting in itself, but singularly touching from the picture which it presents of friendship between two nations in later times so constantly at variance. He tells us how King Oswald of Northumbria, who had himself at an earlier period found a refuge in Ireland, sent thither for missionaries—how St. Aidan came at his prayer—how, while the Saint preached, the King interpreted his discourses—how Aidan was made Bishop of Lindisfarne and was succeeded there by St. Finan and St. Colman, also Irish monks. He tells us how the Irish monk Columba was the first preacher of Christianity among the Picts to the north of the mountains. He tells us how, at a later time, Adamnan, one of St. Columba's successors at Iona, and, thirteen years afterwards, the Irish clergy at Iona, and many elsewhere, adopted the later Roman time for celebrating Easter, which had been introduced into England by the Anglo-Saxon mission of Augustine, but had at first been resisted as an innovation both by the Irish clergy, and by such priests of the early British church (founded, as he records, by missionaries sent from Pope Eleutherus) as survived notwithstanding the rage of the Saxons. His expressions on this subject are striking. This correction, in the Irish, of those two points relating to discipline in which alone they erred, he says, " appears to have been accomplished by a " wonderful dispensation of the Divine goodness, to the end " that the *same nation* which had willingly and without envy " communicated to the *English people* the knowledge of the " true Deity, should afterwards, by means of the English " nation, be brought, where they were defective, to the true " rule of life. Even as, on the contrary, the Britons, who " would not acquaint the English with the knowledge of " the Christian faith, now, when the English people enjoy " the true faith, and are thoroughly instructed in its rules, " continue inveterate in their errors, *expose their heads with-* " *out a crown, and keep the solemnity of Christ without the* " *society of the Church.*" The mode of making the tonsure was the second point in dispute.

Bede is copious in his references also to the continental missions of the Irish, as well as to the multitudes of English, and others, who retired to Ireland " either for the sake of " divine studies, or of a more continent life." The early Irish usage, as regards the time for celebrating Easter, was not, as has been inaccurately stated, the Oriental usage, but the one originally practised at Rome, whence, as Bede tells us, Palladius was sent to the Irish " that believed in " Christ, to be their bishop, A. D. 431." The Irish were at first very naturally reluctant to change even a matter of discipline which they associated with their earlier saints; but this opposition, as Bede tells us, gave way gradually to argument, to a desire to be at one mind with the rest of the Church, and to their respect for the Holy See. He says that the " Scoti which dwell in the south of Ireland had long " since, by the admonition of the Apostolic See, learned to " observe Easter according to the canonical customs." The Irish he invariably calls by their name of "Scoti," for centuries given to them in consequence, as was supposed, of their *Scythian* descent. He describes also the Irish colony from Dalriada, or northern Antrim, which ultimately substituted, in the north of Britain, the name of Scotia for that of Alba.

" The Scoti, migrating from Ireland, under their leader,
" Reuda, either by fair means, or by force of arms, secured to
" themselves those settlements among the Picts which they
" still possess. From the name of their leader they are to
" this day called Dalreadans."—Page 7, Bohn's edition,
edited by J. A. Giles, D.C.L. 1847.

P. 116. *Lit from above, yet fuelled from below.*

An analogous thought, by which this line was probably
suggested, is doubtless familiar to the reader of poetry. It
is in Mr. Patmore's beautiful poem of " The Angel in the
House." It is there applied to love, not poetry.

P. 127. *In Benchorr the holy, in Arun the blest.*

There is no other example of a nation devoting itself to
spiritual things with an ardour and a success comparable to
that which distinguished Ireland. During the first three centuries after her conversion to Christianity she resembled one
vast monastery. Statements so extraordinary that if they
came from Irish sources they might be supposed to have
originated in national vanity, have reached us in such numbers
from the records of those foreign nations under whose altars
the relics of Irish saints and founders repose, that upon this
point there remains no difference of opinion among the
learned. For ordinary readers the subject is sufficiently
illustrated in the more recent Irish histories. Mr. Moore
remarks (Hist. of Ireland, vol i. p. 276): " In order to
" convey to the reader any adequate notion of the apostolic
" labours of that great crowd of learned missionaries whom
" Ireland sent forth, in the course of this century, to all parts
" of Europe, it would be necessary to transport him to the
" scenes of their respective missions; to point out the diffi-
" culties they had to encounter, and the admirable patience
" and courage with which they surmounted them; to show
" how inestimable was the service they rendered, during that
" dark period, by keeping the dying embers of learning
" awake, and how gratefully their names are enshrined in
" the records of foreign lands, though but faintly, if at all,
" remembered in their own, winning for her that noble title

" of the ' island of the holy and the learned,' which through-
" out the night that overhung the rest of Europe she so long
" and so proudly wore.   Thus the labours of the great mis-
" sionary, St. Columbanus, were after his death still vigor-
" ously carried on, both in France and Italy, by those disci-
" ples who had accompanied or joined him from Ireland ; and
" his favourite Gallus, to whom in dying he bequeathed his
" pastoral staff, became the founder of an abbey in Switzer-
" land, which was in the thirteenth century erected into a
" princedom, while the territory belonging to it, through all
" changes, bore the name of St. Gall. * * * This pious
" Irishman has been called, by a foreign martyrologist, the
" apostle of the Allemanian nation.   Another disciple and
" countryman of St. Columbanus, named Deicola, or in Irish
" Dichuill, enjoyed like his master the patronage and friend-
" ship of the monarch Clotaire II. who endowed the monastic
" establishment formed by him at Luthra with considerable
" grants of land."

He proceeds to enumerate many other monuments of early
Irish devotion, as the tomb of the Irish priest Caidoc, in the
monastery of Centula in Ponthieu, and the hermitage of St.
Fiacre, to which Anne of Austria, in the year 1641, made
her pilgrimage on foot.   He records the labours of St. Fursa
among the East Angles, and afterwards in France, and of
his brothers Ultan and Foillan in Brabant; of St. Livin in
Ghent; of St. Fridolin beside the Rhine.   He refers to the
two Irishmen successively bishops of Strasburg, St. Arbo-
gast, and St. Florentius; to the two brothers Erard and
Albert, whose tombs were long shown at Ratisbon; to St.
Wiro, to whom Pepin used to confess, barefooted; to St.
Kilian, the great apostle of Franconia, who consummated
his labours by martyrdom, and who is still honoured at
Wurtzburg as its patron saint.   He proceeds to commemorate
Cataldus, patron of Tarentum, and at one period an orna-
ment of the celebrated school of Lismore, and Virgilius, or
Feargal, denounced to the Pope by Boniface as a heretic for
having anticipated at that early period the discovery of the
" antipodes," and maintained " that there was another world,

" and other men under the earth." This great man propagated
the Gospel among the Carinthians. He then records the
selection by Charlemagne of two Irishmen, Clement and
Albinus, one of whom he placed at the head of a seminary
founded by him in France, while the other presided over a
similar institution at Pavia ; a third Irishman, Dungal,
being especially consulted by the same prince on account of
his astronomical knowledge. This celebrated teacher carried
on a controversy with Claudius, Bishop of Turin, who had
revived the heterodox opinions of Vigilantius against the
veneration of the saints. He bequeathed to the monastery
of Bobio his library, the greater part of which is still preserved at Milan.

Mr. Moore next illustrates the remarkable knowledge of
Greek possessed by the early Irish ecclesiastics, a circumstance
accounted for by the fact that the fame of the Irish churches
and schools had attracted many Greeks to Ireland. Ad-
vancing to the ninth century he records Sedulius and
Donatus, the former of whom had become so celebrated from
his writings that the Pope created him Bishop of Oreto, and
despatched him to Spain in order that he might compose the
differences which had arisen among the clergy there, while
the latter was made Bishop of Fiesole. Of his writings
nothing remains except the Latin verses in which he cele-
brates his native land under its early name of Scotia.

> " Finibus occiduis describitur optima tellus
>   Nomine et antiquis Scotia dicta libris.
>   Insula dives opum, gemmarum, vestis et auri :
>   Commoda corporibus, acre, sole, solo," &c.

He next gives an account of the far-famed John Scotus
Erigena, and remarks upon the influence of the early Irish
writers on the scholastic philosophy.—(Moore's History, vol.
i. p. 276-307.) From the latter part of the fifth century to
the latter part of the eighth was Ireland's golden age.
The Danish invasions reduced her to the comparatively
low condition in which she was found by the Normans in the
twelfth.

The progress of Ireland's Christianity is briefly but comprehensively narrated also in Mr. Haverty's recent History of Ireland:—"Among the great ecclesiastical schools or "monasteries founded in Ireland about this time (the fifth "century), were those of St. Ailbe of Emly, of St. Benignus "of Armagh, of St. Fiech of Sletty, of St. Mel of Ardagh, "of St. Mochay of Antrim, of St. Moctheus of Louth, of St. "Ibar of Beg-Erin, of St. Asicus of Elphin, and of St. Olcan "of Derkan."—P. 78. "* * * The most celebrated of them "founded early in the sixth century were Clonard in Meath "founded by St. Finan or Finian; Clonmacnoise, on the "banks of the Shannon, in the King's county, founded in the "same century by St. Kiaran, called the Carpenter's Son; "Bennchor, or Bangor, in the Ards of Ulster, founded by St. "Comgall in the year 558, and Lismore in Waterford, founded "by St. Carthach, or Mochuda, about the year 633. These "and many other Irish schools attracted a vast concourse of "students, the pupils of a single school often numbering from "one to three thousand, several of whom came from Britain, "Gaul, and other countries, drawn thither by the reputation "for sanctity and learning which Ireland enjoyed throughout "Europe."—P. 91. "* * * Scarcely an island round the coast, "or in the lakes of the interior, or a valley, or any solitary "spot, could be found which, like the deserts of Egypt and "Palestine, was not inhabited by fervent cœnobites and an- "chorites."—P. 92. After various quotations from eminent foreign authorities, as Erie of Auxerre, and Tierry, Mr. Haverty proceeds:—"Stephen White (Apologia, p. 24) "thus sums up the labours of the Irish saints on the con- "tinent:—' Among the names of saints whom Ireland for- "'merly sent forth there were, as I have learned from the "' trustworthy writings of the ancients, 150 now honoured as "' patrons of places in Germany, of whom 36 were martyrs; "' 45 Irish patrons in the Gauls, of whom 6 were martyrs; at "' least 30 in Belgium; 44 in England; 13 in Italy; and "' in Norway and Iceland 8 martyrs, beside many others.' "It has been calculated that the ancient Irish monks "had 13 monastic foundations in Scotland, 12 in England,

" 7 in France, 12 in Armoric Gaul, 7 in Lotharingia, 11 in
" Burgundy, 9 in Belgium, 10 in Alsatia, 16 in Bavaria, 6 in
" Italy, and 15 in Rhetia, Helvetia, and Suavia, besides
" many in Thuringia, and on the left margin of the Rhine
" between Gueldres and Alsatia."—P. 108.　Even after the
Danish invasion Ireland continued to found her religious
establishments in foreign countries:—"A few Irish monks
" settled at Glastonbury, and for their support began to teach
" the rudiments of sacred and secular knowledge.　One of
" the earliest and most illustrious of their pupils was the
" great St. Dunstan, who, under the tuition of these Irish-
" men became skilful in philosophy, music, and other accom-
" plishments. * * * St. Cadroc, the son of a king of the
" Albanian Scoti, was at the same time in Ireland, studying
" in the schools of Armagh."—P. 154.　Mr. Haverty gives
also an interesting account of the Culdees of Ireland, " reli-
" gious persons resembling very much members of the tertiary
" orders of St. Dominic and St. Francis in the Catholic
" church at the present day, or one of the great religious
" confraternities of modern times."—P. 110.　He also ex-
plains those abuses, the cause of so much misconception, by
which the great chiefs occasionally usurped and transmitted,
though not in holy orders, the titles and estates of the richer
bishoprics, the spiritual duties of which were vicariously dis-
charged by churchmen, as has happened more frequently at a
later time in the case of parishes appropriated by lay rectors.

P. 127.　*Not so by the race our Dalriada planted.*

Mr. Moore's History of Ireland, the tone of which is
notoriously sceptical as regards Irish claims which can possibly be considered as legendary, contains a series of citations
from unquestionable authorities, English and Scotch, respecting that remarkable incident in Irish history, the establishment of an Irish colony in Western Scotland, at that time
named Alba—a colony from which that noble country derived
both its present name and its Royal House, and from which,
through the Stuarts, our present Sovereign is descended :—
" From the family of this hero (Con of the Hundred Battles,

" A. D. 164) descended that race of chieftains who, under the
" name of the Dalriadic kings, supplied Albany, the modern
" Scotland, with her first Scottish rulers; Carbry Riada,—the
" son of Conary the Second by the daughter of the monarch
" Con,—having been the chief who, about the middle of the
" third century, established that Irish settlement in Argyle-
" shire,* which, taking the name of its princely founder,
" grew up, in the course of time, into the kingdom of Dal-
" riada; and finally, on the destruction of the Picts by
" Keneth MacAlpine, became the kingdom of all Scotland."—
Hist. of Ireland, vol. i. p. 127. In a note Mr. Moore proceeds, after quoting the testimony of Bede to this coloniza-
tion, " For the truth of this important, and now undoubted
" historical fact we need but refer to the admissions of Scotch
" writers themselves. After mentioning the notice, by Am-
" mianus, of Scots in Britain, A. D. 360, the judicious Innes
" adds, ' This may very well agree with the placing and com-
" ' ing in of Eocha Riada (the same as Bede's Reuda) the first
" ' leader of the colony of the Scots into Britain about the be-
" ' ginning of the third age. It is like he brought over at
" ' first but a small number, not to give jealousy to the ancient
" ' inhabitants of these parts, the Caledonians.' * * * Thus
" Pinkerton, whose observations prove him to have been
" thoroughly well informed on the subject, says, ' Concerning
" ' the origin of the Dalrendini of Ireland, all the Irish writers,
" ' Keating, Usher, O'Flaherty, &c. &c., are concordant, and
" ' say the name sprung from Carbry Riada. Beda, a supe-
" ' rior authority to all the Irish annalists put together, in-
" ' forms us that this very Riada led also the first colony of
" ' Scots to North Britain. So that the point stands clear,
" ' independently of the lights which Kennedy and O'Connor
" ' threw upon it.'—*Enquiry*, part iv. c. 2. ' Chalmers also
" ' concurs in the same view.' * * * But the most ancient
" testimony of the Scots of North Britain to the descent of
" their kings from the royal Irish race of Conary is to be

* In these Scoto-Irish chiefs of Argyleshire, says Sir Walter Scott,
historians " must trace the original roots of the royal line."—*Hist.
of Scotland*, vol. i. c. 2.

" found in a Gaelic Duan, or poem, written by the court bard
" of Malcolm III. (about A. D. 1057)."—MOORE's *Hist. of
Ireland*, vol. i. p. 129. Mr. Moore gives an interesting
account of the political motives which at a later period induced some Scotch writers to oppose the claims of King Edward the First by exaggerated statements respecting the antiquity of the Scotch monarchy. He then proceeds in a note
(vol. i. p. 138):—" It is but fair to observe that by none of
" these writers was so bold a defiance of the voice of history
" ventured upon as to deny that the Scots of Albany had
" originally passed over from Ireland. Even Sir George
" Mackenzie, who endeavours to set aside the relationship
" as much as possible, says, ' We acknowledge ourselves to
" ' have come last from Ireland,' while of all those Scotch
" writers who preceded him in the same track, John Major,
" Hector Boece, Leslie, Buchanan, not a single one has
" thought of denying that the Scots were originally of Irish
" extraction."

After referring further to the attestations of the same fact
by Bishops Lloyd and Stillingfleet, Mr. Moore alludes to the
last attempt to mystify this subject, an attempt now only
remembered to be ridiculed, connected as it is with MacPherson's Ossianic imposture:—" There remained another mode
" of undermining the Scotic history of Ireland, or rather of
" confounding it with that of the Scotia derived from her, so
" as to transfer to the offspring much of the parent's fame;
" and of this MacPherson, with much ingenuity, and a
" degree of hardihood almost without parallel, availed him-
" self." After referring on this subject to the authority of
Dr. W. II. Drummond, and the discoveries of Dr. Young,
Bishop of Clonfert, in the Highlands, A. D. 1784, and alluding
to the innumerable suppressions and falsifications, as well as
to the blunders, chronological, geographical, and relating to
manners, which throw an obvious absurdity upon MacPherson's endeavour to change Irish ballads, still recited in
numberless households of Clare and Mayo, into Scotch
epics of the third century, Mr. Moore continues:—" But the
" imposture of MacPherson was at the least as much his-

" torical as poetical. His suppression (for it could hardly
" have been ignorance) of the true history of the Irish settle-
" ment in Argyleshire, so early as the middle of the third
" century—a fact fatal to the whole groundwork of his pre-
" tended Scottish history—could have proceeded only from a
" deliberate system of deception."

P. 135. *Dead is the Prince of the Silver Hand.*

Nuad " of the Silver Hand " was the leader of the Tuatha
de Danann who are said by the bards to have landed in Ireland A. M. 3303, *i. e.* according to the chronology of the
Septuagint, adopted by the Four Masters. Eochy, the last
of the Firbolgic kings, was slain by them; and a cairn still
shown on the seacoast near Sligo is said to be his grave.
The first proceeding of the invaders was to burn their fleet,
so as to render retreat impossible. " According to the super-
" stitious ideas of the bards these Tuatha de Danann were
" profoundly skilled in magic, and rendered themselves in-
" visible to the inhabitants until they had penetrated into
" the heart of the country. In other words, they landed
" under the cover of a fog or mist; and the Firbolgs, at first
" taken by surprise, made no regular stand, until the new
" comers had marched almost across Ireland, when the two
" armies met face to face on the plain of Moyturey, near the
" shore of Lough Corrib, in part of the ancient territory of
" Partry. Here a battle was fought, in which the Firbolgs
" were overthrown, ' with the greatest slaughter,' says an old
" writer, ' that was ever heard of in Ireland at one meeting.'
" * * * The scattered fragments of his (Eochy's) army took
" refuge in the northern isle of Aran, Rathlin Island, the
" Hebrides, the Isle of Man, and Britain. * * * The victorious
" Nuad lost his hand in this battle, and a silver hand was
" made for him by Credne Cerd, the artificer, and fitted on
" him by the Physician Diencecht, whose son, Miach, im-
" proved the work, according to the legend, by infusing feel-
" ing and motion into every joint of the artificial hand, as if
" it had been a natural one."—HAVERTY'S *History of Ireland*, p. 5.

Twenty-seven years later Nuad was killed in battle by Balor " of the mighty blows," a Fomorian. The sway of the Tuatha de Danann is said to have lasted for 197 years, when it was terminated by the immigration of the Milesian race. Dr. O'Donovan says, (Four Masters, vol. i. p. 24):—" From " the many monuments ascribed to this colony by tradition, " and in ancient Irish historical tales, it is quite evident that " they were a real people; and from their having been con- " sidered gods and magicians by the Gaedhil, or Scoti, who " subdued them, it may be inferred that they were skilled in " arts which the latter did not understand. * * * It appears " from a very curious and ancient Irish tract, written in the " shape of a dialogue between St. Patrick and Caoilte Mac " Ronain, that there were very many places in Ireland where " the Tuatha de Danann were then supposed to live as " sprites or fairies, with corporeal and material forms, but " endued with immortality. The inference naturally to be " drawn from these stories is that the Tuatha de Danann " lingered in the country for many centuries after their sub- " jection by the Gaedhil, and that they lived in retired situa- " tions, where they practised abstruse arts, which induced " the others to regard them as magicians."

The Tuatha de Danann are chiefly remembered in connec- tion with two circumstances. They are asserted to have carried into Ireland the far-famed " Lia Fail," or " Stone of " Destiny," on which the kings of Ireland were crowned for ages, and which was afterwards said to have been removed to Scone in Scotland; and they gave Ireland her name. The three names by which Ireland was called in early years, Eire, Banba, and Fodhla, were assigned to her in consequence of their belonging to the wives of the three last kings of the Tuatha de Danann race, each of whom reigned successively during a single year. These three queens were slain in the battle fought by the Milesians against the Tuatha de Danann at Tailtinn, or Teltown, in Meath; the Irish queens being accustomed in the Pagan times to lead their armies to battle. The Tuatha de Dananns seem to have easily kept the Firbolgs, a pastoral people, in subjection,

being, though inferior to them in numbers, far superior in
civilization. " It is probable," says Mr. Haverty, " that by
" the Tuatha de Dananns mines were first worked in Ireland ;
" and it is generally believed that they were the artificers of
" those beautifully shaped bronzed swords and spear-beads
" that have been found in Ireland, and of which so many·
" fine specimens may be seen in the Museum of the Royal
" Irish Academy. * * * There is evidence to show that
" the vast mounds or artificial hills of Drogheda, Knowth,
" Dowth, and New Grange, along the banks of the Boyne,
" with several minor tumuli in the same neighbourhood, were
" erected as the tombs of Tuatha de Danann kings and chief-
" tains; and as such they only rank after the pyramids of
" Egypt for the stupendous efforts which were required to
" raise them. As to the Firbolgs, it is doubtful whether
" there are any monuments remaining of their first sway in
" Ireland ; but the famous Dun Angus, and other great stone
" forts in the islands of Aran, are well authenticated rem-
" nants of their military structures of the period of the
" Christian era, or thereabouts."—P. 20.

P. 135. *Ere came the Milesians they ruled the land.*

According to Charles O'Connor the last of the three early
invasions of Ireland, that of the Milesians, took place not much
earlier or later than B. C. 760, that is, at about the period of
the foundation of Rome. This computation seems more probably correct than that of the Four Masters, or that of the
Ogygia, which refers it to a period more ancient. Dis-
tinguishing between the main facts, respecting this immigration, and the various adornments which they received from the bardic fancy of later times, we arrive at
these results. The six sons of Milesius King of Spain, or of
the Gadelian portion of Spain, after his death, sailed to Ireland accompanied by his widow Scota, in part to avenge the
death of Ith, a prince of the same race who had some time
previously landed on the coast of Donegal, and been put to
death as a pirate by the Tuatha de Danann. The names of
the brothers were Heber, Colpa, Amergin, Ir, Donn, and

Heremon. From their ancestor, Gaedhuil Glas, this race had
long been known by the name of Gaedhil, Gadelian, and *Gael;*
by the last of these names their descendants in Ireland were
called, as well as by the name of Scoti. The following ac·
count of their earlier fortunes is given by Mr. Haverty:—
" The Tuatha de Danann confessed that they were not pre-
" pared to resist them, having no standing army, but said
" that if they again embarked, and could make good a land-
" ing according to the rules of war, the country should be
" theirs. Amergin who was the Olav, or learned man and
" judge of the expedition, having been appealed to, decided
" against his own people, and they accordingly re-embarked
" at the southern extremity of Ireland, and withdrew the
" distance of ' nine waves' from the shore. No sooner had
" they done so than a terrific storm commenced, raised (as
" the bards affirmed) by the magic arts of the Tuatha de
" Danann, and the Milesian fleet was completely scattered.
" Several of the ships, among them those of Donn and Ir,
" were lost off different parts of the coast. Heremon sailed
" round by the north-east, and landed at the mouth of
" the Boyne (called Inver Colpa from one of the brothers who
" was drowned there), and others landed at Inver Scene, so
" called from Scene Dubsaine, the wife of Amergin, who
" perished in that river. In the first battle fought with the
" Tuatha de Danann, at Slieve Mish, near Tralee, the latter
" were defeated; but among the killed was Scota, the wife of
" Milesius, who was buried in the place since called from her
" Glen-Scoheen."—P. 13. The sway of the Milesians was
soon acknowledged, and they formed alliances with the
races which had preceded them in Ireland. The Firbolgs,
from whom many of the race still existing in the west of Ireland are descended, were allowed to retain some of their
ancient territories. The people of southern Ireland are
regarded as chiefly the descendants of Heber, while many of
the families of Leinster and Connaught, the Hi Nials of
Ulster, &c. claim descent from Heremon.

P. 136. *The Faithful Norman.*

Maurice de Prendergast. This Knight " undertook to " bring the King of Ossory to a conference on obtaining the " word of Strongbow and O'Brien that he should be allowed " to return in safety. Understanding, however, during the " conference, that treachery was about to be used towards " Mac Gilla Patrick, he rushed into the Earl's presence, and " ' swore by the cross of his sword that no man there that " ' day should dare lay handes on the Kyng of Ossory.' " Having redeemed his word to the Irish Prince by conduct- " ing him back in safety, and defeated some of O'Brien's men " whom they met on the way with the spoils of Ossory, he " spent that night with Mac Gilla Patrick in the woods, and " returned next day to the Earl."—HAVERTY's *History of Ireland,* p. 198.

P. 138. *They fought ere sunrise at Tor Conainn.*

This battle, recorded in the legendary lore of Ireland, is the chief memorial of two early races supposed to have ex- isted there before the Firbolg period—that of the Nemedians, said to have come from the borders of the Euxine, and that of the Fomorians. The latter race are thought to have been pirates from Scandinavia. Their memory is preserved in the " Giants' Causeway," the Irish name of which is Cloghanna- Fomharaigh, or " Stepping Stones of the Fomorians." Nearly the whole Nemedian army having been drowned by the sea in this battle, which was fought on the coast of Donegal, about A.M. 3066, the survivors of the Nemedian race escaped over the sea, and Ireland is said to have re- mained nearly a wilderness for 200 years, till the arrival of the Firbolgs. But such narratives belong rather to the ro- mance than the history of Ireland.

P. 158. *'Twas a holy time when the kings long foemen.*

Malachi, who fought under the great Brian Borumha at Clontarf, where the Danish power in Ireland was overthrown for ever, had himself been King of all Ireland, but allowed himself to be deposed, A.D. 1003, and his rival to be elevated

in his place.   Mr. Moore remarks on this subject, (History
of Ireland, vol. ii. p. 101):—" The ready acquiescence with
" which, in general, so violent a change in the polity of the
" country was submitted to, may be in a great degree attri-
" buted to the example of patience and disinterestedness ex-
" hibited by the immediate victim of this revolution, the
" deposed Malachi himself. Nor, in forming our estimate of
" this Prince's character, from a general view of his whole
" career, can we well hesitate in coming to the conclusion
" that not to any backwardness in the field, or want of vigour
" in council, is his tranquil submission to the violent en-
" croachments of his rival to be attributed; but to a regard,
" rare at such an unripe period of civilization, for the real
" interests of the public weal."

P. 160. *Thou son of Calphurn, in peace go forth.*

The following statement is extracted by Dr. Petrie, in his
History and Antiquities of Tara Hill, from the Annotations of
the Life of St. Patrick, by Tirechan :—" And Patrick repaired
" again to the City of Tara to Laeghaire the son of Nial, because
" he (the King) had ratified a league with him that he should
" not be slain in his kingdom;—but he could not believe,
" saying, ' Nial, my father, did not permit me to believe,
" ' but that I should be interred in the top of Tara, like men
" ' standing up in war. For the Pagans are accustomed to
" ' be buried armed, with their weapons ready, face to face,
" ' to the Day of Erdathe, among the Magi, *i. e.* the Day of
" ' Judgment of the Lord.'" Dr. Petrie in the same work
quotes the following passage from the Leabhar Huidhre,
an Irish manuscript of the 12th century :—" Laeghaire was
" taken in the battle, and he gave the Lagenians guarantees,
" that is, the Sun and Moon, the Water and the Air, Day and
" Night, Sea and Land, that he would never during his life,
" demand the Boru Tribute. But Laeghaire went again with
" a great army to the Lagenians to demand tribute of them;
" for he did not pay any regard to his oaths. But, by the
" side of Casi, he was killed by the Sun and the Wind, and
" by the other Guarantees; for no one dared to dishonour
" them at that time."

P. 163. *Thou shalt not be a Priest, he said.*

Conall Creevan, a brother of Laeghaire, King of Ireland, was one of St. Patrick's earliest converts, and became his devoted follower. He asked permission to become a Priest; but the Saint commanded him to remain a soldier. The shield marked with the sign of the Cross was ever after called " Sciath-Bachlach," or the Shield of the Crozier. This is stated by Dr. O'Donovan to be the earliest authentic notice found of armorial bearings in Ireland.

P. 164. *Land which the Norman would make his own.*

Maurice Fitz Gerald, Lord Justice, marched to the northwest, and a furious battle was fought between him and Godfrey O'Donnell, Prince of Tirconnell, at Creadran-Killa, north of Sligo, A. D. 1257. The two leaders met in single combat and severely wounded each other. It was of the wound he then received that O'Donnell died soon after, after triumphantly defeating his great rival potentate in Ulster, O'Neill. The latter, hearing that O'Donnell was dying, demanded hostages from the Kinel Connell. The messengers who brought this insolent message fled in terror the moment they had delivered it;—and the answer to it was brought by O'Donnell on his bier. Maurice Fitz Gerald finally retired to the Franciscan monastery which he had founded at Youghal, and died peacefully in the habit of that order.

P. 167. *Where is thy brother, Heremon, speak.*

Between the brothers who founded the great Milesian, or Gaelic dynasty in Ireland there was strife, as between the brothers who founded Rome. Heremon and Heber divided Ireland between them. A dispute having arisen between them, a battle was fought at Geashill, in the present King's County, in which Heber fell by his brother's hand. In the second year of his reign Heremon also slew his brother, Amergin, in battle. To Amergin no territory was assigned. He is said to have constructed the causeway or *tochar* of Inver Mor, or the mouth of the Ovoca in Wicklow.

There are some excellent remarks in Mr. Haverty's History on the absurdity of disparaging the authentic part of Irish history on account of other portions having been but Bardic Legends:—" The ancient Irish attributed the utmost " importance to their historical compositions for social rea- " sons—every question as to the rights of property turned " upon the descent of families, and the principle of clanship. " * * * Again, when we arrive at the period of Christianity " in Ireland, we find that our ancient annals stand the test " of verification by science, with a success which not only " establishes their character for truthfulness at that period, " but vindicates the records of preceding dates." He refers especially to the eclipses recorded. " * * * Shortly after the " establishment of Christianity in Ireland the Chronicles of " the Bards were replaced by regular Annals, kept in several " of the monasteries."—P. 18, 19.

P. 168. A cry comes up.

In the reign of Edward the First those Irish who lay contiguous to the county lands finding themselves in a position of utter Outlawry, the ancient Brehon Law of Ireland not being recognized by England, and English law not being extended to them, applied to the King for the protection of the latter. The incident is thus narrated by Plowden in his History of Ireland:—" They consequently offered, through Ufford, the " chief Governor, 8000 marks to the King, provided he would " grant the free enjoyment of the laws of England to the " whole body of Irish natives indiscriminately." Edward was disposed to accept the offer; but his intentions were frustrated by his representatives in Ireland, who did not choose to be bound by any laws in their dealings with the Irish. In the words of Plowden:—" These politic and bene- " volent intentions of Edward were thwarted by his servants, " who, to forward their own rapacious views of extortion and " oppression, prevented a convention of the King's barons and " other subjects in Ireland. * * * The cry of oppression was " not silenced; the application of the Irish was renewed, and " the King repeatedly solicited to accept them as free and

" faithful subjects." Edward the First was too much occupied with his schemes for the conquest of Scotland to pay serious attention to affairs in Ireland. In the natural order of things, an amalgamation of races and of interests would have taken place, such as took place in England. This result was prevented by a prolonged Outlawry incomparably more unjust than the original Norman Conquest of Ireland, and also by such laws as the celebrated Statute of Kilkenny, passed A. D. 1362, and thus described by an English historian, Mr. Plowden:—" The substance of that singular statute is offered as " a specimen of the ferocious arrogance with which the Eng- " lish then treated the Irish. It was enacted that inter- " marriages with the natives, or any connection with them " as fosterers, or in the way of gossipred should be punished " as High Treason; that the use of their name, language, " apparel, or customs, should be punished with the forfeiture " of lands and tenements; that to submit to be governed by " the Brehon Laws was treason; that the English should not " make war upon the natives without the permission and " authority of Government; that the English should not per- " mit the Irish to graze upon their lands; that they should " not admit them to any benefice or religious privilege, or " even entertain their Bards," &c. &c.

It is thus that Sir John Davies, an authority not likely to be prejudiced in favour of the Irish, comments on this state of things:—" As long as they (the Irish) were out of the " protection of the law, so as every Englishman might op- " press, spoil, and kill them without controlment, how was " it possible they should be other than outlaws and enemies " to the crown of England? If the king would not admit " them to the condition of his subjects, how could they learn " to acknowledge and obey him as their sovereign? * * * " In a word, if the English would neither in peace govern " them by the law, nor in war root them out by the sword, " must they not needs be pricks in their eyes, and thorns in " their sides, till the world's end?"—DAV. *Disc.*

In justice to the English Sovereigns it should be remembered that although they were of course responsible for that which was done in Ireland by persons acting in their name, and armed with their authority, several of them showed a disposition to govern legally. King John and King Henry III. were of the number of these. The former caused a regular code of English laws to be drawn up and deposited in the Exchequer of Dublin, under the king's seal, "for the common "benefit of the land." In Henry III.'s reign a duplicate of the great Charter was sent to Ireland. Except as regards the Norman Barons these privileges bore little fruit; but they seem to evince a good intention.

P. 179. The statute of Kilkenny.

See the preceding page. A striking, and, in its admissions, a very touching picture of the condition of things in Ireland in the fourteenth century is presented by the following extracts from the remonstrance despatched to Pope John XXII. by O'Neill, King of Ulster, and the other princes of that province. It is given in Plowden's History of Ireland with the following remarks:—" The disastrous prospect of affairs " in Ireland drove the English government to the unchris- " tian and scandalous shift of prostituting the spiritual pow- " ers of the church to the profane use of state policy. * * * " So powerfully therefore did the English agents press the " mutual interests of both courts to resist the erection of a " new Scotch dynasty in Ireland, that a solemn sentence of " excommunication was published from the Papal chair " against all the enemies of Edward II. and nominally " against Robert and Edward Bruce, who were then invad- " ing Ireland for the purpose of securing to the latter the " throne, to which the generality of that nation had called " him."—Vol i. p. 131. He proceeds—" This remonstrance " (sent to neutralize the effect of Edward's appeal to Rome) " produced so strong an effect upon Pope John XXII. that " his Holiness immediately transmitted a copy of it to the " King, earnestly exhorting him to redress the grievances " complained of, as the only sure expedient to bring back the " Irish to their allegiance."—P. 133.

Extracts from the Irish Remonstrance to Pope John XXII.

Copied from Plowden's History of Ireland.

" We have now to inform your Holiness, that Henry, king
" of England, and the four kings his successors, have vio-
" lated the conditions of the Pontifical Bull by which they
" were impowered to invade this kingdom; for the said
" Henry promised, as appears by the said Bull, to extend
" the patrimony of the Irish Church, and to pay to the Apo-
" stolical See annually one penny for each house: now this
" promise both he and his successors above-mentioned, and
" their iniquitous ministers, observed not at all with regard
" to Ireland. On the contrary, they have entirely and
" intentionally eluded it, and endeavoured to force the
" reverse.

" As to the church lands, so far from extending them,
" they have confined them, retrenched them, and invaded
" them on all sides, insomuch that some Cathedral churches
" have been by open force notoriously plundered of half their
" possessions: nor have the persons of our clergy been more
" respected ; for in every part of the country we find
" Bishops and Prelates cited, arrested, and imprisoned with-
" out distinction; and they are oppressed with such servile
" fear, by those frequent and unparalleled injuries, that they
" have not even the courage to represent to your Holiness
" the sufferings they are so wantonly condemned to undergo.
" But since they are so cowardly and so basely silent in
" their own cause they deserve not that we should say a
" syllable in their favour. The English promised also to
" introduce a better code of laws, and enforce better morals
" among the Irish people; but instead of this they have so
" corrupted our morals, that the holy and dove-like simpli-
" city of our nation is, on account of the flagitious example
" of those reprobates, changed into the malicious cunning of
" the serpent.

" We had a written code of laws, according to which our
" nation was governed hitherto; they have deprived us of

" those laws, and of every law except one, which it is impos-
" sible to wrest from us; and for the purpose of extermi-
" nating us they have established other iniquitous laws by
" which injustice and inhumanity are combined for our
" destruction. Some of which we here insert for your
" inspection, as being so many fundamental rules of English
" jurisprudence established in this kingdom.

" Every man, not an Irishman, can on any charge however
" frivolous prosecute an Irishman; but no Irishman, whether
" lay or ecclesiastic (the prelate alone excepted), can prose-
" cute for any offence whatsoever, because he is an Irishman.
" If any Englishman should, as they often do, treacherously
" and perfidiously murder an Irishman, be he ever so noble
" or so innocent, whether lay or ecclesiastic, secular or
" regular, even though he should be a prelate, no satisfaction
" can be obtained from an English court of justice; on the
" contrary, the more worthy the murdered man was and the
" more respected by his own countrymen the more the
" murderer is rewarded and honoured, not only by the
" English rabble, but even by the English clergy and bishops;
" and especially by those whose duty it is chiefly, on account
" of their station in life, to correct such abominable male-
" factors. Every Irishwoman, whether noble or ignoble, who
" marries an Englishman, is, after her husband's death, de-
" prived of the third of her husband's lands and possessions
" on account of her being an Irishwoman. In like manner,
" whenever the English can violently oppress to death an
" Irishman, they will by no means permit him to make a will
" or any disposal whatsoever of his affairs; on the contrary,
" they seize violently on all his property, deprive the church
" of its rights, and perforce reduce to a servile condition that
" blood which has been from all antiquity free.

" The same tribunal of the English by advice of the king
" of England and some English bishops, among whom the
" ignorant and ill-conducted archbishop of Armagh was
" president, has made in the city of St. Kenniers (Kilkenny)
" the following absurd and informal statute,—that no religious
" community in the English Pale shall receive an Irishman

" as novice, under pain of being contumacious contemners
" of the king of England's laws. And as well before as after
" this law was enacted it was scrupulously observed by the
" English Dominicans, Franciscans, monks, canons, and all
" other religious orders of the English nation, who showed a
" partiality in the choice of their religious subjects, the more
" odious inasmuch as those monasteries were founded by
" Irishmen, from which Irishmen are so basely excluded by
" Englishmen in modern times. Besides, where they ought
" to have established virtue, they have done exactly the
" contrary; they have exterminated our native virtues, and
" established the most abominable vices in their stead.

" For the English, who inhabit our island, and call them-
" selves a middle nation (between English and Irish) are
" so different in their morals from the English of England,
" and all other nations, that they can with the greatest
" propriety be styled a nation not of middling, but of extreme
" perfidiousness; for it is of old that they follow the abomi-
" nable and nefarious custom, which is acquiring more in-
" veteracy every day from habit, namely, when they invite
" a nobleman of our nation to dine with them, they, either
" in the midst of the entertainment, or in the unguarded
" hour of sleep, spill the blood of our unsuspecting country-
" man, terminate their detestable feast with murder, and sell
" the heads of their guests to the enemy. Just as Peter
" Brumichehame, who is since called the treacherous baron,
" did with Mauritius de S—, his fellow sponsor, and the said
" Mauritius' brother, Calnacus, men much esteemed for their
" talents and their honour among us;—he invited them to an
" entertainment on a feast-day of the Holy Trinity; on that day
" the instant they stood up from the table, he cruelly massacred
" them, with twenty-four of their followers, and sold their
" heads at a dear price to their enemies; and when he was
" arraigned before the king of England, the present king's
" father, no justice could be obtained against such a nefarious
" and treacherous offender. In like manner Lord Thomas
" Clare, the Duke of Gloucester's brother, invited to his house
" the most illustrious Brien Roe O'Brien, of Thomond, his
" sponsor. * * * * *

" All hope of peace between us is therefore completely
" destroyed; for such is their pride, such their excessive lust
" of dominion, and such our ardent ambition to shake off this
" insupportable yoke, and recover the inheritance which they
" have so unjustly usurped that, as there never was so there
" never will be any sincere coalition between them and us;
" nor is it possible there should in this life, for we entertain
" a certain natural enmity against each other, flowing from
" mutual malignity, descending by inheritance from father to
" son, and spreading from generation to generation.

" Let no person wonder then if we endeavour to preserve
" our lives, and defend our liberties as well as we can, against
" those cruel tyrants, usurpers of our just properties and
" murderers of our persons :—so far from thinking it unlawful,
" we hold it to be a meritorious act, nor can we be accused
" of perjury or rebellion, since neither our fathers nor we did
" at any time bind ourselves by any oath of allegiance to
" their fathers or to them; and therefore without the least
" remorse of conscience, while breath remains, we will attack
" them in defence of our just rights, and never lay our arms
" until we force them to desist.

" Therefore, on account of all those injuries and a thou-
" sand others, which human wit cannot easily comprehend,
" * * * we are forced to carry on an exterminating war;
" choosing in defence of our lives and liberties rather to
" rise like men and expose our persons bravely to all the
" dangers of war, than any longer to bear like women
" their atrocious and detestable injuries; and in order to
" obtain our interest the more speedily and consistently, we
" invite the gallant Edward Bruce, to whom, being de-
" scended from our most noble ancestors, we transfer, as we
" justly may, our own right of royal dominion, unanimously
" declaring him our king by common consent who in our
" opinion, and in the opinion of most men, is as just, pru-
" dent and pious as he is powerful and courageous: who
" will do justice to all classes of people, and restore to the
" Church those properties of which it has been so damnably
" and inhumanly despoiled," &c.

P. 181. *The tanist succeeds when the king is dust.*

According to the Irish law the king, far from being able to alienate his kingdom, had but a life interest in the sovereignty. His son did not by necessity succeed to the crown. The sovereignty was vested in a particular family as representing the clan or race. Within certain limits of kindred in that family the king was chosen by election; and at the same period his Tanist, or successor, was chosen also. Such was the immemorial usage; and the transactions by which Irish princes occasionally pretended to transfer their rights to a foreign power were traitorous proceedings on the part of both the sides concerned in them. These frauds were concealed from the Irish, and the elections to the monarchy went on as before, until some occasion rose supposed to be favourable for the assertion of the new claim.

P. 185. *Fair she stood—God's queenly creature.*

A singularly picturesque narrative of this event is given in an old Irish Chronicle translated by Duald Mac Ferbis, one of Ireland's "chief bards," for Sir James Ware, in the year 1666, and republished in the Miscellany of the Irish Archæological Society, vol. i. 1846. The chronicler thus concludes: " God's blessing, the blessing of all the saints, and every one, " blessing from Jerusalem to Inis Glaaire, be on her going " to heaven; and blessed be he who will reade and heare " this for blessing her soul; and cursed be that sore in her " breast that killed Margaret."

P. 188. *Thus sang thy mission'd bard O'Neill.*

The bards were often selected as ambassadors, and sent to foreign powers. They assumed great state on such occasions; and being men of learning, no doubt adopted a tone in some respects different from that which they used when among their own people.

P. 196. *Florence Mac Carthy's Farewell.*

There is a striking description of Florence Mac Carthy in the Pacata Hibernia. He " was contented (*tandem aliquando*) " to repaire to the president, lying at Moyallo, bringing some " fourty horse in his company; and himself in the middest of " his troope (like the great Turke among his janissaries) " drew towards the house, the nine and twentieth of October, " like Saul higher by the head and shoulders than any of his " followers."—P. 170. The moral indignation constantly expressed by the author of the Pacata Hibernia at Florence Mac Carthy's method of countermining the far darker intrigues of the Lord President, recorded in that work, with intrigues of his own, is curious. Before the period he describes, Florence had been for eleven years detained a prisoner in England. In 1601 he was again arrested at a time when he possessed the " Queen's protection," and sent to the Tower—where he passed the rest of his life.

P. 199. *First at Clontibret they stood.*

This battle was fought in 1595. Sir John Norreys commanded the invading force. The O'Neill led the Irish.

P. 199. *How soon the giant son of Meath.*—SEGRAVE.

P. 199. *Portmore and Bunburb's plain know where.*

This battle was fought in 1597. Lord de Burgh commanding the English.

P. 200. *My prince, my chief, my child on whom*
So early fell the dungeon's doom.

Red Hugh O'Donnell, when but a boy of fifteen, was already celebrated for his beauty, his courage, and his skill in warlike accomplishments. To prevent him from assuming the headship of Tirconnell the following device was resorted to by Sir John Perrot, Lord President of Munster. During the summer of 1587 Red Hugh with Mac Swyne *of the battle-axes*, O'Gallagher of Ballyshannon, and some other Irish chiefs, had gone to a monastery of Carmelites situated on the western shore of Lough Swilly, and facing the mountains of Inishowen, the church of which had long been a famous place of pilgrimage. One day a ship, in appearance a merchant vessel, sailed up the bay, cast anchor opposite Rathmullan, and offered for sale her cargo of Spanish wine. Young Red Hugh was among those who went on board during the night. The next morning he and his companions found themselves secured under hatches. He was thrown into prison in Dublin, where he languished for three years and three months. At the end of that time he made his escape, and flying to the south took refuge with Felim O'Toole, who surrendered him to the English. "He remained again in irons," says the Chronicle, "until the Feast of Christmas, 1592, when it seemed to the Son of the Virgin time for him to escape." Once more he fled, accompanied by two sons of Shane O'Neill, to the mountains of Wicklow then covered with snow. After wandering about for three days and nights O'Donnell and one of his companions (the other had perished) were found by some of O'Byrne's clansmen beneath the shelter of a cliff, be-numbed and almost dead from hunger; for during those three days their food had consisted of grass and forest leaves. On the restoration of his strength O'Donnell succeeded, with the assistance of O'Neill, in making his way to his native moun-tains. From that moment the two great Northern Princes of Tirconnell and Tirone, renouncing the ancient rivalries of their several Houses, entered into that common alliance against the invader, the effects of which were irresistible until that reverse at Kinsale of which the cause has never been ex-plained.

P. 203. She whose marriage couch.

The celebrated picture of an Irish artist, Mr. Maclise, has rendered well known this incident, one of the most touching in history. After the capture of Waterford the King of Leinster led forth his daughter and married her to the Nor-man, Strongbow. This was on St. Bartholomew's Day, 1170. "The marriage ceremony was hastily performed, and " the wedding cortège passed through streets reeking with " the still warm blood of the brave and unhappy citizens."— HAVERTY'S *Hist.* p. 190.

P. 204. *Catch that death-shriek.*

" Another and equally unsuccessful attempt to plant Ulster
" was made in 1573 by a more distinguished minion of the
" Queen, Walter Devereux, Earl of Essex. Elizabeth em-
" barked with that noble Earl in his project of colonizing
" Clandeboy in Ulster * * * Lingard says that the agree-
" ment was that the Queen and the Earl should furnish each
" half the expense, and should divide the colony when it
" should be peopled with two thousand settlers. This bar-
" gain of fraud and crime was sealed by Essex with a des-
" perate act of villany. On his arrival in Ulster he met a
" most formidable opposition from Phelim O'Neill, which re-
" sulted, after a great deal of hard fighting, in a solemn peace
" between them. ' However,' say the manuscript Irish
" Annals of Queen Elizabeth's reign, ' at a feast wherein the
" ' Earl entertained that chieftain, and at the end of their
" ' good cheer, O'Neill with his wife were seized; the friends
" ' who attended were put to the sword before their faces;
" ' Phelim, with his wife and brother, were conveyed to
" ' Dublin where they were cut up in quarters.' "—(*The Confiscation of Ulster.* By THOMAS MACNEVIN, p. 53; James
Duffy.)

P. 204. *Sing the base assassin's steel,*
By Sussex hired to slay O'Neill.

The intended victim was Shane O'Neill, Prince of Tirone,
against whom the Queen supported the pretensions of his
illegitimate brother Matthew, Baron of Dungannon, and of
his sons. Sussex " was concerting at that time, A. D. 1561, a
" plan for the secret murder of O'Neill * * * This chosen
" tool of the Queen's representative was named Nele Gray;
" and after first swearing him upon the Bible to keep all
" secret, it was proposed that he should receive for this
" murder of Shane one hundred marks of land a year to him
" and his heirs for ever."—MOORE's *Hist.* vol. iv. p. 32.

" With regard to the odious transaction now under considera-
" tion there needs no more than the letter addressed by
" Sussex himself to his royal mistress, on that occasion, to

" prove the frightful familiarity with deeds of blood which
" then prevailed in the highest stations."—*Ibid.* The letter,
which is preserved in the State-paper Office thus concludes :—
" In fine I brake with him to kill Shane, and bound myself
" by my oath to see him have a hundred marks of land. He
" seemed desirous to serve your Highness and to have the
" land; but fearful to do it, doubting his escape after. I
" told him the ways he might do it, and how to escape after
" with safety, which he offered and promised to do."

P. 205. *Whom thy country and thy sire.*

The illegitimacy of Elizabeth rests upon authority not
particularly favourable to the opposite side, viz. Archbishop
Cranmer, and an Act of Parliament never repealed even in
her own reign :—" Cranmer, ' having previously invoked the
" ' name of Christ, and having God alone before his eyes,'
" pronounced definitively that the marriage formerly con-
" tracted, solemnized and consummated between Henry and
" Anne Boleyn was, and *always had been, null and void.* The
" whole process was afterwards laid before the members of
" the Convocation, and the Houses of Parliament. The
" former presumed not to dissent from the decision of the
" metropolitan; the latter were willing that in such a case
" their ignorance should be guided by the learning of the
" clergy. By both the divorce was approved and confirmed."
—LINGARD'S *Hist.* vol. v. p. 36. What was the origin
of the Parliament which Elizabeth induced to recognize her
title ? " In the Lower House a majority had been secured
" by the expedient of sending to the sheriffs a list of court
" candidates, out of whom the members were to be chosen."
—LINGARD, vol. vi. p. 5. The court *named five candidates for
the shires, and three for the boroughs!*

P. 205. *Trampling that Faith whose borrow'd garb.*

Not only had Elizabeth repeatedly asserted herself to be a
Catholic in her sister's reign, but for some time after her own
accession she wore the same mask. " She continued to assist
" and occasionally to communicate at mass: she buried her
" sister with all the solemnities of the Catholic ritual; and

" she ordered a solemn dirge, and a mass of requiem for the
" soul of the Emperor Charles V."—LINGARD. Her corona-
tion was conducted with all the ceremonial of the Catholic
Pontifical, and at it she received the Sacrament under one
kind.

The following contemporaneous sketch of Elizabeth's last
year is not commonly known:—" Sir John Harrington, her
" godson, who visited the court about seven months after
" the death of Essex, has described in a private letter the
" state in which he found the Queen. She was altered in
" her features and reduced to a skeleton. Her food was no-
" thing but manchet bread, and succory pottage. * * * For
" her protection she had ordered a sword to be placed by her
" table, which she often took in her hand, and thrust with
" violence into the tapestry of her chamber. About a year
" later he returned to her presence. 'I found her,' he says,
" 'in a most pitiable state. She bade the archbishop ask
" 'me if I had seen Tirone. I replied with reverence that I
" 'had seen him with the Lord Deputy. She looked up
" 'with much choler and grief in her countenanae, and said,
" '" O now it mindeth me that you was one who saw this
" '" man elsewhere," and hereat she dropped a tear and
" 'smote her bosom. She held in her hand a golden cup
" 'which she often put to her lips; but in truth her heart
" 'seemed too full to need any more filling.' * * * At
" length she obstinately refused to return to her bed : and
" sat both day and night on a stool bolstered up with
" cushions, having her finger in her mouth, and her eyes
" fixed on the floor, seldom condescending to speak, and re-
" jecting every offer of nourishment. The bishops and the
" lords of the council advised and entreated in vain. For
" them all, with the exception of the Lord Admiral, she ex-
" pressed the most profound contempt. He was of her own
" blood; from him she consented to accept a basin of broth;
" but when he urged her to return to her bed, she replied
" that if he had seen what she saw there he would never
" make the request. To Cecil, who asked if she had seen
" spirits, she answered that it was an idle question beneath

" her notice. He insisted that she must go to bed, if only
" to satisfy her people. ' Must!' she exclaimed; ' is *must* a
" ' word to be addressed to princes? Little man, little man,
" ' thy father, if he had been alive, durst not have used that
" ' word; but thou art grown presumptuous because thou
" ' knowest that I shall die.' Ordering the others to depart
" she called the Lord Admiral to her, saying in a piteous tone,
" ' My lord, I am tied with an iron collar about my neck.'
" He sought to console her, but she replied, ' No, I am tied,
" ' and the case is altered with me.' "—LINGARD, vol. vi.
p. 315, 16. Edit. 1854.

P. 207. *Than to beard O'More in his lair.*

The celebrated " Owny O'More." Under this chief the
people of Leix recovered almost all their ancient possessions. Having incautiously exposed himself, he was killed
by a musket ball on the 17th of August, 1660, and the
country fell into the hands of the invaders under Lord Mountjoy. Fynas Moryson, Mountjoy's Secretary, remarks, as
quoted by Mr. Moore, " ' It seemed incredible that by such
" ' inhabitants the grounds should be so manured, the fields
" ' so orderly fenced, the towns so numerously inhabited, and
" ' the highways and paths so well beaten.' The writer
" accounts for this prosperous change by adding that years
" had then elapsed ' since the Queen's troops had been among
" ' them.' * * * Among other instances of the wanton havoc
" thus perpetrated, the following is mentioned by the eye-
" witness already cited :—' Our captains, and by their ex-
" ' amples, the common soldiers, did cut down with their
" ' swords all the rebels' corn, to the value of £10,000
" ' and upward, the only means by which they were to
live.' "—*Hist. of Ireland,* vol. iv. p. 119. This mode of
warfare was what the Irish were at that time constantly
exposed to. " About this time the same viceroy (Mountjoy)
" invaded Offaly, and with a kind of harrows named *pracas,*
" constructed with long pins, tore up from the roots all the
" unripe corn, and thus prepared the way for one of the most
" horrible famines which ever visited this unhappy country."

Z

—Haverty's *Hist.* p. 477. In the earlier Desmond war this method of warfare was pursued with a dreadful success, described by Spenser. Leix was subjected, in common with many other parts of Leinster, to another confiscation in the reign of James I. :—" The native septs of the Queen's County " were transplanted to Kerry; and in many instances the " proprietors, as in the case of the O'Ferralls, were dispos- " sessed without receiving any compensation."—Haverty's *Hist.* p. 505.

P. 214. *O Athunree, thy fate o'erhung Kinsale.*

The wholly inexplicable disaster at Kinsale, when, after their marvellous winter march, the two great northern chiefs of Tirconnell and Tirone had succeeded in relieving their Spanish allies there, and when the victory seemed almost wholly in the hands of warriors who till then had never met with a reverse, was one of those critical events upon which the history of a nation turns. But for it Ireland would at the death of Elizabeth have been in such a position that Ulster would have had nothing to fear from James I.

P. 216. *For knights wave-wash'd round Smerwick's base.*

The treachery by which, according to Irish historians, the massacre of the Spaniards at Smerwick was aggravated, is denied by some writers, who maintain that the vanquished force surrendered without terms. About 500 of the garrison were flung into the sea.

P. 231. *The Intercession.*

Dr. Leland and other historians relate that the Catholic clergy frequently interfered for the protection of the victims of that massacre which took place at an early period of the Ulster Rising of 1641. They often hid them beneath their altars. From the landing of Owen Roe O'Neill all such deplorable outrages ceased.

P. 239. *This night they shall sup with the Queen's O'Connor.*

The mode by which Sir George Carew, President of Mun- ster, contrived to separate the " Sugane" Earl of Desmond from his allies is narrated in the Pacata Hibernia, the work of Stafford, Sir George Carew's Secretary, p. 65, 91, 97, 193. Dublin, 1810. The principal allies of the Sugane Earl were Dermond O'Connor, and Redmond Burke. The latter was induced to betray the Earl by the expectation delusively held out to him that in this case his pretensions to the Barony of Leitrim would be recognized. Dermond had married the Lady Margaret, sister of the young Earl of Desmond, who had been from his childhood detained by Elizabeth as a prisoner in the tower, but whom she had sent back to Ireland in order to divide the adherents of James Fitz Thomas. Sir George Carew formed a plot with Dermond O'Connor who agreed to betray the Sugane Earl, p. 67. Dermond O'Connor, however, required two conditions :—First, pledges to ensure the President's fidelity :—secondly, a colourable pretext for his treason. " The hostages agreed on were " Redmond and Brian, sons of Milesius Mac Craghe, Arch- " bishop of Cashell, who himself had before been a principal " actor in the business, and Captain William Power, and " John Power his elder brother, who likewise had been em- " ployed in the action. * * * Therefore that these four should " make a journey from Kilwallocke towards Kinsale, where " Captain Poore his companie were then in garrison ; and the " time of their going been made knowen unto Dermond " O'Connor, he should lie with some of his forces in the Pass " of Ballyhowre, to intercept passengers, where these four " should, as it were, by chance fall into his ambush, and so " they did; where Dermond O'Connor, although for the rea- " sons above mentioned, he saved their lives, yet he could not " restrain the furie of his men, that knew nothing of his pur- " pose, but that they were stripped of their clothes, and left " almost naked."—P. 92.

The pretext by which Dermond was to be apparently justified in surrendering his chief, the Sugane Earl, consisted of a letter supplied by the President, by which it was to be made to appear as if the Earl himself had been the traitor, and was in secret league with the President for the destruction of his own allies. Of this letter Stafford remarks, " foras-

" much as the contents thereof doe manifest the invention, I
" have thought not unfit to bee inserted in the present re-
" lation."

The Lord President's Letter to James Fitz-Thomas
(the Sugane Earl).

" Sir, your last letters I have received, and am exceedingly
" glad to see your constant resolution of return to subjection,
" and to leave the rebellious courses, wherein you have long
" persevered;—you may rest assured that promises shall bee
" kept: and you shall no sooner bring Dermond O'Connor
" to me, alive or dead, and banish his Bownoghs (mercenaries)
" out of the Countrie, but that you shall have your demand
" satisfied, which I thank God I am both able and willing to
" perform," &c.—P. 93. * * * " This letter was sent to
" Dermond O'Connor, which, when time shall serve, hee
" might shew as intercepted by him; and therefore what he
" did was imposed upon him by necessitie, except he
" would suffer himself wittingly and willingly to be be-
" trayed."—P. 94. Dermond O'Connor next invited the Earl
to a meeting where, having managed by a feigned quarrel
among the attendants on both sides to separate him from
his followers, he laid hold on him, exclaiming, " My lord,
" you are in hand." " In hand," answered he; " for whom,
" or for what cause?" " I have taken you for O'Neill,"
saith he, " and I purpose to detain you until I bee certified
" of his pleasure, for yourself have combined with the Eng-
" lish, and promised to the President to deliver me either
" alive or dead into his hands; and for proof thereof, behold,"
saith he, " letters which were intercepted."—P. 98. Dermond O'Connor then carried off the Earl, and imprisoned
him in Castle-Ishin. A slight delay occurred, however, in
completing the treachery, for Dermond did not trust Sir
George Carew, and would not deliver up his prisoner until
the stipulated price had been paid. In the mean time John
Fitz-Thomas and Pierce Lacy collected 4000 men, and rescued
the Earl. Though the attempt failed the chief agents in it were
not defrauded of their promised rewards. The Archbishop

received £121 13s. 3d.; John Power, one of the hostages,
£36 10s.; the Lady Ellis, £33 6s. 8d.; the Lady Margaret,
£100.—*Pacata Hibernia,* p. 193. Shortly afterwards Dermond O'Connor went to visit his brother-in-law, and for this
purpose procured safe-conducts from the Lord Deputy and
Sir George Carew. " But in his route towards Thomond he
" was attacked near Gort by Theobald-na-loug, who had
" the command of a hundred men in the Queen's pay. Der-
" mond and his party sought refuge in a church; but Theo-
" bald set fire to the building, slew about forty of Dermond's
" men as they issued from the burning pile, and having
" taken the traitor himself prisoner, had him beheaded the
" following day. * * * The act greatly annoyed the govern-
" ment, and he was deprived of the Queen's commission."
—HAVERTY'S *Hist.* Theobald's excuse was that he had but
avenged the death of a kinsman, Lord Burke, who was slain
by O'Connor in Munster.

Another plot against the Sugane Earl is related in the
Pacata Hibernia with an equal unconsciousness that it
contained anything unfit to be divulged. A man of the
name of Nugent, who had been servant of Sir Thomas
Norris, deserted the English cause for the Irish, and having
subsequently quarrelled with his new friends, delivered himself up with a view of receiving the Royal protection.
" Answer was made that for so much as his crimes and
" offences had been extraordinary, he could not hope to be
" reconciled unto the State, except he would deserve it
" by extraordinary service."—P. 67. Nugent offered to
assassinate, or, as he called it, to " ruine " either the Sugane
Earl or his brother, John Fitz-Thomas. " The President
" having contrived a plot for James Fitz-Thomas (as is before
" shown) gave him in charge to undertake John, his bro-
" ther.—P. 68. He was next admitted to the council,
where he sued for protection, and where, by a preconcerted
scheme, he was repulsed by Sir George Carew with every
outward demonstration of scorn. The sequel is thus
narrated in Mr. Haverty's History:—" When in the act
" of levelling his pistol at John's back he was seized, and

" being sentenced by the Irish leaders to die, he confessed
" his design, adding that the President had hired several
" others who were sworn to commit the deed."—P. 476.
Eventually the Sugane Earl was delivered up by the "White
Knight," while concealed in a cave. This event and the
capture of Florence Mac Carthy nearly at the same time,
and just before the arrival of their Spanish succours, was a
calamity to Munster soon after consummated by the defeat at
Kinsale.

P. 252. *The Lady turned Beggar.*

This lady was one of the countless victims of Charles the
Second's ingratitude. At the end of the Cromwellian war
more than half Ireland was confiscated, and handed over to a
new race, consisting in a large measure of the Parliamenta-
rian soldiers. The greater number of those thus reduced to
beggary had fought for Charles the First, as well as for their
country and the freedom of their Faith, and on the return of
his son naturally looked for the restoration of their property.
But the celebrated " Act of Settlement" confirmed nearly the
whole of it to the new possessors.

THE END.

CHISWICK PRESS:—PRINTED BY WHITTINGHAM AND WILKINS,
TOOKS COURT, CHANCERY LANE.